right of way

Also by Lauren Barnholdt

Watch Me

Two-way Street

One Night That Changes Everything

Sometimes It Happens

The Thing About the Truth

Through to You

right of way

LAUREN BARNHOLDT

SIMON PULSE
New York London Toronto Sydney New Delhi

SIMON PULSE
An imprint of Simon & Schuster Children's Publishing Division
1230 Avenue of the Americas, New York, NY 10020
First Simon Pulse paperback edition June 2014

Interior designed by Mike Rosamilia
Cover designed by Russell Gordon
The text of this book was set in Cochin.
Manufactured in the United States of America
2 4 6 8 10 9 7 5 3 1
The Library of Congress has cataloged the hardcover edition as follows:
Barnholdt, Lauren.
Right of way / Lauren Barnholdt. — 1st Simon Pulse hardcover ed.
p. cm.
Summary: Told in their separate voices, seventeen-year-old Peyton convinces eighteen-year-old Jace to drive her from a Florida wedding toward her Connecticut home with the intention of staying in North Carolina rather than face her parents' marital and financial problems, while both avoid the obvious attraction they have felt since they met at Christmas.
[1. Love—Fiction. 2. Automobile travel—Fiction.
3. Runaways—Fiction. 4. Family problems—Fiction.] I. Title.
PZ7.B2667Rig 2013 [Fic]—dc23
2012021578
ISBN 978-1-4424-5127-8 (hc)
ISBN 978-1-4424-5128-5 (pbk)
ISBN 978-1-4424-5129-2 (eBook)

For Michelle Nagler, who took a chance on me
and my writing, and made my dreams come true

ACKNOWLEDGMENTS

Thank you so, so much to:

Jennifer Klonsky, Alyssa Eisner Henkin, and everyone at Simon & Schuster for all their hard work on my behalf;

Krissi, Kelsey, Jodi, Kevin, and my mom for all their support;

My husband, Aaron, for everything;

Everyone who read *Two-way Street* and took the time to write me and tell me you loved it—I appreciate it more than you know!

peyton the trip

Saturday, June 26, 10:03 a.m.
Siesta Key, Florida

I'm a traitor to my generation. Seriously. All we hear about these days is how we're supposed to be strong women and not depend on anyone else and blah blah blah. And now look what I've done.

"Are you sure there's no way you can come?" I say into my phone. I'm crouching behind some bushes outside the Siesta Key Yacht Club, which is not comfortable. At all. The bushes are prickly, there are bees floating around, and the ground is kind of wet. Which makes no sense. I thought it never rained in Florida. Isn't it called the Sunshine State?

"I'm sorry," my best friend, Brooklyn, says on the other end of the line. "I'm so sorry, but there's no way I can come now. My parents found out, and they're freaking out. And honestly, Peyton, I kind of think you should just forget the whole thing. I mean, what if my parents call your parents?"

My heart leaps into my throat. "Are they going to?"

"I don't know. My mom said she wouldn't as long as I talked you out of it, but you never know what my mom's going to do. She's a loose cannon." It's true. Brooklyn's mom really is a loose cannon. One time last year she came down to our school screaming about women's equality on the wrestling team. It was pretty ridiculous, since Brooklyn is totally unathletic, and no girls were even trying out for the wrestling team. But her mom had read some article about Title Nine that had gotten her all riled up.

"But what am I supposed to do?" I ask. "My parents already left. I can't call and tell them I don't have a way to get back to Connecticut. They'll be pissed."

Brooklyn and I had this whole thing planned out. She was going to fly down to Florida from Connecticut, and meet me here, in Siesta Key, at my uncle's wedding. Then we were going to rent a car and drive to North Carolina, where we were going to spend the summer. It was a very simple two-part plan. One, she takes a plane down here. Two, we rent a car and go to North Carolina. Leave it to her parents to wreck everything.

"You're going to have to call your mom or something," Brooklyn says. "It'll suck, yeah, but what else are you going to do?"

I don't say anything. My eyes fill with hot tears. There's

a bee buzzing near my face, and I don't even bother to swat it away. I really, really do not want to call my parents. And not just because they're going to be pissed. But because it's going to mean that I have to go home, and I really, really do not want to do that.

Brooklyn sighs.

"Look," she says finally. "Is there any way you can book a flight to North Carolina? And maybe get a ride to the airport?"

"I don't have a credit card. Or any money, really."

"Can you ask Courtney for help?"

"I could ask her, I guess, but I don't know if she has any money either." I stand up and scan the outdoor tables for my cousin. I don't see her dark hair anywhere. I look for her boyfriend, Jordan, but I don't see him either. In fact, I don't see *anyone* I recognize. Most people have already left the brunch and gone home. The wedding was yesterday, and the festivities are over.

I guess I could call Courtney, I think, taking a step back toward the tables that are set up on the lawn of the yacht club. But who knows if she would tell my parents? Or her dad? I mean, I trust her, but—

My eyes stop scanning the crowd as they land on the only person I recognize who's still at the brunch. The only person I don't want to see. Jace Renault. He looks up from the table where he's sitting, talking to some older couple that he probably just met. The old lady is laughing at something

Jace is saying. Which isn't surprising. Jace is charming like that. Ugh.

He catches my eye, and I quickly turn away.

"Brooklyn," I say. "Please, can you lend me the money for a plane ticket? I'll pay you back, I promise."

"Peyton, you know I would if I could, but my mom took my credit card away."

"I can't believe this," I say. "I planned so hard so no one would find out, and now—"

There's a tap on my shoulder. I turn around. Jace is standing there, a huge smile on his face. "Hello," he says.

I turn and start to walk away from him. "Who's that?" Brooklyn asks.

"That's no one," I say loudly, hoping that Jace will get the message to go away. But of course he doesn't. He just starts to follow me as I walk through the grass of the club back toward my room. He's doing a good job keeping up, since I'm having a little trouble walking. My shoes keep slipping on the wet grass.

"You really shouldn't be walking through here," he says conversationally. "I don't think the groundskeepers are going to be too thrilled with all the divots you're making."

"Who the hell is that?" Brooklyn asks. "Is that Jace?"

"No," I say.

"Yes, it is."

"No, it isn't."

"Yes, it is!"

"No. It. Isn't."

"No it isn't what?" Jace asks from next to me. He's caught up to me now.

He really is like some kind of gnat that I can't get away from. I knew there would be pests and bugs in Florida; I just didn't expect them to be six foot two and of the human variety.

"I'll call you back," I say to Brooklyn. I hang up the phone and whirl around. "What do you want?" I ask.

He shrugs. "I don't know," he says. "I saw you staring at me, and you looked upset."

"I wasn't staring at you!" I say. "I was looking for Courtney." I smooth down my dress. "And I'm not upset."

"Courtney and Jordan left a little while ago," he says.

"Do you know where they went?" I ask, my heart sinking.

"I'm not sure." He shrugs like it doesn't matter. And I guess to him, it doesn't. He's not the one who's stranded at some wedding in Florida with no way to get to North Carolina. "Why?"

"None of your business." I'm walking again, looking down at my phone, scrolling through my contacts. I wonder if there's someone I can call—someone who might be willing to help me. Why didn't I make more of an effort to get to know someone at the wedding? Why didn't I befriend some nice old lady who would be able to take me somewhere—preferably a senile one who would be too out of it to ask any questions? *Because you were too busy with Jace.*

"Do you need a ride or something?" Jace asks.

I snort.

"What's so funny?"

"I just think it's kind of hilarious that suddenly you're so concerned about my well-being after what you did to me last night."

"Peyton—" he starts, his voice softening. But I'm not in the mood.

"Stop." I hold my hand up. "I don't want to hear it. And I don't need a ride. So just go away."

"Then how are you getting to the airport?"

"I'm not going to the airport." God, he's so annoying. How can he think that after what happened between us last night that I would get into a car with him? Is he crazy?

Although I guess when I really think about it, it's actually not that surprising.

Anyone who is as good-looking as Jace is usually completely out of touch with reality. It's like they think their looks give them the right to just go around saying whatever they want to say, and doing whatever they want to do. As if the fact that they're six foot two and broad-shouldered with dark hair and gorgeous, deep-blue eyes gives them the right to get away with anything.

"If you're not going to the airport, then where are you going?"

I keep ignoring him, continuing through the grass in these stupid high heels, trying to get back to my room. And he keeps following me, still not having any trouble keeping up. I glance down at his feet. He's wearing sneakers. Of course he is. Jace Renault would never do anything as, you know, *polite* as wearing dress shoes to a wedding. Although technically he's wearing them to the brunch the day after the wedding. But still. Proper attire should be worn. Proper attire that doesn't include sneakers.

I'm so caught up in looking at his feet that I don't realize that my own shoes are sinking farther into the wet grass, and so when I slip, I'm halfway to the ground before I feel his arms grabbing me around the waist.

He's so close that I can feel his breath on my neck as he lifts me up, and it sends delicious little shivers up and down my spine. He looks at me, his eyes right on mine, and I swallow hard. If this were a movie, this would be the moment he'd kiss me, the moment he'd push my hair back from my face and brush his lips softly against mine, telling me he was sorry for everything that happened last night and over the spring, that he had an explanation for the whole thing, that everything was going to be okay. But this isn't a movie. This is my life.

And so instead of kissing me, Jace waits until I'm upright and then he says, "Those shoes are pretty ridiculous."

"These shoes," I say, "cost four hundred dollars."

"Well, you got ripped off."

"I didn't ask you."

He keeps following me, all the way back to my hotel room. What is *wrong* with him? Like it's not enough that he stomped all over my heart? Now he has to keep torturing me with his nearness? When we get to the outside of the suite I'm staying in, I unlock the door and push it open.

"Well, thanks for walking me back to my room," I say, all sarcastic.

But he doesn't seem to notice. In fact, he just peers over my shoulder into the sitting area of my room. "Jesus, Peyton," he says, looking at the mound of bags that are stacked neatly in the middle of the floor. "How long did you plan on staying? A few months? I knew you were high maintenance, but that much luggage is a little crazy, don't you think?"

"I'm not high maintenance!"

He shrugs, as if to say I am high maintenance and everyone knows it, so there's no use denying it. Like he knows anything about me and my high-maintenance ways. (And yes, I am a little bit high maintenance. But not in a bad way. I just like to have things the way I like them.)

"Looks pretty high maintenance to me." He steps into the room, then reaches down and picks up the bottle of water the hotel has left on the desk. He opens it and takes a big drink.

"You owe me four dollars." Plus I wanted that water. But I'm not going to tell him that. Why give him the satisfaction?

"Don't you mean I owe your parents four dollars?"

I narrow my eyes at him then hold out my hand. "Give it to me."

"Fine," he grumbles, reaching into his pocket and pulling out a bunch of crumpled up bills.

"Figures that you don't have a wallet," I say.

"Figures that you would notice something like that, being that you're so high maintenance." He grins at me sweetly.

"I am *not* high maintenance! So stop saying that!"

"Then why do you have a million bags for a weekend trip to a wedding?"

I feel the anger building inside me—he's so damn arrogant I can't even stand it—and before I even know what I'm saying, I'm telling him. "Because," I say, getting ready to savor the look of shock that I know is about to cross his face, "I'm running away."

the trip jace

Saturday, June 26, 10:17 a.m.
Siesta Key, Florida

Peyton Miller hates me. And for good reason—I've been nothing but an asshole to her since we met. And even though I *knew* she was pissed at me because of what happened last night, even though I *knew* she hated me and probably wanted to beat me senseless with those ridiculous shoes she's wearing, I found myself getting up from my table and walking over to her while she was in the bushes.

I wanted to explain to her what happened last night; I wanted to explain to her all the reasons I had for being such an asshole. But when I got close to her, she started being such a brat that I figured it wasn't the time. Either that, or I just chickened out. Probably a combination of both.

Which is probably for the best, since there are a million fucking reasons that things are not going to work out between me and Peyton Miller, even before considering the fact that she hates me.

Some of these reasons are:

1. **She is beautiful and she doesn't know it. This is a very annoying trait for a girl to have, because it makes you want them, while at the same time you can't even hate them for being conceited because they're not.**
2. **She is ridiculously smart—so smart that I sometimes cannot believe it. In fact, she is a horrible mix of beautiful and smart. One second she'll be tottering around in those stupid high-heeled shoes she always wears, and the next she'll be debating me over whether or not there should be universal healthcare.**

2a. **She is way too smart to put up with any of my shit and calls me out on it any chance she gets.**

3. **Right now she's trying to get rid of me, even though I'm trying to help her.**
4. **She broke my heart.**

Number four is obviously the biggest one. She's the only girl who's ever broken my heart, and it's a very weird, uncomfortable feeling for me. I like to be the one doing the heartbreaking. Well, not really. No one ever *likes* to break someone's heart, but sometimes it has to be done. And if I have a choice between breaking a heart and getting my heart broken, well, call me selfish, but I'll take being the heartbreaker.

"You're running away?" I say now. I move into the room so she can't see the shock on my face, mostly because I know she *wants* to see the shock on my face. She wants to see me freak out like a little girl and ask her all kinds of questions. Which I'm dying to do, let's face it. But I don't want to give her the satisfaction.

Instead I head over to the minibar in the corner and start rustling through the contents until I find a Snickers. I rip open the wrapper and take a bite, then hold it out to her. "Want some?"

She wrinkles up her nose. "It's ten o'clock in the morning."

"So? It's never too early for chocolate."

"I don't share food with people."

"What, are you worried about germs? Because I think it's a little late for that after what happened last night, don't you?" I give her a grin.

"Get out," she commands, pointing toward the door. "Or I'm going to call security."

"Ooooh, good idea," I say. I plop down on her bed and take another bite of my candy bar. "And what will you tell them?"

"That an annoying jerk won't get out of my room."

I roll my eyes at her. "Relax," I say. "I'm going." I polish off the rest of the candy bar and drop the wrapper into the trash. I'm halfway to the door and trying to think of an excuse to stay, when she speaks.

"Wait!" she says. "You need to pay for that."

I reach into my pocket and pull out a few more bills, then drop them onto the desk. "You should be careful," I say, "if you really are running away."

There's no sarcasm in my voice because I really am worried about her. She can't run away. She hardly has any street smarts. And I highly doubt her high heels are going to protect her from any robbers and miscreants that she might encounter out on the road.

"Yeah, well," she says. "You don't have to worry about me."

"Oh, I'm not *worried* about you. I just—"

She gives me a look, silencing me. Then she plops herself down on the bed. She bites her lip and pushes her hair out of her face, and then a second later, she's crying.

Shit. I hate when chicks cry. I never know what to do. You can never tell if they're crying about something that's actually important, of if they're upset because their jeans don't fit.

I move back into the room and sit down next to her on the bed, making sure there's a sliver of space between us. I cannot allow myself to get too close to her. If I'm too close to her, something might happen. Thinking about getting close to her and something happening makes me think about last night, about what did happen, after the wedding, after the champagne, after the two of us were alone. And then, of course, I think about how it ended.

"What's wrong?" I ask her gently.

"What's *wrong*?" Peyton yells and then sits up, grabbing for the tissues that are sitting on the nightstand. "What's *wrong* is that I'm supposed to be running away from home, and my friend, the one who was supposed to help me, she . . . she . . . she got caught and now I'm going to have to call my parents and tell them what happened!"

Wow. She's kind of hysterical.

"Why do you have to call your parents?" I ask.

She looks at me like I'm stupid. "Because!" She jumps up and starts pacing around the room, like she has so much energy that she can't take it. I'm a little disappointed that she's not sitting next to me anymore, but it's most likely for the best. I really have no self-control, and I probably would have tried to kiss her. It's one of my character defects. The lack of self-control, I mean. (Although I guess the fact that I want to kiss a girl who completely broke my heart and who hates me could also be considered a character defect.)

"Because why?"

"Because they thought that Brooklyn was flying into Florida, and that we were going to rent a car and drive to North Carolina, checking out colleges on the way, and then fly home to Connecticut together next week."

"But you were really running away."

"Right." She sniffs. "We were going to spend the summer in North Carolina. Brooklyn knows a boy there, and I . . ." She trails off, then shakes her head, obviously not wanting to tell me the reason she's going.

I shrug. "So why not just call your parents and tell them Brooklyn couldn't come and get you, and that you don't want to go by yourself? Tell them you need a plane ticket home. They might be annoyed, but they're not going to be pissed. It's not your fault she bailed."

She puts her back against the wall and slides down until she's sitting in a heap on the floor. "But then I'll actually have to go home," she says.

"So?"

"So!" She throws her hands up in the air, and I'm reminded of another reason why I don't like her. She's overly dramatic, even for a girl. "I was running away!"

"Yeah, I get it. But that plan's changed now. So call your parents. You can run away some other time."

She snorts. "Whatever," she says. "I should have known better than to expect you to understand."

"What's that supposed to mean?"

"Never mind," she says. "Just get out of here." Whatever it was that made her want to confide in me before is gone, and now she's back to being her old, bratty self. Reason number five things won't work out with us: She runs hot and cold. (Obviously I need to stop listing the reasons things won't work out. It's kind of depressing. And at some point, I'm going to lose count.)

"No, I want to know what you meant by that."

"Just that you've never dealt with anything hard in your life."

"I've dealt with hard things before," I say. But even as I'm saying the words, I know they're kind of a lie. My parents are together—happily in love. They're not rich like Peyton's parents, but they make enough money so that I can shop at Abercrombie once in a while and drive around in a (used) Nissan Sentra. I'm the starting forward on the school basketball team. I've never really had a problem getting girls, and I'm going to be valedictorian at my graduation tomorrow. (I have to give a stupid speech and everything, and my mom's all excited about it. I'm actually kind of dreading the speech. The whole graduation thing just seems so pointless, a big charade that's supposed to make you feel good about yourself, when everyone knows that in reality, high school is just one big sham.)

"Oh yeah?" Peyton asks. "Like what?" She smirks. "I'd love to know all these torturous things you've been dealing with."

"Like I'm really going to tell you." I stand up, because I'm starting to realize that this is pointless. Peyton hates me. And I'm not going to put myself out there for a girl who hates me, and who I don't even like. "Well, good luck."

"Thanks." She's still sitting there, her dress in a pool around her on the floor. She looks small and vulnerable, and I remember what it was like to kiss her last night, how her hair felt in my hands, how soft her skin was. What the fuck is wrong with me? I just said I was done with her, and now I'm thinking about kissing her again? I sigh.

"Listen," I say, kneeling down next to her. "Let me take you home."

She looks up at me, her eyes shining. "What?"

"I'll drive you home."

"You'll drive me *home*? I live in Connecticut."

"I know where you live," I say, rolling my eyes.

"You have your car?" she asks.

I nod. "Yes."

"And you'd drive all that way for me?"

"Not *for* you." I shake my head. "I wanted to check out a college up there anyway. This gives me an excuse." It's a lie, of course. But I can't let her know that I'm desperate to keep her with me, that once I leave this room, once we're apart, I don't know when I'm going to see her again, and that the thought is too much for me to take.

"But I thought you were going to Georgetown in the fall."

"How did you know that?"

"Facebook." She blushes, but points her nose in the air, all haughty. "What?" she asks. "I'm not allowed to look at your Facebook page? It's not like it's private or anything."

"I don't care if you look at my Facebook." I shrug. "And Georgetown's not definite." Another lie.

"So you'll drop me off somewhere along the way?" she asks. She pulls at the bottom of her skirt nervously. "Because like I said, I wasn't really planning on going home."

"No." I shake my head. "I'll drive you home, but that's

it. I'm not getting involved in any kind of weird running-away plan. Your parents would kill me. Not to mention, I'd be kidnapping a minor."

She rolls her eyes, already wiping her tears away, already standing back up and smoothing down her dress. "Fine," she says, biting her lip. "But first I have to change." She crosses to the middle of the room and starts going through her suitcase, pulling out clothes and setting them on the bed until she finds what she wants, and then packing everything back up.

"Do you have to call your parents or anything?" she asks as she walks into the bathroom and shuts the door.

I try not to think about what she's doing in there, mainly taking off her clothes. "Call my parents?"

"Yeah," she yells through the door, "so that you can tell them you're not going to be home for a while."

"Oh, right."

"Are they going to be okay with it?"

"My parents don't run my life," I scoff. "They'll be fine with it."

And the lies just keep on coming.

peyton before

Saturday, May 22, 12:23 p.m.
Greenwich, Connecticut

Here are the reasons I hate going shopping with my mom:

1. **She always wants me to buy things I don't like.**
2. **She's always insisting I show her how the clothes look on me, even when I tell her they're hideous and don't need to be seen outside of the privacy of my dressing room.**
3. **It makes me feel fat.**

"Peyton, please tell me you don't need the size eight," my mom calls from the dressing room across from me. We're in Nordstrom, which is one of the worst stores in which to try on clothes, because they have this whole area where you can come out and twirl around in front of a four-way mirror. That is just wrong.

"I don't need the size eight," I call back. "The six fits just fine." I open the door and hold the dress out to the salesgirl, who gives me a wink as she takes it out of my hand.

"I'll be right back with the eight," she mouths.

"Thank you," I whisper back gratefully. She's just out of sight when my mom emerges from her dressing room.

"What do you think?" she asks. She's clad in a tight black dress that hits just above the knee. It's sleeveless, but classy, with a cowl neck and a sexy zigzag pattern worked into the fabric.

"You look great, Mom," I tell her. And she does. My mom's body is amazing, especially for someone who's had two children. Of course, she works hard at it, with tons of pilates and spinning and Zumba and those crossfit groups that are oh-so-trendy right now. Every morning at five she's out the door, clad in spandex, a towel thrown over her shoulder, a water bottle in her hand, ready to spend the next two hours sweating at the gym. She's always trying to get me to go with her, but I refuse. What kind of crazy person is up at five in the morning? There are worse things in the world than being a size eight.

"But do you think black is too somber for a wedding?" She turns this way and that, inspecting herself in the mirror, admiring the way she looks.

For about the tenth time since we started shopping, I wish my older sister Kira was here. Kira's into fashion, and she always knows what to say to my mom in these situations. Plus Kira makes shopping fun, joining me as we roll our eyes behind my mom's back and sneak the clothes we really want up to the cash register. But Kira's away at college, and so I'm stuck fielding my mom's questions by myself.

I don't really know a ton about the rules of fashion, but I do know that my mom expects me to answer, even if I don't really know what I'm talking about. And I also know enough that, since we're shopping for an outdoor summer wedding, in Florida, black might not be the best choice. "Well," I say slowly, "it *is* a summer wedding, and the ceremony's outside, so maybe you should look for something a little brighter."

Her face falls for a moment, but then she's back to smiling. "You're right!" she says. "Maybe something in tangerine. Although it would be shame not to get this one, too. I can always find somewhere to wear a little black dress!" She laughs like this is some kind of joke, and I giggle along with her, even though it's not really that funny.

The salesgirl reappears holding a size eight of the fluttery grey dress I just tried on. She looks back and forth between my mom and me nervously, like she's worried my mom is going to catch her with the bigger dress. But my mom's already forgotten about what happened a few moments ago.

"Nora," she says, even though the salesgirl's name is Nicole. "Nora, please fetch us some dresses in bright colors. I want tangerine, green, pink, yellow . . . but nothing peach.

It washes my daughter out." She flutters her hand at all the dresses that are littering the floor and bench of the dressing room. "And take these things away. They're all wrong. Wrong, wrong, wrong!" She giggles again.

"Of course," Nicole says, scurrying into the dressing room to gather the clothes.

"I think I'm going to go out and choose some things myself," I yell to my mom. I'm back in my own dressing room now, changing into my jeans and T-shirt. There's silence from the other side of the door, and I can tell I've said the wrong thing.

"Honey, they have people to do that sort of thing for you," she says. "This is Nordstrom, not JCPenney."

"I know," I say, keeping my voice light. "Sometimes I just like to do it myself."

"Okay," she says. But I can hear the disappointment in her voice. The disappointment that means I'm not doing what she wants. The disappointment that seems to be directed at me more and more lately.

I walk out of the stuffy air of the dressing room and back into the store, where Nicole is busy flicking through a rack of pale-green sundresses.

"Sorry about my mom," I say, rolling my eyes. "I wish I could say that's not like her, but it totally is."

Nicole smiles. "Oh, no," she says. "It's no problem at all. I always want to make my customers happy."

I smile back, even though I'm sure it's a completely

canned response and that she secretly wants to throttle us and then start wandering the aisles, looking for something that's both bright and fun and won't make me look like a sausage.

My phone starts vibrating in my purse, and I fish it out. Courtney. My cousin. It's her dad, my mom's brother, who's getting married in a few weeks.

"Hey," I say. "What's up?" Courtney's a year older than me, just finishing up her freshman year at Boston University. Her family lives in Florida, and so we've never gotten the chance to be super close, but we're still pretty good friends. It's never uncomfortable to talk to her, and whenever I see her we always have an amazing time.

"Hey, Peyton," she says. "What's going on?"

"Just out shopping for your dad's wedding," I reply, watching as Nicole disappears into the dressing room holding an armful of outfits that my mom is sure to veto. "What's up with you?"

"Not much," she says. "Are you finding anything good?"

"Not yet," I say. I move a couple of more steps away from the dressing room, just in case my mom can hear. "We're in Nordstrom and my mom's acting like she's in Prada or something. She keeps making the salesgirl go out and fetch things for her."

Courtney laughs. "That sounds like Aunt Michelle."

"Yeah, well, I'm picking out my own stuff, thank you very much."

"Good for you," Courtney says. She clears her throat. "Um, so the reason I'm calling is that I need to talk to you about something."

"Okay," I say. Sure enough, Nicole's coming out of the dressing room, her arms loaded up with the dresses she just brought in there. My mom, I'm sure, sent her right back out, saying that none of them were right without even trying them on. I swear, sometimes I think she does things like that just to be a diva.

"Well," Courtney says, "remember when the invitations came out for my dad's wedding? And you sent me that Facebook message asking me if Jace was coming?"

As soon as she says his name, my heart skips from my stomach up into my throat. "Yes," I say, trying to sound nonchalant. "I remember."

"Well, at the time I said no, because my dad told me that the Renaults were going to be out of town. I guess they'd had some big trip to Europe planned for, like, years. And since my dad's wedding was slightly spur-of-moment, it was really too late for them to cancel."

"Right," I say. "I remember you told me that." I remember everything Courtney told me about Jace's Europe trip, because I remember everything about Jace. The way his hair flopped over his forehead. The way his smile curled up more on one side than on the other. The way he loved to debate me on everything from politics to the difference between McDonald's and Burger King. The way he smelled like peppermint and shaving cream, even though when I was kissing him it always seemed like his face was slightly scruffy.

"Well, it turns out the Renaults are coming after all. Something about the dollar not being strong enough, and figuring out a way to waive the cancellation fees. Or something." Courtney pauses, and my world stops. "Peyton?" she asks. "Are you there?"

"Yes." I lick my suddenly dry lips, and then sit down right there in the middle of the floor.

"Listen," Courtney says. "I'm sorry to spring this on you. I know how it feels to have to see a guy you have a weird thing with. If this same thing had happened to me and Jordan a year ago then I'd—"

"No," I lie, cutting her off. "It's not weird. It's totally fine. And me and Jace are nothing like you and Jordan." This part, at least, is true. Courtney and her boyfriend Jordan were together for like, months before he broke up with her and totally broke her heart. They got back together after that, but to compare what Courtney and Jordan have with what Jace and I have (had? never had? should have had?) is ridiculous. Jace and I have only met once, when I was in Florida over Christmas. And yeah, it was the most intense experience I've ever had with a guy, but still. That isn't saying much, since he lives hundreds of miles away. (And since my experience with guys is pretty limited.)

"Okay," Courtney says, not sounding so sure. "But if you decided you didn't want to come to the wedding, I would totally understand. And my dad would too. I could just tell him that—"

"Oh, no," I say. "It's fine, I promise. I'm still going."

"Okay." She pauses. "Well, I just thought I'd let you know."

"Thanks."

"So what else is new?"

"Not much. I'm just waiting for—"

"Ta-da!" my mom yells, waltzing out into the middle of the store. She's wearing a long yellow dress that's so tight it looks like it might be cutting off her circulation. The bottom flares out, mermaid style. The dress looks amazing on her, but I don't know if it's really appropriate for a wedding.

"Peyton?" Courtney asks.

"Yeah, I'm here," I say. "Can I call you back?"

"Sure."

I hang up the phone and walk slowly over to my mom. "Wow," I say. "It's very . . . different."

"Isn't it?" She's raising her voice now, and I can tell it's because she wants everyone in the store to start looking at her. Which people are. Sort of. And not necessarily in a good way. "Nora, darling, do you think I should wear a hat with this?"

That's when I notice that Nicole is standing behind her, looking a little dazed. "Ummm . . ." She looks at me for guidance, knowing she better give my mom the answer she wants. I nod my head slightly.

"Yes, definitely," Nicole says, smiling. "A hat would set this dress off just beautifully. And it would be perfect for an outdoor wedding."

My mom beams. "Thank you, Noreen," she says. "Can you please go and pick out an assortment of hats for me to try on?"

Nicole scuttles away.

My mom looks at me, finally realizing that I'm not holding any dresses. "Peyton!" she says. "You haven't even picked out one dress!"

I sigh, suddenly feeling defeated. This wedding is turning into kind of a debacle. I mean, let's assess the situation, shall we?

First, if I'm being completely honest, I kind of hate weddings. All those people celebrating a couple that most of them don't even really know that well, and who will probably be divorced in less than ten years. It's more depressing than happy when you really think about it.

Second, I'm going to have to buy some stupid dress that I don't really want, mostly because my mom wants me to have it.

And third, Jace Renault is going to be there. Jace Renault, the only boy I've ever dared to let myself care about. Jace Renault, who I've only seen once in my life, and who still somehow managed to break my heart.

"Mom," I try, "I was thinking, maybe I should stay home while you guys go to Florida. I could watch the house and you wouldn't have to worry about buying me a plane ticket. That way—"

"You most certainly will not stay home!" she says. "This is a big day for your uncle, and I know he would be hurt if you weren't there."

I sigh. "But, Mom," I say, "I'm going to be so bored. And you and Dad—"

"Peyton," she says. "You're going. And that's final."

"Fine," I say. I consider adding, *You'll be sorry,* but I'm old enough to realize that would be pretty immature. Of course, if I thought it would make a difference, I'd say it anyway, immature or not. But it won't. She's made up her mind, and that's that.

So instead, I walk toward another rack of dresses. If I'm going to have to see Jace Renault, I might as well make sure I look amazing.

jace before

Saturday, May 22, 1:21 p.m.
Sarasota, Florida

I'm hanging out at my friend Evan's house when my phone rings. The caller ID flashes a number I don't recognize, and so I hesitate. Usually I don't pick up numbers I don't recognize. It's almost never a good idea. Bill collectors, girls you don't want to talk to . . . these are the kinds of people who call from blocked numbers.

But since Evan just informed me that he wants to jump off the roof of his house and into the pool, and I don't necessarily feel like dealing with that, I answer it.

"Jace?" a girl's voice asks.

"Who's this?" I ask, deciding it's best not to give too much away just yet.

"Who is it?" Evan asks. He's busy fastening some kind of ramp together on the other side of the pool. I have no idea why he needs a ramp if he's going to be jumping off the roof, but whatever.

"Who is this?" I ask again, motioning for Evan to be quiet. Like it's going to do any good.

"It's Courtney," the girl says.

"Oh," I say, relieved. "Hey, Courtney."

"Courtney!" Evan abandons his ramp and runs over to where I'm sitting on the patio. Cold water drips from his hair onto the pavement. He's wet because he cannonballed into the pool as soon as I got here, so he could "figure out how deep I'll end up."

"Dude," I say, shaking my head at him. "No offense, but you're kind of disgusting."

"Courtney," Evan says, grabbing the phone away from me without even asking. "Do you want to come over? I'm building a ramp and I'm going to either skateboard off it into my pool or possibly jump off the roof, and then I'm going to send the tape into MTV so they can—What? No, this is Evan. . . .Yeah, I know you have a boyfriend, but didn't that douchebag Jordan break up with you?" He snorts. "Right, and you really think he's changed, huh? . . . Well, whatever. If you change your mind, let me know."

He throws the phone back to me and then does another cannonball into the pool. Freezing water splashes into the air and lands all over my shirt.

"Hey," I say to Courtney. "Sorry about that."

"That's okay," she says. I guess you could say Courtney

and I are friends—her parents and my parents have been best friends for like five years. They tried to hook us up once when we were fourteen, but it didn't work out. At all. Mostly because it just wasn't right. Courtney's cute and smart, but we just didn't click in that way. There were no hard feelings, though, and we've always been friendly. But we're not the type of friends who just call each other out of the blue, so there must be something she wants to talk to me about.

"So what's up?" I ask. I stay on the patio but move as far away from the pool as possible. I need to be able to see Evan just in case he needs to be rescued from some sort of calamitous situation.

"So this might be weird," Courtney says, "and I really don't want to come across like I'm being a bitch or getting involved in your business."

"Is your mom still mad about the Christmas party?" I ask, sighing. I really do not want to get all caught up in *that* again.

Courtney's parents got divorced not that long ago, which was this huge scandal, because *my* mom wanted to stay friends with *Courtney's* mom, but then Courtney's mom said she wouldn't be friends with my parents unless they stopped hanging out with Courtney's dad. Everything came to a head when Courtney's dad threw this Christmas party, and my parents went, and Courtney's mom got all mad at them. The whole thing is completely ridiculous, if you ask me. Which, of course, nobody ever does.

"No, no, it's not about that," Courtney says. "It's, um . . . look, I know this is probably none of my business, and you can feel free to tell me to screw off. But Jace, what happened between you and Peyton?"

"Peyton?" I take in a deep breath through my nose. I don't want to think about Peyton. I don't want to talk about Peyton. I don't even want to hear Peyton's name.

"Yeah."

"Nothing happened." I shrug, even though Courtney can't see me. "I hardly even remember her. What's she up to now, anyway?"

"Okkkayy," Courtney says, not sounding convinced. And who would blame her? I'm not even convincing myself.

"Hey!" Evan calls from somewhere over my head. "Up here! Look at me!"

I shade my eyes from the sun with my hand and peer up at the roof. Evan's standing there in a bathing suit and a pair of neon-green goggles, a huge grin on his face. "What the hell are you doing?" I ask. "Are you fucking crazy? Get down from there."

"Go get the camera!" he yells, pointing over to the side of the pool where he's left the camcorder.

"No way." I shake my head. "You're going to split your head open."

"Courtney!" he screams. "This one's for you!" And then he starts pounding his fists against his bare chest like he's Tarzan or some shit.

"What's going on over there?" Courtney asks, sounding worried.

"Nothing," I say, sighing. "It's too much to get into right now. But, um, I kind of have to go. Is there anything else?"

"Yeah," she says. "I just wanted to let you know that Peyton's going to be coming to the wedding."

"Whatever," I say, shrugging again. Apparently this has become my thing. Shrugging without anyone there to see it. I am now shrugging for my own benefit. What will be next? I wonder. Shaking my head no when I want to get a thought out of my head? I try it. But I'm still thinking about Peyton. Her long hair. The way she would bite her lip when she was thinking about something. The way her body was curvy and perfect and made me want to hold her close and protect her. Jesus. All this for a girl I've only met once.

"So it's all good then?" Courtney's asking. "You don't mind that she's coming?"

"Of course I don't mind that she's coming," I lie. "She's your cousin."

And then something occurs to me. If Courtney's calling me to see how I feel about Peyton being at the wedding, she's probably called *Peyton* to see how Peyton feels about *me* being at the wedding. It only makes sense. It's like girl code or whatever. (Which I've never understood, by the way. Girls going around screaming about girl code, when girls are the ones who'll stab each other in the back the first chance they get. Dudes aren't like that. Take Evan, for example. He's up on the roof, shirtless, wearing green goggles and getting ready to possibly kill himself, and what am I doing? I'm sitting here, like a good friend, trying to talk him out of it, while at the same time being willing to film the whole thing if it comes down to it. Now that's what's called being a good friend.)

"Why?" I ask Courtney. "What did Peyton say about me?"

"Nothing."

"Nothing?" From up on the roof, there's the sound of something sloshing around, and then a bunch of water comes sliding down and onto the patio.

"Yes," Courtney says simply. "Nothing."

"Are you sure?" I ask accusingly. "She said *nothing*?"

"She just said she didn't care if you were there."

"She didn't *care* if I was there?"

"That's what she said." I want to ask Courtney what *exactly* Peyton said, but then I realize that hearing Peyton doesn't care is probably enough, especially if I want to protect my mental state.

"Well, whatever," I say. "I'm coming to the wedding. And you don't have to worry about me and Peyton."

"Great," she says, sounding relieved.

We hang up and I look toward the roof warily. Water is still pouring down in rivulets, pooling on the patio in front of me. "Evan?" I call.

"Yes?" He appears at the top of the roof, dripping wet, an empty plastic milk jug in his hand.

"What the *hell* are you doing?"

"I told you," he says. "I'm going to be jumping off this roof and you're going to be filming me."

"But why are you soaking wet? And why are you holding an empty milk jug in your hand?"

"Because," he says, looking at me like I'm the stupid one, "I needed to get my body accustomed to the water by wetting myself with it. I can't just jump in without knowing what I'm getting myself into it. I might get hypothermia or something."

"So you brought a jug of water up and poured it over your head?"

"A jug of pool water," he reports proudly.

"But you were already in the pool," I say. "Why did you have to wet yourself all over again?"

He frowns. "I don't know."

"Listen," I say. "I think you should—"

But before I can stop him, he jumps off the roof and into the water. He does a huge cannonball, and the splash soaks me.

He surfaces at the side of the pool. "Holy shit," he says. "What a rush!" He hoists himself up and onto the patio. "That was just practice, of course."

"Oh, of course." I ring out the bottom of my T-shirt.

"Now you'll film me, right?" He picks up the camera

and shoves it into my hands, then starts heading back to the front of the house so he can get back on the roof.

I flip the camera's power switch to on, and the little red light starts blinking. I sigh. Maybe there's something to that girl code bullshit after all.

peyton — the trip

Saturday, June 26, 10:47 a.m.
Siesta Key, Florida

Jace is so obviously trying not to let me hear the phone call with his mom, but I can still tell that it's not going so well.

The conversation, a summary:

Jace: Oh, hi, Mom, I just wanted to let you know that I'm with Peyton in her hotel room. The thing is—
Jace's mom: What?! You're with a girl in her hotel room? What are you doing in there? Leave at once!
Jace: No, no, it's fine, we're not doing anything. The thing is, Mom, her parents kind of abandoned her here, and so I'm going to be driving her home.
Jace's mom: Oh, okay, honey. That sounds fine. Where does she live?

Jace: Connecticut.

Jace's mom: WHAT?! **(Begins to freak out and maybe even swear.)**

At this point, Jace leaves the room and walks outside. Of course I can't really be sure of what his mom is saying since I'm hearing it through Jace's cell phone from where I'm changing in the bathroom. So that conversation is pretty much made-up. But still. It's what I imagined, and it's probably scarily accurate.

I look at myself in the huge mirror that's mounted over the double sinks, then run a brush through my hair before changing into a pair of shorts and a soft pink tank top. I take a deep breath, then another and another, trying to calm down and force my heart to stop beating so fast.

It'll be fine, I tell myself. *You'll have Jace drive you where you need to go, and then you can ditch him at a rest stop or something and take a cab to the place you're going to be staying in North Carolina.*

Of course, it's definitely kind of weird to be going without Brooklyn, since I don't know anyone in North Carolina. But there's no way I can go home. Not now. Maybe not ever.

I grab my purse and set it down on the marble countertop, then pull out the brochure from the rental condo that the listing agent sent us a few days ago. The condo was one of the only places that would let you rent if you were under twenty-one, and even then Brooklyn had to sign the rental agreement, since she's eighteen and I'm not.

CREVE COEUR it says on the front of the brochure, and I run my fingers over the letters, over the name of my new building. "Creve Coeur" means broken heart in French. Brooklyn and I both agreed that was a weird name for a condo complex, especially one that's touted as "relaxing and tranquil; only a short drive to the shore!" But whatever. In a way, it was actually pretty fitting. Almost like a sign or something.

When we came up with the plan to go away, Brooklyn had just broken up with her boyfriend, Trevor, who she'd been with for a year and a half. She broke up with him because she said the two of them had nothing to talk about anymore. She cried in her room for two days straight, and I comforted her, although I couldn't figure out how broken her heart could have been when she was the one who broke up with him. If she was so hurt, then why didn't she just call him up and tell him she wanted to get back together?

It wasn't like me and Jace. He had been the one who wanted to end things—not that there was even a thing to end, because it wasn't really like that—so I always felt like my broken heart was a little more serious than Brooklyn's.

Not that I ever told her that. And to her credit, she *had* been with Trevor for a year and a half, while I had only ever seen Jace, um, once. Which is horribly embarrassing when you think about it. That I'd gotten all worked up over a guy I'd only ever spent time with once.

But I read a very smart thing in a self-help book (don't judge—they can actually be very comforting) about how sometimes the people you don't spend that much time with are actually the ones you can end up getting the most hurt by, because you can get attached to the *idea* of them, as opposed to who they really are. You don't get enough time to really get to know them and their flaws, which is why you can sort of create this fantasy of who they are, and therefore indulge all your hopes and dreams of who you wanted them to be.

It was a very smart book.

Anyway, Brooklyn had just broken up with Trevor, and even though I didn't exactly understand how she could be so upset, it ended up working out to my advantage. Because when I came up with the idea of going away for the summer, Brooklyn immediately jumped on it, getting all excited, and even suggesting North Carolina. Which was fine with me. I didn't have a preference about where we went, just as long as it was far away from Connecticut.

Brooklyn knew a boy in North Carolina, a boy she'd met on a vacation to Myrtle Beach a couple years ago, a boy she'd somehow kept in touch with. They'd been talking a little since she broke up with Trevor, and I think she was looking for a rebound.

So North Carolina became the plan, and I let Brooklyn

believe I wanted to go just so I could get away from thinking about Jace.

She still has no idea what the real reason is that I wanted to leave home. I thought about telling her, I did. I thought about telling Brooklyn, or my sister, or maybe even my dad. But I didn't. I *couldn't*.

"Peyton?" Jace knocks on the bathroom door.

I shove the Creve Coeur brochure back into my purse. "Yes?" I open the door.

"We're all set!" he says with a smile. "I'm ready to drive you back to Connecticut."

"Are you sure?" I push by him and into the room. "Because it didn't sound like your mom was all that thrilled about it."

"My mom was fine with it."

"Really? Because it sounded like you two were fighting."

"We weren't fighting," he says. "And why were you spying on my phone call?"

"I wasn't eavesdropping on your phone call." I sit down on the bed and then slide my feet into the flip-flops that are sitting on the floor. I really want to wear my sparkly sandals with the low heel, but they're probably not road-trip appropriate. Not to mention I don't want Jace to think I'm trying to impress him. Or that I'm high maintenance.

"If you weren't listening, then how do you know what my mom was saying?" Jace asks.

"I don't know for sure," I say. "But I could hear her voice all the way in the bathroom, so I kind of got the gist."

"I'm a grown man," Jace says, puffing out his chest. "I can take my car wherever I want."

"Really?" I ask. "And who pays for that car?"

Jace glares at me. "Whatever," he says. "Forget it. You can find your own way home."

And that's when I panic. "Hey," I say. "Look, I'm sorry." But he's moving toward the door, and as much as I don't want to, I follow him. I grab his arm just as he's about to walk out, and little sparks zip up my fingers. "Don't go."

He stops, and then, after a beat, he turns around. "Are you going to stop being such a brat?"

"Yes," I say. "I'm sorry." It's not the complete truth. I'm kind of sorry I was a jerk to him, but at the same time, he really does deserve it. On the other hand, just because he broke my heart doesn't mean I should be a bitch to him. I should rise above it, two wrongs don't make a right, you catch more bees with honey or whatever and blah blah blah. Besides, like it or not, right now I need him to take me to North Carolina.

"Truce?" I say, and hold my hand out.

He takes it, his fingers wrapping around mine, making the electricity that's already zinging through me multiply. "Truce," he says.

He holds my hand for a few seconds longer than is really necessary, and we're just standing there, staring at each other, my hand in his, and oh, my God, I want to kiss him so badly it's almost painful.

"Peyton," he says, and he's running his finger over my hand in a little circle, and it's making my body freak out in all the best ways. And for a second, I think he's going to tell me that he's sorry, that he can't believe he ever let me go, that he thinks we should just start over and maybe even be together, that he made a mistake and can I ever forgive him? But then he drops my hand.

"Are you ready to go?" he asks.

I nod, and he moves past me and back into the room, picking up the bags that are sitting on the floor. I feel like a balloon that has been deflated. *Get yourself together, Peyton,* I tell myself as I shoulder my bag and follow Jace out of the room. *Jace Renault is not for you. He's bad news. And thinking anything different, even for a second, is just going to get you hurt.*

the trip jace

Saturday, June 26, 10:59 a.m.
Siesta Key, Florida

Peyton is shady. And not just because she was listening in on my phone call, either. Which, by the way, was none of her business. I'm a grown-ass man. If I want to take my car up to Connecticut, it's none of my mom's business. And it doesn't matter that my mom pays for my car. That's a completely inconsequential fact.

I'm eighteen, and the car is in my name. Which means that if we were in a court of law, she couldn't legally stop me from doing anything I wanted with it. I know my rights. I watch those law shows on TV. (What? They're good. And sometimes there's nothing else on, especially when I'm skipping school.)

Of course, my mom did flip out, mostly because I have graduation tomorrow night and I'm supposed to give a speech since I'm valedictorian. And my mom got all freaked out and started screaming because she thought I wasn't going to be back in time to attend. And so I told her very calmly that I probably wouldn't be. I never wanted to give that stupid graduation speech, anyway. That's when she started screaming some more, and so that's when I hung up on her.

But anyway.

Peyton is shady for lots of reasons, but right now she's shady because she's running away. I don't know much about her family life—she never wanted to let me in on that kind of thing, which is a completely different story—but her mom seems nice enough, if you like those MILF types. Not that I want to bang her mom—cougars aren't really my thing—but I bet Evan would be all over it. So then why is Peyton running away? The summer right before she's supposed to start her senior year? What could be so bad that she can't last at home for one more year before she goes off to college?

I know she has a nice house. I know because I've seen pictures of it—pictures that she sent me. One is of her and her friend Brooklyn, sitting by the fireplace around Christmastime, wearing elf hats, their arms thrown around each other, beaming at the camera. And a couple of, um, more risqué ones she sent me of her in a bathing suit out by her pool. The whole place looked pretty nice.

So then what's her problem? Is she just one of those girls who writes people off without any real reason? Like maybe she and her parents got into some dumb fight about something, and now she's running away?

"Be careful with that one," she instructs as I load one of her suitcases into the trunk of my car. "It has a lot of important things in it."

"Yeah?" I say, tossing it into the trunk. "Like what?"

She glares at me and then starts rearranging all her bags, putting them just so. "Like my computer."

"Oh," I say. "Right. Your computer. We wouldn't want your Twitter log-in getting lost or anything, that's for sure."

"Sorry," she says. "But I don't go on Twitter anymore. Twitter is the new Myspace. I mean, how totally 2011." She wrinkles up her nose, like she's talking about some stupid website for tweens instead of a multibillion dollar website that has become the center of the social media network and changed our culture and the world forever. What a snob.

"Right." I nod and slam the trunk shut. "Well, then, we wouldn't want anyone getting access to any of your personal pictures."

She nods, looking confused for a second. And then understanding dawns on her face. She looks at me in horror. "You better have deleted those."

"Deleted what?" I give her a fake innocent look, which seems to infuriate her.

"You know what I'm talking about." For a second, I think she's going to hold her hand out or something and demand I give them back. Which would be ridiculous. You can't give someone back a digital picture. "Those pictures I texted you."

I pull my phone out and scroll to the one of her in the elf hat. "Oh, you mean this one?" I chuckle and shake my head. "But you look so cute in it!"

She reaches for my phone and I'm so caught off-guard that she's actually able to take it away from me. I'm All-State in basketball, and this chick is actually somehow able to get my phone.

She starts scrolling through the pictures. "I'm deleting the one of me in the elf hat!" she announces.

"Give me that," I say, reaching for it. The thing is, I did delete her stupid bathing suit photos a day after she sent them to me, just like she made me promise. Of course, that was when I was acting like some lovesick schoolboy instead of a grown-ass man who drives his own car wherever he wants.

"No!" she says. "Not until I make sure you deleted those pictures."

I reach for the phone again, but she runs away from me, around toward the front of the car. Now she's standing in front of the hood, and I'm in the back, trying to get at her—it's like some kind of new game, halfway between chicken and freeze tag. An older couple goes walking by and gives us disapproving looks, like they can't believe what the youth of America are up to these days.

"Peyton Miller," I say real loud, "you better give me my

phone back! It's your own fault that you were sexting me inappropriate pictures. If you didn't want me to have them then you shouldn't have sent them."

The older couple looks at us, horrified.

Peyton glares at me and then holds my phone up over her head, like she's going to smash it.

"Put that down!" I yell.

"Ooh, what's wrong?" she says. "Mommy and Daddy won't buy you another one?"

"You can't just go around smashing other people's property!" I say.

The old man and woman are past us now, and I can hear the old man asking his wife what sexting means.

"Take back what you said about me sexting you," Peyton says.

"I take it back." She lowers the phone. "Even though you did."

The phone goes back up over her head.

"Okay, okay," I say, holding my hands up in surrender. "I'm sorry, you're right, you didn't sext me."

She lowers my phone slowly, giving me a chance to take back what I just said. But I don't. "Good," she says. "Because a bathing suit picture hardly counts as a sext." Her face is flushed red, though, and I can tell she's embarrassed thinking about it. I'm a little flushed, too, thinking about it, although not because I'm embarrassed.

I walk around the car toward her and hold my hand

out. But when I get there, she's looking down at the screen.

"Is that her?" She holds it up, and I swallow hard. There's a picture of Kari on the screen, her hair all blond and wild in a ponytail after one of her lacrosse games.

"Yes," I say, taking the phone from her and shoving it in my pocket. "That's Kari."

"She's pretty," Peyton says. For a second, I see the flash of hurt in her eyes, but it's so quick that I wonder if I imagined it.

"Thanks," I say, which makes no sense. Why should I thank her for telling me that Kari is pretty? It's not like I'm responsible for Kari's prettiness.

"Are you ready to go?" Peyton asks. She looks up at me, and my heart catches. I want to explain to her, about what happened last night, about what happened over Christmas, about Kari, about everything. I open my mouth, and she rolls her eyes. "Well?" she demands. "Are you ready or not?"

"Yes," I say. "I'm ready. I just have to get my stuff out of my room. And Hector, too, of course."

She shakes her head. "Hector," she mumbles. "He's probably going to be the only good part of this trip."

before   peyton

Saturday, May 22, 4:37 p.m.
Greenwich, Connecticut

So once Courtney called and informed me that Jace was going to be at the wedding after all, I somehow ended up with a very sexy dress. It's this gorgeous turquoise color and it plunges down in the front, making my boobs look bigger than they already are. It's tight and short and has spaghetti straps and it makes my waist seem tiny.

I started grabbing dresses left and right after I hung up the phone, not even looking at prices. Which is why Nicole was ringing us up before I realized that the dress I picked out was eight hundred dollars. Eight hundred dollars. For a dress. My mom's dress was only five hundred. Of course, her hat was another two hundred, so really she ended up spending seven hundred, but still. That's a lot of money for dresses we're probably only going to wear once.

Then, of course, we had to get shoes, and by the time we left the mall, we'd spent close to two thousand dollars.

"Damn," Brooklyn says from my bed as I turn this way and that. It's later that afternoon, and she's come over to inspect my purchases. "That might have been the best eight hundred dollars your mom ever spent."

"You think?" Now that I'm home, I'm starting to feel that this dress might be a little too scandalous for a family wedding. That, and it maybe makes my butt look big.

"Yeah." Brooklyn nods. "You got it going on in that thing."

"Thanks." I run my hands over the shimmery material, not being able to stop myself from wondering what Jace is going to think when he sees me in it. He always told me how much he liked my body. But that could have been a lie. The same way everything else he told me was a lie.

"Uh-oh," Brooklyn says. "You're thinking about him again, aren't you?" She sighs, then reaches over and pinches me hard on the arm.

"Ow!" I say, pulling away from her. "What the hell was that for?"

"That was aversion therapy," she says. "Every time you think of Jace, I'm going to pinch you. And that way, after a while, you won't think about him anymore."

"Either that or I'll just be pissed off at you," I say, rubbing my arm. "And how do you know I was thinking about him?"

"Weren't you?"

"Yes," I admit. I throw myself forlornly down on the bed and stare up at the ceiling. "I was thinking about what he was going to think when he saw me in this dress."

"He's going to think that you look hot and that he made a huge mistake," Brooklyn says. "And he's not going to know what to do with himself."

"Really?" I smile, even though I know in my head that stuff like that only happens in movies and books. More than likely I'll end up at the wedding, looking absolutely phenomenal, and Jace will end up there too, and he'll see me in the dress, but he won't care.

Probably he'll have a new girl with him, or even worse, he'll find another girl at the wedding that he'll dance with all night. She'll be wearing the same dress as me, only hers will fit her even better because she'll be a lot skinnier than me, and it will turn out that Jace doesn't love my body as much as he said. That it was just a ruse to get me to send him a bikini picture.

The two of them will dance all night, and then they'll sneak off into the tropical night air of Florida so that they can—

"I told you that I needed to get a new dress for the wedding!" The sound of my mom's voice comes up the stairs, and I sit up, straining to hear what she's saying. Not like it's hard. She's practically screaming.

"And you couldn't wear one of the millions of dresses

you have in your closet?" my dad yells back. "Christ, Michelle, you spent two hundred dollars on a hat! Two hundred dollars! Do you even understand what money is?"

"Of course I understand what money is!" my mom screams. "How can I not when you keep reminding me of it every single second?"

"Then I don't understand how you could be confused," my dad says, and I hear the sound of them moving toward the back of the house. "If I say it as much as you think I do, then how can you not . . ."

Their voices fade away as my dad follows her around the house. I've seen this dance before. My mom spends money. My dad gets upset with her about it. She knows this, and so sometimes she'll come home and try to hide the stuff she's bought before he sees it. Sometimes he catches her, and then he flips out, following her around the house yelling at her.

The thing is, my parents are technically separated. Well, in the middle of a divorce, really. But they're still living in the same house, mostly because they can't afford to sell it right now—they owe more on the mortgage than it's worth. I'm not sure why my dad doesn't just move out and get an apartment, but I'm pretty sure his lawyer told him not to.

Brooklyn looks at me, her eyes anxious. "You okay?"

"Yeah." I sigh, feeling even more guilty about spending so much on a dress. I reach out and finger the material. "Maybe I should take this back."

Brooklyn stands up and shakes her head. "You know what you need?" she asks. "A burger from McGreedy's."

"No way. I'm not going to start eating a ton of fattening food before the wedding. I need to make sure I look like my most fabulous self."

Brooklyn rolls her eyes. "You've been watching too many Jennifer Hudson Weight Watchers commercials." She picks her purse up off my nightstand. "You already look fabulous. And there's no way you're going to let some guy—no, some *loser*—stop you from eating what might be the world's perfect burger."

I think about it. She is kind of right. I mean, it's not going to matter if I don't eat anything but lettuce from now until the wedding. Jace is probably going to act like a jerk no matter what I do, and then not only will I be all upset about it, but I won't even have been able to enjoy any really good food in the meantime.

"Can we get fries, too?" I ask, perking up.

"Yes."

"And afterward can we go and look at lip glosses?"

"Yes," Brooklyn says. She grins. "Just because you don't care enough about what Jace thinks to change your eating habits doesn't mean we shouldn't use him as an excuse to buy beauty products."

jace before

Saturday, May 25, 3:56 p.m.
Sarasota, Florida

Fucking Peyton Miller. Ever since Courtney called me earlier, Peyton is all I can think about. I keep looking at the dumb picture of her that I have in my phone. It's her and her friend Brooklyn sitting in front of the fireplace on Christmas wearing these goofy Santa hats. She has her hair pushed back from her face and she looks so adorable I almost can't take it.

"So then I jumped off the roof," Evan's saying, "and right into the pool."

"You didn't," Kari McAfee says.

"I did." Evan nods. "Jace got it all on video, didn't you, Jace?"

"Unfortunately, yes," I admit. I did get the whole thing on video. If it ever gets out I'll probably get sued or something.

Okay, that's going a little too far. But I would definitely get in trouble with Evan's parents.

"Next I want to do a prank." Evan takes a big bite of the hot dog he's eating. We're sitting on the bleachers at our school, watching one of the last baseball games of the season. Actually, I guess it's one of the last baseball games of my whole high school career. The thought should make me sad—I am valedictorian after all—but somehow, it doesn't. "You up for a prank, Jace?"

"What kind of prank?" I ask warily.

"I dunno." Evan shrugs and then shoves the rest of his hot dog into his mouth. "I saw this one on YouTube that had like a million hits. This dude filled his parents' house with bottles of water while they were on vacation. You know, he like, moved all the furniture out, everything. It was hi*lar*ious!"

"That sounds lame," I say. "And besides, your parents never go on vacation."

"We wouldn't have to do that exact one," Evan says, like it should be obvious. "We'd come up with something better."

"I think it sounds cool," Whitney Blue says. She scoots a little closer to Evan on the bleachers, and I tune them out as they start to talk about all the different pranks they might be able to do.

I shove my phone back into my pocket and try to get Peyton out of my thoughts. It's been three months since we've spoken. Three months. Three months is a lifetime.

She could be doing anything right now. She could have a boyfriend. A boyfriend who she's bringing to the wedding. A boyfriend I'll have to see her with. A knot forms in my stomach and I feel my fists clench as I think about having to see some asshole with his hands all over Peyton. Not that I would ever punch someone out. Well, that's not that true. I would if someone was hurting her.

"Penny for your thoughts?" a voice says. I turn to see Kari scooting closer to me on the bleachers. She holds out her container of nachos and I take one.

"Thanks," I say, grateful for the distraction. I drag the chip through the melted orange cheese and pop it in my mouth.

"So what's new?" she asks. Kari and I have been friends ever since sophomore year, when she transferred to our school from New York City. Everyone was afraid of her at first because she showed up wearing black jeans and a black sweater. Yes, we wear black in Florida, but not all black, and not with knee-high boots. Half the school thought she was going to fight them. Well, the girls at least. And maybe some of the boys.

"Not much," I say. "What's new with you?"

"Same old," she says. She flips her head over and gathers her long blond hair up in a ponytail. Kari totally assimilated to Florida, dying her hair blond and ditching the black clothes for the jeans-and-tank-top uniform of the Gulf Coast. She even joined the soccer team.

We lapse back into silence. "What's wrong with you?" she asks.

"Nothing," I say. "Why?"

"Because you're being all quiet," she says. She elbows me playfully in the side.

"I'm fine," I say, and shrug. "Just tired." I look out onto the field as Ian Walker strikes out. Everyone on our side of the bleachers groans. I roll my eyes. Ian Walker is a douche, and everyone knows it.

"Late night last night?" Kari asks.

"Not really," I say. I'm not much of a partier, and Kari knows it, so she's teasing me.

"Well, you should hang out with us tonight," she says. "Me and Whitney are having a slumber party, aren't we, Whit?" She turns and looks over her shoulder to where Whitney and Evan are sitting on the bleachers behind us.

"If you call just the two of us a slumber party," Whitney says.

"Oh, I definitely call that a slumber party," Evan says, raising his eyebrows up and down suggestively.

"You can come too," Whitney says to Evan. "We're having it at my house."

"Oh, really?" Evan licks his lips and rubs his hands together, like there's going to be all kinds of debauchery happening. Which is ridiculous. And kind of creepy.

But Whitney doesn't seem to mind. She giggles. "You

guys can't sleep over, though. We'll just watch movies or something."

Evan looks a little disappointed, like he thought he was going to actually be able to spend the night. Which is stupid for a few reasons, not the least of which is that Evan's mom is the strictest parent I know. I think that's maybe why he's always trying to do crazy stunts—it's like he's rebelling, only instead of doing drugs or alcohol, he takes chances with his safety.

"I'll watch movies," Evan says. "I'll bring some scary ones."

Kari looks at me. "You in?"

"Sure." I shrug. "Why not?" It will give me something to do to get my mind off Peyton. Although with the way I'm feeling right now, that's going to be a tall order. I hope Evan brings a really, really good movie.

"Do I look okay?" Evan asks me as we walk up the driveway of Whitney's house later that night. He's wearing jeans and a black sweater. "I just bought this sweater," he says proudly. "It's Gucci."

I roll my eyes, then reach over and pull the Old Navy tag off the back. "You left the tag on."

"Oh." Evan frowns, then rips it in half and throws it on the ground.

"Jesus," I say, picking it up. "You like this girl and you're disrespecting her property like that?" I shove the tag back into his hand. "Throw it in the garbage when you get inside."

He looks aghast. "No way. What if she sees it?"

"What if she sees it out here?"

"Jace, she's not going to see some random tag out here on the lawn. And if she does, maybe she'll think it blew over from a neighboring house."

"A neighboring house?" I shake my head. "Why are you talking like that?"

"I'm trying to seem more refined." He squares his shoulders. "I think it's important to cultivate a good vocabulary."

We're not even inside yet and this is already turning into a debacle. "Look," I say. "Whitney likes you. Otherwise she wouldn't have invited you here tonight. Now you should just be yourself."

Evan looks horrified. "I would never be myself," he says.

"Why not?"

"Because myself isn't really all that likeable."

"That's not true," I say, even though it kind of is. If I were a chick, I doubt I'd be that interested in Evan. Although all those guys from *Jackass* seem to get a lot of women, so maybe he's onto something. Besides, what the hell do I know?

Up until this Christmas, when I met Peyton, I'd been doing pretty well with the ladies. It seemed like every month I had a new one. (I was starting to get a little worried about myself, honestly, wondering if maybe I was turning into a male slut.)

And then I met Peyton at the Christmas party, and it was like I got sucker punched. Suddenly, I didn't want any other girls. I didn't even want to *look* at another girl or *talk* to another girl, much less hook up with one. It was pretty intense. And then after Peyton and I stopped talking, I never really recovered. I could still appreciate when a girl was good-looking, of course. It just wasn't the same.

"Look," I say to Evan now, "you should just be yourself. Otherwise you're going to get stuck playing a part the whole time you're around her."

He frowns, considering what I've just said. "You think?"

"Absolutely." I reach out and ring the doorbell. "Don't go changing just because of some chick."

"Yeah!" he says, nodding his head. "I'm not going to go around changing for *any* chick."

"Just be honest and be yourself." I meet Evan's outstretched fist with mine for a pound.

"Hey," Whitney says when she opens the door. "Come on in, guys. Kari's in the kitchen ordering pizza."

Evan holds his hand out to Whitney and she looks at him, puzzled. "Can you throw this away?" He uncurls his fingers to reveal the ripped Old Navy tag. "I bought this sweater at Old Navy today in an effort to impress you and I forgot to take the tag off."

"Um, sure," Whitney says, taking it. She looks at me as I brush by her and into the house.

"Don't ask." I shake my head. Maybe that wasn't the best advice, telling Evan to be himself. After all, I was myself with Peyton, and look where that got me.

jace the trip

Saturday, June 26, 11:23 a.m.
Siesta Key, Florida

"Is this car even safe?" Peyton asks as we pull out onto the road.

"Of course it's safe," I say. "I'm very good about upkeep." That's bullshit. I'm good about keeping the inside of my car clean just in case I happen to have a girl in here or something, but other than that, I'm pretty lax. I'm not the best with oil changes. One time I heard from a mechanic that you don't have to have your oil changed more than once every five thousand miles, and if you do, you're just getting ripped off. I took the advice to heart.

"Somehow I doubt that." She scans the backseat, looking for something she can call me out on, some misplaced fast-food wrapper or empty soda can. But there's nothing. The only thing back there is Hector. My dog.

Well, not *my* dog exactly. A few days ago, Evan showed

up at my house with Hector, a golden retriever mix, and somehow conned me into letting the dog stay. Hector was supposed to be a present for Whitney, but it turns out she's allergic. So now Evan's trying to find a new home for him, and since Evan's parents are super strict and wouldn't let the dog stay at their house, I got stuck with him.

And since I couldn't leave Hector at home while my family went to the wedding, he was with me in my hotel room last night. Which means he's now coming on this road trip.

Peyton gives Hector a scratch on the chin, and he licks her hand. "Good boy," she says, all gentle. "You're so beautiful."

I snort.

She glares at me. "Only a jerk hates a dog."

"I don't hate him," I say. "I just don't understand why everyone loves him so much. Yes, he's cute, but looks aren't everything now, are they?"

"I don't know," she says, all snotty. "You tell me."

She leans back in her seat and closes her eyes before I can come up with a witty comeback. I sneak a glance at her. God, she's beautiful. I shake my head, disgusted with myself for having these thoughts, and pull the car down the curving road of the yacht club and toward the exit. When I get through the gate at the end of the winding drive, I pull my car onto the main road and start to coast toward the highway.

"Um, hello?" I say to Peyton.

"What?" she snaps, her eyes still closed. She reaches down and hits the lever on the side of the seat and drops it back. Hector moves forward and rests his chin next to Peyton's head, then gives a happy little sigh. Great. Now it's two against one. Figures.

"Do you have directions?" I ask.

"To where?"

"Um, to Connecticut?"

Her eyes pop open. "No," she says, looking a little panicked. "I don't have directions."

"So then how are we supposed to get there?"

She bites her lip, thinking about it. "Can't we just drive north?" she asks. "Connecticut's north. We're bound to hit it eventually."

"Oh, yeah, that's a really great plan," I say. "Just keep driving north until we 'hit it eventually.'" I shake my head. "For someone who was so worried about the safety of my car, you're not really that prepared."

"Sorry I don't have directions to my house in Connecticut," she says, rummaging around in her purse. "But I thought I was going to North Carolina. And besides, don't you have a GPS?"

"No."

"No?"

"No! Why would I have a GPS? Until this morning, I was planning on going home right after brunch, which is a fifteen-minute drive that I know very well, not a fifteen-*hour* drive that is going to take me God knows where."

"Twenty-seven," she says.

"What?"

"Twenty-seven-hour drive."

"It's *twenty-seven hours* to your house?"

She shrugs. "I thought you knew."

"And how would I have—?" I cut myself off. Nothing good is going to come of us arguing the whole time. Besides, it's way too early in the trip for us to be fighting at all. Shouldn't our fights be reserved for later in the day, when things have gone wrong and we're tired and cranky? "Look, never mind," I say, shaking my head. "We need to stop and buy a GPS."

"Hold on," she says. "I think I have one on my cell." She has her phone out, and she's looking down at the screen. "What the hell?" She frowns, then turns it off and then back on again. "My phone's not working."

"Did you drop it or something?" I ask.

She shakes her head.

"Well, I hope you backed up all your pictures," I say. "We wouldn't want you losing any of those now, would we?"

But she's not listening. She's just staring down at her phone, with a look of understanding on her face. "What?" I ask. "What is it? What's wrong?"

"My phone's shut off," she says. "It . . . it's not broken, it just . . ."

"What, you forgot to pay the bill or something?"

"Yeah, or something." She sighs, then rubs her temples with her fingertips. She looks so small just sitting there like that that I start to feel a little bad for her.

"Look, don't worry about it," I say. "We're going to stop and get a GPS. And if you need to use my phone to make calls, you can. It's not a big deal."

She shakes her head slightly, and gets a faraway look in her eyes, and I'm afraid that maybe she's going to start crying again. "Peyton," I say softly. "It's okay. I'm going to take care of everything. Don't worry, all right?"

And after a second, she nods.

When we pull into a parking lot of a Target about fifteen minutes later, Peyton seems to have calmed down a little bit. She slides her sunglasses down over her eyes and walks with me through the parking lot toward the store, still not saying anything.

She grabs a basket when we get inside. "A basket just for a GPS?" I ask.

"I need a few things that I forgot," she says. "Um, shampoo, stuff like that." She doesn't say it bratty, though.

"Okay."

"You might want to get some stuff, too," she says. "You know, just in case we have to spend the night somewhere."

The thought of spending the night with her makes my pulse race. Just the two of us. Alone in a motel room. Maybe there will only be one room left, with one bed. I'll try to sleep on the floor of course, but then in the middle of the night it will be bothering my back too much and I'll have to sneak up—

"Hey!" a voice booms out in front of me. I look up to see a guy standing in front of us. For a second, I can't really place him, but then, when I do, my heart sinks. B.J. "Peyton and Jace! Nice to see you two crazy kids!"

"Nice to see you, too," Peyton says. Which I really wish she wouldn't have done.

B.J. has a screw loose. He's Courtney's boyfriend Jordan's best friend, and he's definitely not all there. Who knows what kind of shenanigans he's up to?

I give him a slight smile, then take Peyton's arm and start trying to steer her past him.

"I'm B.J.!" B.J. says. "Don't act like you don't remember, Jacey! Not after what we talked about last night." He gives me a wink, and I pray to God he doesn't bring up what we were talking about last night. Not in front of Peyton. "We're friends. At least, I thought we were." He opens the box of Twinkies he's holding and pulls one out, breaks it in half, and licks out some of the frosting.

"Yeah," I say. "I know, I remember. That was fun, haha." I try to steer Peyton around him again, but he follows us.

"You want some Twinkie?" He holds it out to Peyton, probably because he can tell there's no way in hell I would take it. He obviously doesn't know Peyton that well, because there's no way in hell she's going to take it, either. She's way too uptight.

"Thanks," Peyton says. She reaches out and grabs the Twinkie half and takes a bite. "I'm starving."

B.J. nods. "Me too," he says. "You know you're allowed to eat food in the store as long as you pay for it when you check out?"

"No," I say, "I didn't know that." Not only is this dude really fucking annoying, he's also kind of disgusting. He has frosting smeared all over his lips, which isn't really the best look for anyone.

"I did," Peyton says. "Whenever I go grocery shopping with my mom I always open up a bag of Oreos."

B.J. nods. "So smart," he says. "It's like I'm always telling Jordan—"

"Yeah, okay," I say. "Sounds good, but we're actually in a bit of a hurry."

"How come?" B.J. asks conversationally.

"It's kind of classified," I say. "Sorry."

"Jace is driving me home to Connecticut," Peyton reports. "My ride totally bailed on me."

"That sucks," B.J. says. He's reaching into the box for another Twinkie. He breaks it in half and hands one piece to Peyton. "Hey, you know that Jordan and Courtney drove from Florida to Boston once, right? It was cool; they ended up getting back together on that trip. Well, not exactly *on* the trip, but—"

"Well, that will definitely not be happening to us," I say, cutting him off. I give him a look, a look that says, "go away and don't you dare bring up what we were talking about last night."

"Definitely not," Peyton agrees.

"But last night—" B.J. starts, sounding confused.

"No," I say, giving him a firm look. And somehow, miraculously, it seems like he gets the message.

He nods. "Yeah," he says. "I guess that makes sense." He turns to Peyton. "You're so cool, Peyton, and Jacey's a little . . ." He trails off, maybe because he realizes that I'm standing right there.

"Can we just get the GPS please and get out of here?" I ask.

"What do you need a GPS for?" B.J. asks, following us.

"Because I don't really know the way home from here," Peyton explains.

I pick up my pace until I'm a few steps ahead of them, listening as they babble about Jordan and Courtney and road trips and a bunch of other nonsense. I'm about to lose my shit when B.J. says, "All right, well, I'll see you guys later. I have to go look at some costumes."

"Costumes?" Peyton asks.

He nods. "Yup. We're going to have a big costume party on the beach tonight. At least, I'm trying to get it to be a costume party. I love costumes." He takes another bite of Twinkie. "They're just so *fun*."

"Okay, well, I hope you have a good time," I say. "See you later." Or not.

Peyton says goodbye to B.J, and then he disappears into the aisles.

"That dude is crazy," I say.

"I like him," Peyton says. "He's different."

I snort. "Yeah, if by different you mean totally out of his tree."

She rolls her eyes. "It figures you would say something like that."

We're in the electronics aisle now, and those moments of vulnerability she had in the car, when she was leaning back with her eyes closed, and then again when she was upset about her phone being turned off are long gone. Now she's back to acting like she's totally in control with a little bit of brattiness thrown in for good measure.

"What's that supposed to mean?" I ask, following her to the display of GPSs.

"Nothing." She shrugs. "Just that you don't like anything that's not cookie-cutter." She surveys the display and then shakes her head. "Why are these things so expensive?"

I follow her around the corner of the aisle while she looks at the rest of the units. "I like things that aren't cookie-cutter," I say, sounding defensive.

"Ha!" She kneels down and starts looking at the GPS units in a glass case. "Name one band you like that they don't play on the radio."

"Guru Steve."

"Guru Steve?" she repeats, tilting her head. "Isn't that . . . isn't that your *friend's* band?"

"Yeah, so what?"

"Oh, my God." She rolls her eyes. "You're hopeless."

"Just because I don't like all kinds of crazy indie music, now I'm hopeless?"

"Yes." She's standing up now, looking around and sighing loudly. "How come I can never find a salesperson when I need one? Someone needs to open this case."

"I'll have you know," I say, "that I am into a lot of things that people aren't into at first. For example, I was the first one out of all my friends to have a Twitter account."

"Only counts if you have your name."

"What?"

"Were you able to score the Twitter user name Jace?"

"Well, no," I say, "that would be impossible. And besides, I wouldn't want that name anyway. Too much pressure."

"Too much pressure?"

"Yeah, like if you don't tweet interesting things all the time, people think you don't deserve the name and that you should give it up to some other, cooler Jace."

"Whatever." She shakes her head. "Are you going to find me a salesperson or not?"

"Fine." I stomp off, wondering if what she said is really true. But there's no way I'm cookie-cutter. And the fact that she said that just proves that Peyton Miller doesn't know anything. I scan the aisles, looking for a salesperson, but of course there aren't any.

I sigh. Peyton's right about one thing: You can never find a salesperson when you need one.

the trip peyton

Saturday, June 26, 12:07 p.m.
Bradenton, Florida

I cannot believe my phone got turned off. Actually, that's a lie. I *can* believe my phone got turned off, and I know exactly why it got turned off too. Because my mom didn't pay the bill. And I know why she didn't pay the bill. Because she doesn't have any money.

I'm so frustrated that I almost kick at one of the shelves in the electronics section. Which would be a disaster because I definitely don't have the money to pay for those kind of damages. So instead, I punch the air as hard as I can. Just like that, the anger's gone, and for a second, I feel like I'm going to cry. But then *that's* gone, too, and now I just feel really depressed.

I open my purse and look through my wallet. I have three hundred dollars. I figured that would be enough traveling money to get me to North Carolina, since everything was mostly already paid for. Brooklyn was going to use her mom's credit card to pay for the rental car, and I was going to pay her back once we got to North Carolina and I found a job.

But now that I'm going to have a buy a GPS, I'm not sure how much money I'm going to have left over. The cheapest GPS they have here is almost a hundred bucks. And with tax, that's going to leave me barely enough to support myself in North Carolina until I can find a job. Not to mention that at some point I'm going to have to figure out what I'm going to do about my cell phone. I need to get it turned back on, but who knows how much that's going to cost? And what if Jace and I need to get a hotel?

By the time Jace finally returns with the salesperson, I feel like maybe I'm going to have a nervous breakdown.

"I finally found someone," Jace says. "Someone" is a pimply-faced guy who looks like he's around twenty-one, and that the last place he wants to be spending his Saturday morning is here, selling me a GPS.

"Is that the cheapest one you have?" I ask, pointing to some no-name brand GPS that looks like it's definitely going to break in about two weeks. But who cares? If it can last a couple of days, I'll be happy.

"I dunno." The guy shrugs.

"Well, do you sell maps here?" I don't know how to fold a map, much less read one, but desperate times call for desperate measures.

"Hey, don't worry about it," Jace says to me. "I'm paying for the GPS."

I shake my head. I'm no one's charity case. If there's one thing this whole situation with my mom has taught me, it's that I need to stand on my own two feet. Which is one of the reasons I'm running away. Well, that and the horrible thing she did to me. The horrible thing I'll never get over, the horrible thing I'm not going to think about right now, and maybe not ever, thank you very much.

"No way," I say. "You're not buying it."

"Relax," Jace says, rolling his eyes like I'm stupid for thinking he was trying to do something nice for me. "I need one for my car anyway. This way I can keep it after I drop you off. I'm going to have to get home somehow."

"Oh." In that case, I guess it's okay.

I step back while Jace looks through the case. I watch his eyes move over each GPS—watch as he asks a bunch of questions. I think about what happened last night in his hotel room, and close my eyes for a second, wishing I were back there, before Brooklyn bailed on me, before I found out Jace was a big liar after all, before I was dealing with any of this.

After a few minutes, Jace settles on the GPS that he wants, and then we split up. I fill my basket with shampoo (generic), conditioner (generic), and a bottle of water (generic). Then we meet back up at the register, where I pay for my stuff, and Jace pays for the GPS and some bones for Hector. So I guess he's not completely heartless.

As we walk back out to the parking lot, my stomach is in knots. The warm Florida air is helping a little bit, though, and I raise my face to the sun, willing the vitamin D to help my mood.

Jace unlocks the car and I slide into the passenger seat. Hector immediately starts licking my face, glad that we're back, glad that he hasn't been abandoned in the car.

"Good boy," I say, giving him a scratch on his chin and burying my face in his soft fur.

We have a GPS. Now I just have to figure out how I'm going to get Jace to bring me to North Carolina while thinking he's taking me to Connecticut.

before peyton

Saturday, May 22, 7:07 pm
Greenwich, Connecticut

I'm just about to finish my frozen yogurt when my cell phone rings.

"It's my mom," I tell Brooklyn. "She's probably wondering where I am." I left my house without telling my mom or dad where I was going, mostly because they were still fighting about those stupid dresses when I left, and I didn't want to have to deal with it. Sneaking out was a good decision. The burgers we ate were amazing, and the frozen yogurt we got for dessert is even better.

"Hello?" I say, swirling the rest of my peanut butter cup yogurt around the last piece of Oreo cookie that's in my bowl.

"Peyton!" my mom yells. "Where are you?"

"Getting frozen yogurt with Brooklyn," I say.

"Well, you need to come home immediately." In the background, there's a frantic rustling noise.

"Why?" I ask warily.

"Because we need to take these dresses back! And the shoes! And the hat! Your father is acting ridiculous about it and so now I have to spend my Saturday night back at the mall, returning things!" At the last part of her statement, her voice raises, I'm assuming so that my dad will be able to hear her. Not that it's necessary. I'm sure she already told him all of this while they were fighting.

"Mom," I say, "you're freaking out about nothing. Just wait a little while until this blows over and then I'm sure you'll be able to keep the dresses."

She should know this. It's a total pattern that my parents have. My mom goes out and spends a lot of money, my dad freaks out about it, they get into a fight, then my mom freaks out about it even more and starts ranting and raving about how she's going to just take everything back and can you believe her husband did this to her and blah blah blah. Then my dad relents and shakes his head and says that's why they're getting divorced and then goes into his home office and slams the door and doesn't come out for hours.

"No," my mom says. "We're taking them back. Meet me at the mall in fifteen minutes." The line goes dead.

"What was that all about?" Brooklyn asks.

I sigh, then eat my last spoonful of frozen yogurt. "I have to meet my mom at the mall," I say. "Can you drop me off?"

"Of course." She looks at me across the table sympathetically. Brooklyn's the only one I've ever told about my parents fighting about money the way they do. She's super understanding about it, even though her parents' relationship is, like, as normal as you can get.

But for some reason, I still haven't told her about my parents getting divorced. In fact, I haven't told anyone. I don't know why. Maybe it's because I don't really believe it's really going to happen, since my parents don't ever follow through on anything.

Of course, I could just be in denial.

I push that thought out of my mind, then get up and toss my empty yogurt cup into the trash before following Brooklyn out to the parking lot.

By the time I get to the mall, my mom is all smiles again. "Hello!" she says when she sees me. "I worked it out with your father, and so we get to keep the dresses."

I sigh. "Then, Mom, why did you make me come all the way down here? I was out with Brooklyn, and we were—"

"Because part of the deal was that I would return the hat." I look down to the register kiosk she's standing in front of and see the hat there, thrown haphazardly on the counter.

Nicole comes scampering over. "Can I help you?" she asks brightly, but her smile falters as she realizes it's me and my mom, back to torture her some more.

"Yes," my mom says, wrinkling up her nose. "We need to return this hideous hat."

"Okay." Nicole picks it up and looks at the price tag. "Do you have your receipt?"

"Of course I have my receipt, I just bought it this morning." My mom slides it across the counter toward her, and Nicole gets to work entering the information for the return into the cash register.

"I'm sorry you had to return your hat, Mom," I say.

She waves her hand like it's nothing, even though she was just freaking out about it at home. "It's okay," she says. And then she lowers her voice. "Whatever you do, Peyton, make sure you don't marry for money." She sighs and looks wistfully at the hat. "Because money comes and goes."

I resist the urge to roll my eyes. My mom makes no secret of the fact that she married my dad for his money. My mom is adopted, and she grew up in a house where they didn't have a lot of material things. They weren't poor—just average middle class. They lived in a nice house, but scrimped to be able to afford it and to send my mom to a nice school. My mom was friends with all the popular, rich kids, and she confessed to me once that she always felt like she needed to keep up with them.

And I think—and this is my own idea, not something I've ever heard my mom say—that along the way, my mom somehow took the fact that she was adopted and extrapolated that into the idea that she was meant to be rich. Almost like she thought that her biological family had come from money, and so that was the kind of person she was supposed to be. Never mind that she knew nothing about her birth mom, and never really showed any interest in finding her. (Probably because she was afraid she'd find out she wasn't wealthy after all.)

Anyway, when she graduated college, she became determined to marry a man who had money. Right after she turned twenty-three, she married my dad, who was thirty at the time. He was a real-estate developer, and was making millions flipping properties and investing in commercial buildings.

They had my older sister, Kira, a year later, and my theory is that my mom didn't want to work and thought it would be easier to get away with that if she had a kid. When Kira was five and ready to start kindergarten, my mom had me, and by the time *I* was ready to go to school my mom was thirty-three and had been out of the workforce for ten years and so it was just easier for her to stay home.

Somewhere along the way, I think my dad started resenting her for it. And as the real-estate market started getting progressively worse, and my dad started making less and less money, my mom refused to—or couldn't?—cut back on her spending. And their marriage started falling apart.

Which is why I would never, ever let myself get all worked up about some guy because of his money. I mean, that's really the last thing my mom needs to be worrying about. In fact, if there's one thing this whole thing with Jace has taught me, it's that guys in general shouldn't be your focus. Ever.

"Come on," my mom says as Nicole hands her the slip showing her credit card has been refunded for the cost of the hat. "Let's go have dinner."

"Do you think that's a good idea?" I ask. I'm not sure we should really be spending more money, but I'm not going to come right out and say that because I know that's not what my mom wants to hear.

"Of course," she says, and rolls her eyes. "We're not destitute, Peyton." From behind the cash register, I see a slight smile tug at Nicole's lips, and I know she knows that my mom had to return the hat because she couldn't afford it. And I also know that Nicole kind of likes that.

I know my mom was a total jerk to her, and I know Nicole has to deal with horrible, demanding people all day, but still. It makes me hate her a little. Which then makes me hate myself a little because come on—who hates a salesperson? And then I start to feel bad that I feel bad for hating her, because shouldn't my loyalties always lie with my mom? Ahhh!

By the time we're finished eating dinner at the sushi place across the street (I barely have three pieces since I'm full from my burger and frozen yogurt) I'm exhausted from all the emotional upheavery, and so as soon as I get home, I decide to take a nap. I'm a big fan of naps, especially late-night ones. I don't think they really count as time spent sleeping because you always end up waking up and then staying up later than you would have if you hadn't napped.

So really it's more like displaced sleeping.

My dad's car wasn't in the driveway when we pulled in, which meant he was probably off at some job site or scoping out a property. The weird thing about my dad and his job is that even though it doesn't seem like he's making much money, he's never—at least as far as I know—considered looking for some other kind of work. He just keeps pumping money into the business, taking out different loans and mortgages, making it almost impossible to turn a profit unless he gets an immediate sale. It seems crazy if you ask me, but of course, no one ever does.

Once I'm in a tank top and leggings, I snuggle into bed with my phone next to me. I run my finger over the Internet icon, willing myself not to do it. But I already know I'm going to. I'm like a junkie.

I pull up Jace's Facebook page. I hardly ever go on here anymore. I did a lot in the beginning, when we first stopped talking. But I made a promise to myself that I would stop, that it was just too hard to see his pictures, to read his status updates, to know what was going on his life.

But it's like a drug, and today, I can't stop myself. I flick through his pictures. The ones I know almost by heart. Jace with his friend Evan at a Rays game. Jace with his dad on vacation at Daytona Beach. Jace with his basketball team after a game.

I stay on each picture for a few moments, running my eyes over his face, his clothes, his hands, looking for any new detail I can find. I hold my breath when I get to the last pictures, wondering if there's going to be any new photos, any new images that will give me details about what Jace has been up to.

But there aren't.

I put my phone down on the pillow and stare up at the ceiling, wondering what he's doing right now. Is he with another girl? Is he doing homework? Is he eating dinner, out with friends, getting ready to take a nap like me?

You could text him, I think. The thought sends a delicious, dangerous little shiver up my spine.

I tiptoe out of bed, feeling like a thief in the night, and open the top drawer of my desk. Inside, there's a scrap of paper with Jace's phone number scrawled on it. I wrote it down after I deleted his number from my phone, just in case I ever needed it again. The paper is folded into a tight square and wrapped with Scotch tape, and on the front, I wrote "DO NOT OPEN THIS UNDER PENALTY OF DEATH."

Which was a really stupid thing to write, since of course I wasn't going to *die* if I opened it. No one even knew it existed except for me. I run my finger over the words on the front. Part of one side of the Scotch tape is pulled up, from a near miss I had a month or so ago.

Of course, I think as I put the folded square back into my desk, the paper is pointless. I know Jace's number by heart.

I crawl back into bed and tap the number into my phone, staring at the numbers on the screen. Then I type Hey—am going to Courtney's dad's wedding, I hope that's okay.

No, sounds too lame, like I'm asking his permission. I erase it immediately, then try something else.

Hi—know we haven't talked in a while, but didn't want it to be awkward when we saw each other at the wedding so thought I would say hi ☺

Hmm. I read it over, then erase the smiley face. What I really need to do is call Brooklyn and ask her for advice. She comes up with the best texts and emails. It's like her hidden talent. But there's no way I can do that, because she would tell me not to text him at all. And now that I've made the decision to do it, there's no going back.

I delete the part about me saying hi. Because that sounds really fake and also like maybe I'm just looking for an excuse to talk to him. Which I am, but still. There's no way I want him to know that.

I decide I'm thinking about this way too much, and so before I can stop myself, I delete the whole last text and then quickly type something else.

I hit send before I can obsess about how it sounds, and then slide my phone under my pillow. I'm not going to check to see if he wrote back until I wake up.

jace before

Saturday, May 22, 8:35 p.m.
Sarasota, Florida

"See?" Evan yells, standing up and pointing at the TV screen. "Do you see how amazing that was? How cool it looked when I jumped into the pool?"

We're at Whitney's house, and instead of watching a scary movie, we've somehow ended up watching the video of Evan jumping into his pool. He's already loaded it up onto YouTube, I guess this afternoon, despite his busy sweater-buying schedule.

And when he found out that Whitney had Apple TV, he insisted that we watch it. YouTube really shouldn't allow you to post videos so quickly, I think, watching as Evan beams at his own craziness.

"It looks cool, doesn't it, Jace?" he asks.

"It does." I'm not lying. It does look cool, if you can get over the craziness of it. When Evan jumps off the roof, he sort of scissors his legs in the air. I don't think he did it on purpose—I think he was just scared and a little panicked—but it still looks badass.

"I can't believe you did that," Whitney says, and shakes her head. "I mean, weren't you scared you were going to hit your head and die?"

"Courage," Evan says, and takes a bite of his pizza, "is doing things you don't want to do even when you're scared. Bravery isn't about not being scared; it's about facing your fear and doing it anyway."

I resist the urge to roll my eyes, then get up and head to the kitchen for another soda.

While I'm in there, my cell phone vibrates and I look down. A text. From someone who's not in my contacts. From an 860 area code. **Hey Jace, it's Peyton. Courtney told me you were coming to the wedding so I just wanted to reach out in case it was going to be awkward.**

I blink my eyes, not really sure I'm seeing what I'm seeing. *Peyton* is texting me? Peyton has the *nerve* to be texting me? Is she crazy? *Just wanted to reach out in case it was going to be awkward.* Ha! Of course things are going to be awkward.

Why is she going to the stupid wedding, anyway? She lives in Connecticut for God's sake. Only one of us should be allowed to go to the wedding, and it should be me because of geographic desirability. Who cares if she's family and I'm just the son of the couple's friends?

"Who texted you?" Evan asks, walking into the kitchen behind me.

"No one," I say, shoving my phone back in my pocket. I'm not replying to that. If Peyton thinks she can just text me out of nowhere, and pretend like everything's okay with us, then she has another thing coming.

Evan gives me a look.

"What?" I ask. I open the fridge and grab another soda. Although now that Peyton texted me, I feel like I want something harder. A beer, a shot, anything. I scan the shelves of the refrigerator, but there's nothing. Either Whitney's parents don't drink, or they know enough to keep their booze out of their teenage daughter's reach when they're not at home.

"Come on, Jace," Evan says. "Who texted you?"

I think about lying, but to do that would give Peyton more power. So I reach into the refrigerator and pull out a soda and uncap it. "Peyton."

"Peyton?" Evan exclaims. "What the fuck?"

I give him a dirty look.

"Screw her," he says.

I don't say anything.

"Right, Jace?" he asks, not sounding so sure.

"Right."

"Do you want to talk about it?"

"No."

"Okay." He hoists himself up onto the counter and looks

at me. "But maybe you will at some point, right? Maybe at some point you'll tell me what happened between you guys?"

"Probably not."

"How come?"

"Because nothing happened," I say, starting to get really annoyed. I start opening cabinets in Whitney's kitchen, looking for anything I can eat or drink to distract myself.

"Um, I don't think you should be doing that," Evan says. "It's not your house; you shouldn't just be going through the cabinets like that."

"Oh, now you're the morality police?" I say grumpily.

"You don't have to freak out, dude."

"Look, I'm sorry," I say. I close the cupboard and run my fingers through my hair. "I just didn't want to get that text, you know?" Why the fuck did she text me? I'd just stopped thinking about her, and now, in one day, I've had two reminders of her. First Courtney, and now Peyton herself.

Maybe I shouldn't go to the wedding. I'm obviously emotionally fragile.

"You sure you don't want to tell me what happened?" Evan asks. "It might help you to talk about it."

I sigh. Maybe I should tell him. It would be good to get it off my chest. "Well," I say. "We—"

"Hey!" Whitney says, appearing in the kitchen. "What are you guys doing in here? Because if you're looking for alcohol, I keep it in my room." She grins.

"We were just talking," Evan says. "If you could give us—"

"We were just finishing up," I say. "And I'd love a beer if you have one."

"Sounds good." She grins. "Let's go up to my room."

Thirty minutes later, we're in Whitney's room, and I have a good buzz going. There's a movie playing on the big flat-screen TV she has in here, but I'm not really watching it.

None of us are really watching it. We're just kind of hanging out and talking.

"Let's tell secrets," Kari says. She reaches over and grabs another drink off Whitney's nightstand. I had no idea she was such a lush. Not that I'm judging, but she's had two beers in half an hour and is now apparently going for a third. The weird thing is, it doesn't even seem to be affecting her. Maybe it's because she's from New York. In movies, kids in New York are always getting into bars without getting ID'd.

"No way," Whitney says. "I already know all your secrets." She's sitting in a beanbag chair in the corner of the room, and Evan has his head in her lap. A few minutes ago she started stroking his hair, which just kind of seemed wrong. Not that she's stroking his hair, but just that she's doing it in front of us. It's like . . . I don't know, weirdly intimate.

I pull my phone out of my pocket and read Peyton's text for the millionth time. Maybe I should text her back. Maybe I should tell her it won't be awkward, maybe I should tell her that I'm looking forward to seeing her, or at least ask her what she's been up to.

But then I think about what happened, and I get filled with anger. Forget it, I tell myself. And this time, I delete the text. As soon as it disappears from the screen, I'm filled with regret. I shouldn't have done that. Now how am I going to read it over and over?

God, I really shouldn't have started drinking. I don't drink all that often, and so when I do I start getting all emo and shit.

"I'll go first," Kari says. She grins. "When I was thirteen, I stole a lip gloss from Duane Reade, and I got caught and the police came."

Whitney rolls her eyes. "Lame."

"That is not lame!" Kari picks a pillow up off Whitney's bed and tosses it at her playfully.

"Yes, it is."

"Fine, then you tell one."

"I will," Whitney says. She clears her throat like she's getting ready to make some really big revelation. "You know how finals are coming up?"

We all nod. How could we forget? It's all anyone's talking about, even though they don't really matter. In fact, I could technically bomb all my finals and still be valedictorian. It's already been decided.

Whitney looks over at her desk, a mischievous smile playing on her lips. "Well, I have a copy of the math test in my top drawer."

"You do not," Kari says. She takes another pull of her beer.

"I do," Whitney nods. "Hannah Hewitt gave me a copy."

Evan sits up and looks at her seriously. "How much do you want for it?"

"No way." Whitney shakes her head, her short blond curls bobbing up and down. "I'm not selling it."

"Are you crazy?" Evan says. "You have to sell that shit. You'll get rich!" I can already see him working the math out in his head—how much they could charge for each copy of the test times how many people will actually buy it.

"I'm not going to sell it," Whitney says. "I don't want tons of people using it. I need it. I'm not doing so well in math."

Evan looks disappointed.

"But you can look at it if you want," she says. "It's in my top drawer."

"Can I make a copy of it?"

"No." She shakes her head. "You have to come over here if you want to use it." She licks her lips and smiles.

Kari and I look at each other, raising our eyebrows, and I can tell that we're both thinking the same thing. Whitney and Evan are going to hook up.

"Okay," Evan says agreeably. Then he gets up and goes over to her desk. "Where is it?" he asks.

"In the top drawer." She watches as he opens it and then starts rummaging around in there. "It's all folded up."

He pulls out a paper. "This is it?"

"Yup."

We all watch as he unfolds a picture of David Beckham, shirtless and in some kind of tighty-whitey looking underwear. Evan looks at it, shocked. Whitney collapses back on the beanbag chair in giggles.

Kari rolls her eyes. "That was so stupid," she says. "I knew you were lying the whole time."

"You did not!"

"I totally did," Kari says. "Your math average is an eighty-eight."

"So?" Whitney says. "You know I want an A."

Kari rolls her eyes again. "Ridiculous."

"Whatever, Kari," Whitney says, still giggling. "Why don't you tell a real secret then if you think fake secrets are so dumb?"

"I did." Kari props herself up on Whitney's bed. "I told you about the time I stole something from Duane Reade."

"That was lame."

This conversation is kind of lame, if you ask me. I'm in a bad mood about the whole Peyton thing, and the beer I drank is definitely not helping.

"It wasn't lame," Kari says. God. I hope these two aren't going to start fighting or anything. The last thing I need is girl drama. I can't stand girl drama. It's just so unnecessary. Which is why I'm not going to text Peyton back. She's obviously just trying to get drama going. Well! I am not going to be privy to that. I don't do drama. And if she thinks she's going to suck me, in, well, then she's got another thing coming.

"It *was* lame," Whitney says.

"At least it was true," Kari shoots back.

"So what? Stealing something when you were thirteen? Who cares?" She stares right at Kari, a smile playing on her lips. "Why don't you try telling us a real secret? One that actually means something?"

"I don't have any real secrets." But Kari's sitting up now, giving Whitney a death glare, which makes me think that she does have a real secret. A real secret that she doesn't want to tell.

"Why don't you tell Jace your secret?" Whitney giggles.

"Shut up, Whitney," Kari says.

"What secret?" Evan asks. "What, do you want to bang him or something?"

He laughs, but Kari flushes.

"Oh, shit," Whitney says. But you can tell she likes it.

"Whatever," Kari says. "So what? I had a crush on Jace for, like, a week when I first moved here. Big fucking deal." She looks at me. "I was over it in like, a day."

"How come you never said anything?" I ask, racking my brain for clues that she might have liked me. But I can't come up with any.

"I did," she says. "Remember? I sent you that—"

She cuts off as the sound of a door opening and closing downstairs echoes through the house. "Whitney?" a man's voice calls.

"Shit!" Whitney says, her eyes widening and her skin turning pale. "It's my dad."

"I thought he wasn't going to be home until late!" Kari starts gathering up all the beer bottles and dumping them in the closet.

"He wasn't supposed to be," Whitney says.

"Is he going to flip out?" Evan asks. "Because if he calls my mom, I'm never going to be able to—"

"Yes, he's going to flip out!" Whitney says. "I'm not supposed to have people over, much less boys drinking in my room."

"Whitney?" her dad calls, the sound of his footsteps coming up the stairs. "Are you home?"

"Jesus," Evan whispers.

"Quick!" Whitney says. "Everyone hide."

Evan dashes under the bed, and Kari grabs my hand and pulls me into the closet. She shuts the door behind us just as Whitney's dad opens the door to Whitney's room.

"Ah," he says, "there are you are. I was calling your name."

The closet is kind of cramped, but I'm afraid to move because I don't want to make any noise. My parents probably wouldn't really care if they find out I was over here, but I don't want to get Evan in trouble if it can be avoided. The last time something even remotely like this happened, he got grounded for two months, and it was horrible. He got super depressed. He's like a puppy. He needs socialization.

"Sorry," Whitney says. "I must have fallen asleep."

"With the lights on?" her dad asks.

"Yeah, I just . . . I fell asleep studying for my math final."

Kari starts to laugh, and I put my finger to my lips, signaling her to be quiet. She buries her head against my shoulder to muffle her laughter, and before I know it, I'm also trying not to laugh.

We get ahold of ourselves a couple of seconds later, and when we do, she pulls away and looks at me.

And then, before I know what's happening, she kisses me.

the trip peyton

Saturday, June 26, 12:34 p.m.
Bradenton, Florida

"So I'll be in charge of the GPS," I say, pulling it out of the box and plugging it into the cigarette lighter. I hope I can get a really good look at the map before Jace notices what I'm doing. Otherwise I have no idea how the hell I'm going to be able to get Jace to drop me off in North Carolina. North Carolina is a big state. I need to get dropped off in Raleigh, and if he drops me off in, like, Wilmington or something, that's not going to be good.

Actually, I don't even know if Wilmington is close to Raleigh. Not even a little bit. This is why I need to look at the map. Why didn't I try to figure these things out before I left? I should at least have a little working knowledge of geography if I'm planning on uprooting my life to a new state. I mean, that's so irresponsible.

"Okay," Jace says.

I tap through the GPS screen, accepting the agreement that basically says if we crash the car and die because we're looking at the GPS, then it's our own fault. Then it asks me the address of where we're going. What to do, what to do . . .

And then I have a brilliant idea.

"I think we should probably stay in North Carolina for the night," I say. "That will be a good place to stop, don't you think?"

"I guess." He shrugs.

"Good." I enter us to Main Street in Raleigh. Now we'll be in the middle of the town, and how hard can it really be to get from there to Creve Coeur? Even if I have to take a taxi, that won't be too bad. Things are looking up!

I slide the GPS into the holder and affix it to the windshield, then reach into the backseat and rummage around in my bag until I find my pink fleece blanket. I push my seat back and cuddle up under the blanket, getting ready to sleep. Hector assumes his normal position, with his head on the seat right next to mine. How cozy!

"What are you doing?" Jace asks.

"Having a nap."

"Having a *nap*? Nuh-uh, no way." He shakes his head.

"Why not?"

"Because we're supposed to be sharing the driving. I'm not just going to sit here and drive the whole time while you get a free ride."

I feel like telling him that there's no way this is a free

ride, that I am definitely paying for this ride, if not with money then with my pride. But I don't say that. Instead I just say, "Of course I'm going to share the driving with you. I'm not a freeloader."

"Good," he says.

"You do the first couple of hours, though. While I take a nap."

"Why do you need a nap?" he asks. "You just woke up not that long ago."

"It's noon."

"So?"

"So the brunch started at nine."

"So?"

"So! Some people wake up early before things like that. You know, to shower, get ready, that kind of thing?"

Jace is one of those lucky people who looks amazing even if he hasn't showered, shaved, whatever. I used to think it was so sexy—that he could just roll out of bed and still look perfect. But now I just find it annoying.

"Whatever." Jace shakes his head, and I lean back and close my eyes. He turns the radio on and starts flipping through the channels.

"Can you turn that down?" I ask.

"No." He shakes his head and stares straight out the front windshield. "Whoever's driving is in charge of the music."

"Fine," I grumble, deciding not to argue with him. I'll

torture him with Taylor Swift later. Jace hates Taylor Swift, which makes no sense. How can you hate Taylor Swift? She's so innocent and cute. Not to mention talented. Everyone loves her. Look at the way America totally rallied around her that time Kanye West was mean to her. Jace thinks Taylor Swift is too modest, that it's all some big act. Like how every time she wins an award she acts all surprised.

"Welcome to the Dr. Laura show," comes through the speakers, and Jace goes, "Oh, perfect, I love this show!"

"Dr. Laura?" I moan. "Please, please do not make us listen to this."

"Why not? She gives good advice."

"Sure," I say, "if you believe all women should stay home with their children and that no one should have sex before marriage."

"I didn't say I agree with her on everything, but she does give good advice. She cuts through people's bullshit."

I snort.

"What was that for?"

"What was what for?"

"You snorted."

"No, I didn't."

"Yes, you did."

"Jace," I say, sighing. "I don't snort."

"Whatever."

"Whatever," I say. "Can we please just not talk? In a few

minutes, I will be asleep, and then in a couple of hours, we can stop to go to the bathroom and then we'll change places. Okay?"

"Fine."

But I don't fall asleep. No matter what I try, I can't. I just lie there with my eyes closed, pretending to be asleep. And I hate to say it, but Jace is kind of right. Dr. Laura gives okay advice.

Like when she tells the woman whose daughter watched another girl getting bullied that her daughter was just as much to blame as the bullies.

And when she tells a man that he should stop supporting his deadbeat father who doesn't have a job and has been married four times.

Or when she tells a mother that it's okay to not let her son hang out with his cousin because the cousin is a terror and slammed the son into a bookshelf and made him start bleeding all over.

And then, right after she reads a commercial for some kind of at-home business that sounds like it's definitely a scam, she takes another call.

"Sarah, welcome to the program," Dr. Laura says.

"Hi, Dr. Laura, thanks for taking my call," Sarah says. She sounds nervous, like a lot of people do when they call Dr. Laura, probably because they know they're about to get yelled at. "My question is about my boyfriend. Um, he lives in Colorado, and I live in Washington. And I'm just wondering at what time does it become ridiculous for us to stay together?"

"How old are you and how old is he?" asks Dr. Laura.

"We're both in college. I'm a sophomore and he's a junior."

"Well," Dr. Laura says, "in my opinion, that is way too young to be in a serious relationship. But if you do make the choice to do so, you need to give yourself the chance to really get to know the person, and there's no way you can do that when he's hardly ever around."

"Okay," Sarah says. But she doesn't sound convinced. And then she does something that makes me groan. She says, "But we see each other at least once a month."

"Yes, but once a month does not allow you to really get to know a person," Dr. Laura says, firmer this time.

"But we talk on the phone every day, sometimes for hours."

I squirm in my seat, wanting to yell at the radio and tell Sarah to stop contradicting Dr. Laura. Dr. Laura doesn't like that, and now Sarah's really going to be in for it.

"Well, miss, if you want to spend your college days holed up in your dorm room with a cell phone talking to some guy you're most likely not going to end up with, then that's your business."

"But I haven't met any guys at college who are even close to being as good as Brant."

Jace guffaws. "Brant!" he says. "What a tool name. She should dump that loser."

"You would say that," I mumble, before I remember that I'm supposed to be asleep.

"What?" He glances at me.

"Nothing."

"No, what did you say?"

"Nothing," I say. "Just that you would think it was stupid to have a long-distance relationship. I mean, isn't that what you decided?"

I see his Adam's apple bob as he swallows. He shakes his head and frowns. "That's not what I said. I never wanted—"

"Stop," I say, realizing my mistake. I shouldn't have even brought this up. The last thing I want is to get into some big explanation of our relationship, where Jace tries to tell me why he ended things, and how it has nothing to do with me and blah blah blah. "I don't want to talk about it."

"Peyton—"

"I don't want to talk about it."

"Yeah," he says. "That figures."

"What does?"

"That you don't want to talk about it," he says. "You never want to talk about anything."

"Ha!" I push Hector gently back into the backseat, then reach down and pull the lever on my seat so that it shoots up. "What a crock! I'll talk about anything, anytime, anywhere."

"Oh yeah?" he challenges. "Then why are you running away?"

"That," I say, "is none of your business."

He nods in satisfaction. "That's what I thought."

I reach over and pull the lever on my seat again, sending it back down. "You know what?" I say. "Don't talk to me." Then I reach up and push the button on the radio, turning it off. "And I don't want to listen to this anymore. It's giving me a headache."

I lie back down, waiting for him to say my name, to tell me he's sorry, to try to talk to me again. But he doesn't say anything. He doesn't even turn the radio back on. He just keeps driving.

A couple of hours later, my bladder is dangerously close to overflowing, and so I'm the one who's forced to break the silence. I pretend that I'm just waking up, that I haven't been just lying there the whole time, trying to fall asleep. I made a big mistake when I turned the radio off because after that I had nothing to distract myself.

"Do you want to stop soon?" I ask, reaching up and stretching, as if I was sleeping and not just giving him the silent treatment.

"Fine," Jace says. "There's a Bojangles coming up in a few miles."

"Sounds good," I say nonchalantly, even though I'm about to explode.

Jace pulls off the highway at the next exit, and drives an agonizingly slow two miles to Bojangles. When he pulls into the parking lot, I rush out of the car and into the restaurant, hoping he can't tell it's because I really have to go to the bathroom, and instead thinks it's because I'm sick of him and can't wait to get out of his presence.

When I come out of the bathroom, Jace is standing in line, and I step in behind him, scanning the menu, looking for the cheapest items.

"Have you ever had Bojangles before?" he asks.

"No." I shake my head. "We don't have them in Connecticut."

He nods. "It's good. Like KFC, only better. But when we stop tonight in North Carolina we can go to the grocery store and stock up so that we don't have to keep eating fast food."

"Sounds good," I say, trying not to let him in on the fact that we're definitely not going to need much food tonight, since I'm going to be ditching him as soon as we get to North Carolina.

The line inches forward. "We'll have two number twos," Jace says. "Cheddar cheese on both, one with a Sprite, one with a Diet Coke." He turns to me. "That okay?"

I nod, then rummage in my bag for money. The food does sound good, and my heart does a little dance over the fact that he remembered I like Diet Coke, but I wish he'd picked something a little cheaper. I thought the South was supposed to be cheaper than the Northeast. Haven't they ever heard of the Dollar Menu? Disgusting, greasy, artery-clogging food for a buck?

But when the cashier adds everything up, Jace hands over his debit card without even asking me. "I got it," he says. "Don't worry about it, you can get me back later."

I think about protesting, but I'm afraid that if I do, he'll take me up on it. And I need to save my money. So instead I just say, "Thanks," and put my money back in my bag. Hopefully, whenever I get him back, it will be someplace a little cheaper.

We take the food over to a table in the corner and dig in.

"It's good, right?" Jace asks. He opens a little cup of ketchup, and sets it on the table between us so we can share.

"It is," I say, dipping a fry in the ketchup. He goes for it at the same time, and our hands brush against each other. "Sorry," I say, flustered. It's starting to feel a little hot in here.

"I knew you'd like it," he says.

"How?"

"Because everyone does."

"Oh." I keep eating, not sure what to say.

After a few minutes, he puts his sandwich down and regards me over the table. "So, seriously, are you going to tell me why you were running away?"

I sigh, "No. So stop asking me that. And I'm not running away anymore, so you can stop being so dramatic about it." I cross my fingers under the table, hoping he buys my lie.

"You're the one who was making it all dramatic back in your hotel room."

"Only so you would wipe the smarmy look off your face."

He opens his mouth, like he's going to protest the fact that he's smarmy, but then he changes his mind. "Fine," he says.

I take a bite of my chicken sandwich, although I'm suddenly not really that hungry anymore. I'm thinking about my mom. And about what happened. My eyes start to get all hot and prickly, and I blink hard. *I will not cry, I will not cry, I will not cry.*

"Sorry," Jace says. "I didn't mean to upset you."

I don't say anything.

He sighs. "Seriously, I'm really sorry, Peyton. I know you had your reasons, and it's not really any of my business. But if you ever want to talk about it, I'm here."

Somehow, the fact that he's suddenly being nice about it is making it even worse. And that he's not pushing me to talk about it is somehow making me *want* to talk about it. Because the thing is, no one knows the whole truth. Not Brooklyn. Not my dad. Not even my mom knows that I know. It's kind of too horrible to even say out loud.

"It's okay," I say. "You were just trying to be nice."

He nods, then takes another fry. "They have really good milkshakes here," he says, probably because he thinks I want to change the subject. "You can even get a chocolate peanut butter one."

Chocolate peanut butter is my favorite, and the fact that

he remembers this makes me lose it. I start to cry, right there at the table.

"Peyton," Jace says, his voice softening. "What's wrong?"

"Nothing," I say. "It's just . . . the reason I wanted to leave home, it's just . . . it's really horrible."

He doesn't say anything, and then after a second, he moves over to my side of the booth and wraps his arms around me. I melt into him, leaning my head against his shoulder. We stay like that for a few moments until I lean back, wiping my eyes.

"Peyton," he whispers into my ear, "I need you to know that I'm really sorry. About everything."

I don't know if he's talking about what happened with my parents, or what happened with me and him. He pushes my hair out of my face and he's looking right into my eyes and I really, really want him to kiss me.

But then a man walks down the aisle and sits down at the table next to us and starts slurping his soda noisily, and the moment is broken.

Jace pulls away and then, after a second, he moves over to the other side of the table. And I miss him. I don't want him to be back on his own side of the table. I want him over here, with me. Feeling that connection with him, for the first time in a long time, felt good, and I'm not ready to have it taken away.

Which is why I say, "Okay. I'll tell you why I was running away."

If he's surprised, he doesn't show it. He just nods, and I'm reminded of one of the reasons I liked him so much—he's completely nonjudgmental.

"Okay," he says, his eyes on mine. He leans back in the booth. "I'm listening."

And so I start to talk.

peyton before

Saturday, June 12, 1:02 p.m.
Greenwich, Connecticut

"He's an asshole," Brooklyn declares. We're at the beach, lying on our towels and soaking up the sun. I kind of hate the beach, but Brooklyn loves it, so every once in a while, I do my duty as a best friend and go with her. I slather myself with sunscreen, get nervous that everyone's judging the way I look in my bathing suit, and try to avoid the water so that I don't get stung by a jellyfish or some equally disgusting sea creature.

"I know," I say, flipping through the new issue of *Cosmo*. All the articles are about how you can please your man in bed. Which obviously I won't be needing, so I don't know why I'm even reading this stupid magazine in the first place. "I just don't understand how I could have been so fooled by him."

"What do you mean?"

"I mean, he made me feel like he was such a nice guy, and then to not even respond to a text that I sent him? I mean, that's just common courtesy."

"Please tell me you're joking," Brooklyn says. She doesn't move from where she's lying on her lime-green towel, her face pointed up at the sun. "He completely blew you off after Christmas, are you forgetting that? How can you be surprised that he's not responding to your text?"

I decide to ignore this fact, and just keep on with the conversation we were just having. "Not to *mention* that he's going to be seeing me in a couple of weeks. Isn't he worried that I might go crazy on him or something? Like, what if I start to scream at him and make a big scene in front of all the guests? What if I scream, 'Jace Renault, you are a horrible womanizer, and I am here to say that in front of God and your family!'"

"Do you plan on doing that?" Brooklyn asks, her voice tinged with worry. She props herself up on one elbow and looks at me, her eyebrows raised over the huge black sunglasses she's wearing.

"Of course not," I say, even though the idea is kind of tempting.

"You know what you need," Brooklyn says, pulling her sunglasses off. Her eyes light up with excitement. "You need a new guy!"

"No." I shake my head. "Absolutely not. The last thing I need is a new guy. Guys are trouble. All they do is cause misery and heartbreak."

"Yeah, but think about all the fun you're missing out on," she says, grinning. "You could make a pact with yourself that you aren't going to get emotionally attached. You'd have a good time, and maybe you'd even get over Jace."

"You think?" I ask doubtfully. The thought of making out with some guy I'm not that into doesn't seem like the way to get over Jace. But maybe it would be. Don't they say that once you hook up with a guy, your hormones take over, making you emotionally attached to him? It's, like, the curse of being a woman.

"Oh, definitely," Brooklyn says, nodding. "It's hard to be upset about someone when you're making out with someone else. Now, who do you want to have a crush on? This is so fun!" She reaches into her bag and pulls out our yearbook.

"I don't know," I say. "Can't I just wait until I go away to college? Then I'll definitely be able to forget about him."

"That's a year away!" Brooklyn says. "Way too long. Plus it's not that fun."

"But it's summer," I point out. "How am I supposed to get a crush on someone now?" Having a crush on someone during the school year sounds a lot easier. That way you can lust after them in the halls. You know, from afar. I throw myself back onto my towel and close my eyes, watching the imprint of the sunlight flash and move on the backs of my eyelids.

"Good point," Brooklyn says, flipping through the pages of our yearbook. She pushes a strand of her blond hair behind her ear. "Maybe we should start going to more parties. Or maybe you should get a summer job at a place where lots of guys will be working. Like a sporting goods store."

"Oh, yeah, because that's not depressing or anything," I say. "Spending my summer dressed in some dorky polo shirt trying to sell people golf clubs."

"Think of all the flirting you could do! Actually, forget about the customers—think about the other employees! They'd all be guys." She bites her lip. "Maybe we should both get jobs there."

My phone starts ringing, and I know it's ridiculous and pathetic, but every time it rings, I think maybe it's going to be Jace. Which is so stupid. If he was going to respond to my text, he would have done it. I mean, it's been three weeks. I glance down at the caller ID, but the call is from a number I don't recognize. I pick it up.

"Hello?" There's a beat of silence on the other end of the line, and my heart slides up into my chest. Jace? "Hello?" I try again.

"Hello," a bright female voice chirps in my ear. "This is Maria Valerio from Visa, how are you today?"

"I'm fine," I say, my heart sinking. It's just a stupid telemarketer.

"Is this Peyton Miller?"

"Yes," I say. "But I'm not—" I start to tell her that I'm not interested, but before I can, she cuts me off.

"Good afternoon, Ms. Miller, I'm calling because your

account with us is currently thirty days past due, and we'd like to offer you a chance to rectify the situation before it gets put on your credit report."

"I'm sorry," I say as Brooklyn holds up our yearbook and points at a picture of Matt Swift. I shake my head. No way. Matt Swift is cute, but he's also really stupid. One time when I told him my grandparents lived on Cape Cod, he told me he always wanted to visit that state. "I'm not interested."

I'm talking to both Brooklyn and the lady on the phone. Brooklyn frowns and then goes back to looking.

But the lady on the phone says, "You're not interested in what, Ms. Miller? Paying your bills on time?"

"I'm sure I would be able to handle paying my bills on time," I say, rolling my eyes, not sure why I'm still on the phone. "But I don't want a credit card right now, thank you."

"Well, you should have thought about that before you opened an account with us," she says, getting all snotty.

"I didn't open an account with you," I say. I've been looking for someone to take all my Jace rage out on, since he's not calling me back and letting me yell right at him. Maybe this lady will fit the bill. I hate to get all angry at some random, but honestly, she started with me first.

"Yes, you did," the woman says. "And your account is currently thirty days past due, almost sixty, which will affect your credit report when this information gets sent to the credit bureaus at the end of the month."

"What are you talking about?" I ask as Brooklyn holds up another picture. But I shake my head at her and then stand up and move away toward the snack bar so that I can hear the lady on the phone better.

"Your Capital One Visa," she says. "You have a current balance of ten thousand dollars, and with late fees and back payments, you owe us five hundred and twenty-eight dollars in order to get your account back up-to-date."

"But that's impossible," I say. "I don't have a Visa. That's what I've been trying to tell you."

All the picnic tables at the snack bar are taken, so I sit down on the curb of the sidewalk. The pavement warms my skin through the bottom of my bathing suit, and I slide my feet into the sand and wiggle my toes.

"We did receive one payment from you when you first opened the account," she says, totally ignoring the fact that I just told her I don't even have a stupid credit card. "But since then, there's been nothing, despite a bevy of letters and phone calls."

"But I haven't received any phone calls!" I say. "And how did you get this number, anyway?"

"This phone number was provided to us by DataTrax, a company that allows us to find phone numbers of people who have skipped out on their bills."

"But I haven't skipped out on my bill," I say. "That's what I've been trying to tell you."

"Are you saying that this account isn't yours?"

Is this woman for real? *"Yes."*

"So you didn't open it?" Her tone is skeptical, like she's used to people running up big bills and then trying to pretend they didn't do it.

"Yes!" I say. "I mean, no, I didn't open it!"

"Then who did, Ms. Miller?" she asks.

"I don't know!"

My heart is beating fast now. Because even as I'm saying it, there's a sinking feeling in my gut. A sinking feeling that maybe I do know who opened that account.

A person who likes to spend money.

A person who knows all my personal information.

A person who gets the mail every day and would be able to intercept any envelopes that were addressed to me.

A person who's my mom.

I tell Brooklyn that I don't feel good, that my stomach is bothering me, that I need to get home. She believes me, which makes me feel bad, but I can't tell her what's happening. I can't say the words out loud, can't say anything about it until I know for sure that it's true.

I don't remember much about the ride home, just that the whole time we're driving, rage was boiling up in my body, worse than anything I've ever felt toward Jace or anyone else. It bubbles and simmers the whole way, and by the time Brooklyn pulls into my driveway, my anger is so all encompassing that I feel like I'm going to explode.

"Mom!" I scream as I come barreling into the house. But there's no answer. "Dad!" I scream. Again, no answer. I stomp through the house, yelling their names as I go.

I peek back out the front window, realizing their cars aren't in the driveway, that they're not home. I don't know where they are or when they're coming back, but I don't care. I push my way into their room and pull open the drawer of my mom's nightstand so hard that it comes right off the track and lands on the floor with a thud.

My mom is horrible with organization, and so there's all kinds of stuff in the drawer. Old address books, old bills, lots of credit card offers, a bunch of flyers for gyms and stores and other things. My parents' room is very clean and neat, thanks to the cleaning service that comes twice a week. But if you look beneath the surface, it's actually a mess. Cleaning services can't help you when it comes to organizing. Especially if you don't want their help because you have something to hide.

I've become a banshee, tearing through every paper, my eyes not even really registering what I'm seeing. So I force myself to calm down a little bit and go through each piece slowly, opening anything that looks remotely like it could be from Visa.

But there's nothing.

I leave the mess on the floor, then fling open the closet and start pulling down the bins that line the top shelf. There are papers and things in here too, and I start methodically going through them. I don't care how long it takes—I'm going to find something. If there's nothing in here, I'll go to my dad's office. I doubt she'd leave anything in there, since it's my dad's work space, but if she's trying to hide something, who knows?

But it doesn't come to that.

I find what I'm looking for in one of the purple bins marked SHOES. There aren't any shoes in there, needless to say. And it's a really stupid thing to label a secret bin with, since my mom has a huge shoe rack and therefore wouldn't need to store her shoes on a shelf.

Instead, there are credit card statements. Dozens of them, all addressed to me. I start opening them one by one, my hands shaking the whole time, tears spilling down my cheeks, my heart pounding so hard in my chest I can't hear anything else.

I lay them all out, constructing the picture of what my mom's been doing.

Three credit cards.

Two Visas.

One MasterCard.

All in my name.

With a combined balance of around twenty thousand dollars.

the trip jace

Saturday, June 26, 3:01 p.m.
Ocala, Florida

"Wow," I say, once Peyton's done talking. I stay quiet for a second, wanting to make sure I choose my words carefully. She's finally trusted me with something, and I don't want to give her any reason to regret that. At the same time, I think it's a little crazy that she's running away. "I can't even imagine what that must have felt like."

"It felt like a betrayal," she says simply. "Like the worst betrayal ever. Like my mom would rather have expensive shoes than a relationship with me."

"Yeah." I pick up my cup and take a sip of my soda, mulling over what she just said. "But you know it's not that simple, right? I mean, don't get me wrong, it was horrible what she did. But your mom has issues with money, obviously. It's not as simple as she likes her shoes more than she likes you."

It's the wrong thing to say. Peyton's eyes narrow, and for a second, I think she's really going to lay into me. But she just shakes her head and lets out a little laugh. "It figures that you'd take her side."

"I'm not taking her side," I say quickly. And I'm not. All I was doing was trying to point out that maybe her mom cares about her more than she thinks. "I was just trying to make you feel better."

"By telling me I'm overreacting?"

"I didn't say you were overacting! I was just saying that there might be a deeper explanation, that's all. You're not overreacting. I'd be freaking out if one of my parents did that to me."

"You still think I shouldn't be running away?" she challenges. I can tell what she wants me to say. She wants me to tell her that she *should* be running away, that she should be extremely pissed, that she should hurt her mom as much as her mom's hurt her, that I wouldn't blame her if she never went home again.

But honestly, I think the fact that she's running away is a little bit insane. I mean, when you think about it, it doesn't really make that much sense. What is running away going to accomplish? It doesn't help her to fix things with the credit card companies, it doesn't help her relationship with her mom, and it doesn't help her to feel like she's back in control. In fact, I can't think of one single good thing that it does.

But all I say is, "What does your dad think about it?"

"I didn't tell him."

"Why not?"

"Because it's . . . I don't . . ." She trails off, looking out the window, seemingly frustrated.

"Listen," I say gently. "I know it's a horrible situation. But did you ever think that maybe you should have stayed there for the summer, tried to work things out? I mean, going to North Carolina can't really be the best way to handle all of this."

She takes in a big breath, and when she talks again, her voice is shaky. "I don't want to deal with it," she says. "Why should I have to?"

"Because it's happening?"

"But it's not my fault."

"Peyton, a lot of things are going to happen to you that aren't your fault but still suck and have to be dealt with." Her eyes water, and I reach out and take her hand. "I mean, Peyton, this is serious. You might end up being responsible for this money."

"So you think running away is the easy way out?"

"I didn't say that."

"But do you?" She leans back in the booth and crosses her arms over her chest.

I take a bite of my sandwich in an effort to stall. I think about lying to her and just telling her what she wants to hear. But I don't want to do that. Finally I settle on, "I think that a normal reaction to what you're going through is to try to hurt your parents and to get as far away from everything as you possibly can. But I don't think that turning away from the problem is, in the long run, the best idea."

But she's not giving up. "Answer. The. Question."

I rub my eyes. "What was the question again?" It's a last-ditch effort to confuse her.

"Do you think running away is the easy way out?"

I sigh. "Honestly?"

"Yes, honestly!"

"Honestly I think it's always better to face things straight on and deal with them."

She shakes her head and then moves her straw up and down in her drink. It makes an angry squeaking noise as it slides through the plastic cover. "I should have known better than to talk to you about something like this." She cocks her head, and her eyes focus on the wall over my shoulder.

"Hey," I say, starting to get a little annoyed. "I've been nothing but nice to you. And if you didn't want my opinion, then you shouldn't have asked for it."

"Whatever." She picks up her sandwich again and starts to eat. And after a second, I do the same.

When we get out to the parking lot, Peyton holds her hand out to me.

"What?" I ask.

"The keys."

"Oh. Right." I pull them out of my pocket and hand them over, wondering if it's the right decision. It was one thing to tell her she was going to have to share the driving with me when I was tired and hungry; it's quite another once I'm recharged and she's mad at me. But still. I could use a nap. I know I gave Peyton a hard time about sleeping, but that brunch *was* a little early, especially since I was up so late last night.

We both climb into the car. Hector immediately starts nudging my hand, and I reach into the paper Bojangles bag and pull out the chicken sandwich I ordered him on the way out.

I feed him, and he slobbers all over my hands happily. "Hey, hey, chill," I say. But of course he doesn't listen. After about two seconds, the food is gone, and he licks my hands until he's sure there's nothing left. I pour some bottled water into my empty soda cup, and Hector laps it up, then flops back down in the backseat and sighs happily.

I wipe my hand off with a napkin, then put the napkin in the empty bag and drop the bag on the floor. I'll have to remember to throw it out the next time we stop.

"This feels weird," I say as Peyton slides the key into the ignition.

"What does?"

"Sitting in the passenger seat of my own car."

She doesn't say anything, just rolls her eyes and then starts the car. I know what she's thinking. That I'm complaining about being in the passenger seat of my car while she's dealing with her life falling apart. I decide I need to keep my mouth shut for a little while. Maybe she just needs some time to herself.

I lean back against her pillow and close my eyes. It feels nice and soft. I wonder how she gets it so soft. Mmm. It smells good, too. Girls are always keeping their stuff nice and soft and good-smelling. It smells like her, like vanilla and—

"Hey!" I scream as the pillow gets yanked out from under my head. "What are you doing?"

"Putting my pillow in the backseat," she says, and places it back there gently, like it's a child. Hector immediately claims it, laying his head down and giving another happy sigh.

"Putting your pillow in the backseat?" I repeat, shocked.

"Yes," she says. "It's my pillow. And that's where I want it right now."

"But I was lying on it!"

"But it's not yours." She shrugs, then reaches into her purse and pulls out a pack of gum, then pops a piece into her mouth. She looks down at the pack, considering, and then holds it out to me. "Gum?"

"No," I say. "I don't want any *gum.* I want you to let me use your pillow. I was really comfortable!"

"You can't use my pillow."

"Why not?"

"Because you have a dirty head."

This girl is unbelievable. "So you'd rather have Hector on it?" I say. "He's a dog! And besides, my head is very clean."

She starts to giggle. "Oh, is it?" she asks. "Is your head very clean, Jace?"

"Real mature." I shake my head and then reach into the back and pick up her pillow. "I'm using it."

She pulls it from my hand. "You're not."

"I am."

"You're not."

It's in between us now, and we're yanking it back and forth, acting like children. But it's not really about the pillow. It's about the principle of the thing.

"Listen," I say, "you are riding in my car. So you have a choice. Either give me the pillow, or give me back my car, and I'll be happy to drive my ass back home. Where I won't need a pillow, because I will be curled up all warm and cozy in my bed."

Her eyes widen, like she's shocked that I would say such a thing. For a moment, I'm afraid she's going to tell me "Fine," and get out of my car and stomp away. I'd have to go after her, of course. I can't just leave her at some random Bojangles in the middle of . . . wherever it is we are.

"Fine," she says. "You can use the pillow." She looks at me out of the corner of her eye, shaking her head like she can't believe she's allowing such a thing. "I'll just have to wash the pillowcase before I use it again."

"Thank you," I say. "I appreciate it."

I place the pillow back under my head.

Peyton puts the car in reverse, takes her foot off the brake, and starts to back out of the parking spot. I close my eyes and settle in. I never realized the passenger side of my car was so comfortable. How nice. I wouldn't even mind if Hector wanted to cuddle a little.

And then there's a huge crashing sound as Peyton slams into the car behind us.

before jace

Thursday, June 24, 6:17 p.m.
Sarasota, Florida

"Did you even hear what I said?" Evan asks. "I said that we're going to have to up our marketing campaign!"

"Our what?" I repeat.

We're sitting outside of the Crazy Cow ice cream shop, eating hot fudge sundaes and killing time before we're supposed to meet Kari and Whitney to go bumper boating. Bumper boating is completely lame, and I'm in kind of a shitty mood, but whatever. Evan wanted to do it, and so did the girls, and I wasn't going to be the one to tell them it was stupid. I might be cranky, but I'm not a total asshole.

"What marketing campaign?" I lick up the last of my hot fudge sundae, then drop the container into the trash can next to our table.

"The marketing campaign for my pranks."

I resist the urge to put my head in my hands. "Why do you need a marketing campaign?"

Evan shoves his spoon into his sundae like a pitchfork and leaves it there. "Seriously, have you been listening to one thing I've been saying?" He leans back on the picnic table and looks at me, accusing.

"Of course I have," I lie.

"Then you would *know* that none of the good shows take unsolicited tapes. Apparently it's for legal reasons." He wrinkles up his forehead, like he can't even fathom the idea that a network might not want a bunch of kids sending them tapes in which they're risking their lives doing crazy, stupid things.

"Well, it makes sense," I say. "They don't want kids getting hurt because they think that they can get on TV."

"I guess," Evan says, frustrated. "But it doesn't help me any."

"I thought you were going to start posting your stuff on YouTube."

"I have posted some stuff on YouTube," Evan says, "but there's too much competition. We have to figure out a way to make it go viral. Which is why I need a marketing campaign."

"Viral," I repeat, distracted.

"Okay," Evan says, pulling his spoon out of his ice cream and waving it all around. Drops of liquid fly through the air and land on the picnic table. "What's going on with you? You've been all spacey ever since school ended. Are you getting nervous about graduation?"

"Why would I be worried about graduation?"

"Because it means that the real world is starting. No more messing around. We need to start getting serious about our future."

"You're going to start getting serious about your future?" I ask him skeptically.

"Eventually," he says. "I have hopes and dreams, too, you know."

"I know."

"So are you going to tell me what's been up?" All sound of joking is gone from his voice, and now he's just looking at me with concern.

"I don't know," I say, shaking my head. "It's this . . . it's this stupid Peyton thing. I thought I was over it, but lately I can't stop thinking about her."

"Oh, man," Evan says, letting out his breath in one big sigh. "I know what's going on here."

"What?"

"In fact, I was afraid this was going to happen."

"What?"

"Think about it, Jace. Think about it real hard."

I think about it real hard. *"What?"* I ask, trying not to lose my patience.

"Don't you think it's a little weird that just when you

start getting close to another girl, your obsession with Peyton kicks into high gear?"

"I don't have an obsession with Peyton," I say, even though it's a lie. "And I wouldn't say that Kari and I are getting close."

Ever since that night Kari and I kissed a few weeks ago, we've been kind of an item. After Whitney's dad almost caught us, the four of us all stayed quiet in her room until he left again, and then we snuck out the front door and went to see a movie.

While we were at the theater, Kari and I made out the whole time. It was nice, don't get me wrong. She's cute and I'm a guy—of course it was fun. And it was a nice distraction from Peyton. But when I got home, I wasn't thinking of Kari; I was thinking about Peyton and why she chose that night to text me and what it meant and what it was going to mean when I saw her at the wedding.

And then I started feeling guilty because Kari is really nice and fun and cute and it was a really shitty thing to do to hook up with her all night and then end up thinking about some other girl. And of course I didn't *set out* to hook up with Kari just to get over Peyton, and Kari was the one who kissed me first, but still. It made me feel like a shit. Obviously Kari likes me because (as Evan pointed out to me later) she pushed me into a closet and hid from Whitney's dad that night even though Kari was the only one who was actually allowed to be at Whitney's house.

"You guys have been hanging out for a few weeks," Evan says. "Doesn't that kind of constitute getting close?"

"I guess." Like I said, it's been nice. But not anything amazing. And the weird thing is, I kind of get the sense she feels that way too. That we enjoy each other's company, but that there's nothing deeper going on.

"So what's the problem, then?" Evan asks. "Forget about Peyton, man. Girls like that are bad news."

"Girls like what?"

"Girls who break your heart."

"Good point."

"And who live hundreds of miles away," Evan goes on. "If you ask me, you need to make this thing with Kari work. She's a great girl."

"Maybe you're right." Kari *is* a great girl. And she has one thing that Peyton doesn't have—Kari's never broken my heart.

"Of course I'm right." He finishes his sundae, then tips the plastic bowl up to his mouth and slurps down the rest of the melted ice cream. "See, the problem with you, Jace, is that you always want to make things more complicated than they are. You always want to analyze things and think about them. It's simple. One girl doesn't like you and makes you feel miserable; one girl does and makes you feel good. End of story."

I look at him in shock. "That actually might be the smartest thing you've ever said."

"Really?" He grins at me. "Thanks, man." He tosses his plastic bowl into the garbage. "Come on," he says. "It's time to meet the girls."

When we get to the bumper boat place, Kari and Whitney are already there, waiting. I give Kari a hug when I see her, determined to give this a real shot. Peyton Miller who?

"Evan," I say as I hand the cashier money for two admissions, one for me and one for Kari, "why is your camera in your back pocket?"

"It's not," he says.

"Yes, it is. I can see your pocket cam right in your back pocket."

The cashier gives me two paper bracelets, and I hand one to Kari.

"Thanks," she says and wraps it around her wrist.

Evan sighs. "Okay, fine," he says. "I was going to wait until we were actually on the boats to tell you this, but I was thinking that we could all do a flash mob."

Oh, dear God. I close my eyes and force myself to take a couple of deep, cleansing breaths.

"What's a flash mob?" Whitney asks, grinning. Apparently she likes the fact that Evan is completely crazy, which is good for Evan, but not so good for the sane people on this trip.

"It's when people all do a dance or something at the same

time," Kari says. "Like out in public. And people look at them like they're crazy. Right?"

"Right." Evan nods.

"No." I shake my head. "I'm not doing a flash mob. No way."

The girl at the gate checks my bracelet and gives me a smile. "Hey," she says as I push through the turnstile. She's cute. Long blond hair. Nice smile.

"Hey," I say, grinning back. And then I instantly feel guilty. I'm here with Kari. Kari, who is perfectly nice and cute and fun. Kari, who I've been making out with for weeks. Kari, who is here with me, on this date, and probably doesn't appreciate the fact that I was just semi-flirting with the girl working the gate.

Although if Kari minds, she's definitely not showing it.

"I think a flash mob could be fun," she says. "But how can we really do it at a bumper boat place? And besides, aren't you supposed to plan those things out way in advance?"

We all file into the line that's forming in front of the entrance to the boats, waiting for the ride that's going on right now to be over. I take Kari's hand in mine, to make up for smiling at the girl working the gate. Kari seems a little surprised that I'm holding her hand. Probably because we haven't really done that much PDA.

And honestly, it's kind of awkward. We just kind of stand there, holding hands like kids or something. We're not relaxed, or loose, or romantic or anything. We're just gripping each other's fingers, like we're thirteen again or some shit. Very strange.

And then Peyton's face floods into my mind. Peyton. Who I'm going to be seeing tomorrow night at the wedding.

"Yes, technically you're supposed to plan things out in advance, but I didn't want to bring it up before because I knew Jace would flip out," Evan says. And then he starts going on and on about flash mobs.

I tune him out, trying to figure out why I'm so tense. Can it really be just because I'm going to see Peyton tomorrow? Or is it because of graduation on Sunday? *It's just a dumb speech,* I tell myself. *And she's just a dumb girl.* As soon as I think it, I instantly feel guilty. Yes, it is a dumb speech. But Peyton is not a dumb girl.

"Jace?" Evan's asking.

"What?" I ask, struggling to pay attention to what he's saying.

"Are you listening?" He's holding Whitney's hand as the line moves forward, but unlike me and Kari, they actually look like they want to be holding hands. Whitney's leaning into his chest, and he's rubbing his thumb against the outside of her hand. Who knew Evan could be so comfortable around girls?

Although I guess when you have a girl that you really like, who you can be yourself around, it's easy. Not that I can't be myself around Kari. I mean, why wouldn't I be able to? It's not like I'm hiding something from her. Well, besides the fact that I can't stop thinking about another girl. Another girl that I'm going to be seeing tomorrow.

"Of course I'm not listening," I say, shrugging and trying to make light of it. "You're talking about some kind of flash mob at a bumper boat place. Why would I want to listen to that?"

"Because you might get famous from it," Evan says. "I'll bet Peyton would be sure to notice *that.*"

He realizes his mistake as soon as he says it.

"Who's Peyton?" Kari asks, frowning.

"No one," Evan says quickly.

Whitney's eyes narrow, and I can tell she's going to be grilling Evan about this later. Girls are always so protective of their friends. Guys would never do shit like that. Yeah, we look out for each other, but we also know when to stay out of each other's business. Damn. I'm going to kill Evan.

"Okay, fine," Evan says. "I'll tell you."

"Evan—" I start, but he cuts me off.

"It's Peyton Manning."

Kari laughs, but Whitney looks confused.

"He's a quarterback," Evan explains. "He keeps getting injured, and he's, like, kind of old, so . . ."

"Right," I say, surprised that Evan was able to come up with such a good lie so quickly. "I'm obsessed with him."

Evan nods sadly. "Poor little Jacey here keeps writing him letters and tweeting at him, but Peytie Pie just won't pay him any attention, will he, Jace?"

"Nope." I say, and shrug. "So anyway, about the flash—"

"Jace was even thinking about pretending to be a Make-A-Wish kid, weren't you, Jace?"

"No," I say through gritted teeth. "I wasn't."

"Yes, you were," Evan says. "It was right after that time you wanted me to film you with I LOVE PEYTON MANNING written across your chest while you ran up and down the hallways at school."

"You were going to do that?" Whitney asks, giggling.

"Of course not," I say. "It was just, um, a thought. I was joking."

"It seemed serious to me," Evan says, and shrugs.

Luckily, at that moment the line lurches forward and we all start to get herded into our boats. I slide onto the seat next to Kari. "You can drive," I tell her.

"Oh, no." She shakes her head. "I'm kind of horrible at it."

I shrug as she climbs over me and into the passenger seat.

"You're going down!" Evan screams from the boat next to us and honks his horn a bunch of times. A dad with two kids looks at us nervously, and I can tell he's thinking that he shouldn't have come to the bumper boats on a Thursday night, and that he can't believe how crazy teenagers are these days.

"Evan," I say, "relax. There are kids here."

"Sorry." He looks sheepish, and then he whispers, "You're going down."

"Sorry Evan's being crazy," I say to Kari.

She smiles. "I like it," she says. "At least he keeps things interesting."

She's right next to me, and even though the boat is really small, there are still a couple of inches of space between our legs. She's sitting up ramrod straight, and I realize that I'm sitting up straight, too. Which isn't really how you should be sitting when you're on a date.

I shift my leg over a little so that it's touching hers, but now we're just sort of sitting there with our legs touching. After a few seconds, she shifts away.

The ride begins before I have a chance to think about what that even means, and we immediately start chasing Evan around the big pool of water. He's definitely acting crazy, driving the boat back and forth in looping circles, slamming into the wall and seemingly not caring if he and Whitney get completely soaked.

Whitney doesn't seem to think there's anything wrong with this, and in fact, she seems to actually like it. I wonder if maybe she's secretly as crazy as Evan.

"You're going down!" Evan yells again, and then slams into us. The other people in the bumper boats look at us kind of in disgust. But at least we're leaving them alone and just focusing on each other. That should count for something, especially since not everyone does that. One time I saw this guy wearing a Budweiser tank top begin terrorizing the children on the boats, getting them all wet and laughing gleefully. He even made a girl cry.

"No, we're not!" Kari yells at them. "*You're* going down!"

"Oohh, this girl wants a fight!" Evan turns the boat around, driving the wrong way around the pool, and tries to smash into us head-on, which he knows is against the rules.

We're about to hit, but at the last moment, I yank the steering wheel hard to the left so that we miss them. Instead, we slam into the wall.

"Ha ha!" Evan yells from behind us, happy that he won his game of chicken. "Suckers!"

"Why'd you do that?" Kari asks me, sounding disappointed.

"I didn't want to crash into them that hard," I say. "We would have gotten all wet."

"It's bumper boats," she says. "That's kind of the point."

"Yeah, but you're not really supposed to be slamming into people like that."

"I guess."

There's an awkward silence, and I wonder why it was so important to her that we win the game of chicken. Then I wonder why I'm acting like kind of a dick about it. It's probably just my bad mood. I do that sometimes—get into a bad mood and then just not want to have any kind of fun.

But fuck that. I'm done letting myself get all worked up about Peyton. So I'm going to see Peyton. Big fucking deal. It's a stupid thing to be getting all weird about. Sunday is graduation, and then I'll have the whole summer in front of me before I'm off to college in the fall. And once I'm at

Georgetown, I'm not going to be thinking about Peyton. She'll be just some girl that I knew in high school.

"It's okay," I say to Kari, shifting into reverse and backing our boat out from where it's wedged in the corner of the pool. "We'll get them now."

It's a sneak attack. We come up behind Evan and Whitney and slam right into them, shooting a spray of water over the back of their boat and soaking both of them instantly.

"Oh, that's it," Evan says, glaring at me as Whitney shrieks in glee. "Now it's on."

We spend the next hour riding the bumper boats over and over, and I do my best to get into it and to forget about Peyton. By the end of the night, it seems to be working.

Well. Almost.

peyton before

Thursday, June 24, 5:02 p.m.
Greenwich, Connecticut

"Did you bring a bathing suit?" my mom asks as I slide my suitcase down the hall toward the front door. It's the night before the wedding, and we're about to head to the airport for our flight to Florida. My dad was supposed to be in charge of bringing our bags out to the car, but he and my mom got into some huge fight a few minutes ago, and so now he's just sitting out in the car, pouting and waiting for us to load up our own stuff.

"Yes, I brought a bathing suit." I brought three bathing suits, actually. Because I'm going to be spending the summer in North Carolina, although my mom doesn't know that yet.

Brooklyn and I have spent the past two weeks crafting a plan. A plan to get away from Connecticut for the summer. A plan that will allow me to spend my summer away from my parents and their maybe-divorce, away from my mom and her lies, away from my obsessive Jace thoughts. (Not that I know for sure I won't be having obsessive Jace thoughts in North Carolina, but I figure it can't hurt.)

Here is our brilliant plan:

Stage One: I will go to the wedding and pretend nothing weird is going on. I will pose for pictures like a good girl and act like I'm having a great time. If Jace approaches me, I will smile and then act as if we are just acquaintances, and not like he is a boy who broke my heart. I will be like a Peyton made of stone, smiling and pretending everything is okay.

Stage Two: The morning after the wedding is over, Brooklyn will fly to Florida to meet me at the Sarasota Airport. We will then rent a car and drive to North Carolina, where we've rented an apartment for the summer. (Well—where Brooklyn's rented an apartment. She had to put it in her name, since she's eighteen, and I'm not. But I'm on the lease as a tenant.)

It's a surprisingly simple plan. And it was surprisingly easy to get Brooklyn on board with it. I just told her that I wanted to get away—that my parents had been fighting more, and I needed a break from being upset about Jace. North Carolina was even her idea—she knows a boy there, and I think she wanted an adventure.

Of course, we're going to have to find jobs when we get there, and figure out how to get around—we can't afford to keep the rental car for more than a few days.

But I can't think about any of that right now. I can't worry about the long term. Right now I just need to focus on the short term, on getting through this wedding and getting to North Carolina. I can worry about the rest of it later.

"Why do you have so much luggage?" my mom asks, staring at my bags. "You have more than I do." She says it slightly accusingly, like not having as much luggage as her daughter is going to make her seem like a loser or something. Which is completely ridiculous. Who cares who has more luggage?

"I just wanted to make sure I have enough for my college visits," I say. My parents think that after the wedding, Brooklyn and I are going to spend some time looking at colleges in Florida. They have no idea that I'm going to North Carolina and not coming back.

"I thought we went over what you're going to wear," my mom says, sighing. She and I spent almost two hours the other day going through a bunch of my clothes so that my mom could pick out what she thought I should wear when I make these imaginary college visits. It was a completely pointless exercise, but I pretended to go along with it, turning this way and that as she dressed me up in a bunch of business casual clothes as if I was her own personal Barbie doll.

The whole time I was resisting the urge to come out and yell at her about what she did. If I ever do confront her about it, I'm not sure what will happen. Maybe she'll deny it, maybe she'll beg my forgiveness, maybe she'll tell me I'm being silly, maybe she'll offer to pay it all back. But who really cares? The bottom line will still be the same. I need to get away from her.

"We did pick out what I was going to wear," I say, "but I packed a few other things, too. Casual stuff, in case me and Brooklyn end up hanging out with any of the students."

My mom nods, like this makes sense. "All right. Just make sure you don't drink." She shudders. "College kids these days are always getting drunk and making fools of themselves. And don't even get me started on college boys. They'll drop a roofie in your drink like it's nothing."

"Thanks for the moral lessons," I say sarcastically. It comes out sharper than I intended, and she looks up from tying her shoes. (Which, by the way, are these ridiculous Coach sneakers that cost two hundred dollars, and which she bought just for the plane. Who buys shoes just for a *plane ride*?)

"What's that supposed to mean?" she asks.

"Nothing." I shrug. Actually, come to think of it, I probably bought those plane shoes for her. Get it? Since she probably put them on her/my credit card? The thought sends me into hysterical giggles.

My mom frowns and then opens her mouth to say something, but before she can, the front door opens and my dad reaches in and picks up a bunch of our bags, then slams the door behind him as he heads back out to the car. Yikes. I guess he got sick of waiting.

"Thanks, Joe!" my mom calls after him sarcastically. She shakes her head. "Well, that was the last of them," she says. "So I guess we're all ready."

"Yup," I say. "I guess we're all ready."

I traipse out to the car, stick the earbuds of my iPod into my ears, and zone out until we get to the airport.

I've never been a fan of flying. Being stuck in the airplane, never knowing if it's going to hit turbulence, wondering what will happen if it crashes, not having any leg room, worrying that the person next to you is going to fall asleep and drool all over your shoulder . . . it's a whole big thing.

Unless you're flying first class, which my mom always wants to do, and which we *used* to do until the economy tanked and my dad got all concerned about money. Sure enough, my mom starts as soon as she gets on the plane.

"I really wish you would have let us fly first class, Joseph," she says. My dad hates being called Joseph. It's what my mom does when she's trying to shame and/or annoy him.

"Well," my dad says, giving her a tight smile, "if you'd like to earn the money to pay for the first-class tickets, I'd be more than happy to fly that way."

I tune them out, something I'm getting quite good at doing. I don't know why my dad even came on this trip—actually, that's a lie. I do know why my dad came on this trip. He came on this trip because my mom knew it would look weird to her family if he didn't come. People would ask questions.

Whatever. Not my problem anymore. *North Carolina, North Carolina, North Carolina,* I chant quietly to myself as I head toward my seat. It's a window seat that's, fortunately, a few rows up from my parents. I guess by the time they booked our flight, there weren't any seats left that were together. *Un*fortunately, my seat is next to two little girls, whose parents are sitting behind us. I guess they couldn't get their seats together either.

But the fact that they're letting two kids who appear to be no older than three or four sit together, while the two of *them* sit together, doesn't really make that much sense. Wouldn't it be a better idea to have one parent sit with each child?

"Sorry," their mom says from behind me, almost as if she's reading my mind. "They wanted to sit together."

"They're sisters," the dad explains. "Not twins, but Irish twins." He gives me a big grin and an expectant look, like he's waiting for some sort of reaction.

I look at him blankly.

"You know, Irish twins?" he asks. "They were born only eleven months apart."

I guess that's supposed to be some kind of joke about how Irish people are always having sex or something? So they're always having tons of kids are super close in age? I don't really get it, but whatever. It's actually kind of a prejudiced comment, when you think about it. Not to mention that this family definitely doesn't look Irish—they have dark hair and dark eyes and olive skin.

"I'm Sophia," one of the girls says.

"I'm Aleah," the other one says. They're wearing matching purple gingham sundresses, with purple shoes and purple bows in their hair.

"I'm Peyton." I stow my bag into the overhead compartment and then push past them toward my seat.

I flop down and turn my iPod back on, cranking up the volume and trying to calm myself down. It's not just the flying and the twins that are making me nervous. It's everything. This wedding. Jace. My plan to run away.

Why didn't I just get a Xanax or an Ativan the way normal people do when they're all tense and on the verge of a nervous breakdown? It would have been so much easier. But I have this weird aversion to any kind of pill that makes you feel like you're losing control. Although they say those pills don't actually make you feel like you're losing control; they just allow you to be calm, which obviously would be helpful right about now. Of course, I'd probably be freaking out about having some kind of weird reaction and/or allergy to the pill. Am I too anxious for anxiety pills? Hmmm. The thought is extremely alarming.

"Peyton?" One of the twins is tapping me on my shoulder. I quickly close my eyes and pretend to be sleeping. Tap, tap, tap. "PEYTON!" Then there's a poke. And then, to my complete shock and dismay, one of those twins pulls my earbud out of my ear. What the *hell*?

I turn and glare at her, but she's giving me the cutest smile ever. "Sowwy," she says. "But you couldn't hear me." Then she holds out her juice box. "Can you open this for me?" She wrinkles up her little nose. "The straw is stuck."

"Sure." I take the juice box and deal with the straw problem.

I replace my earbud, but five seconds later, it's yanked out again.

"Peyton?" the other twin says. "Can you help me? I lost my purple crayon. Purple is my favorite color. What's your favorite color, Peyton?"

I sigh. This is going to be a long flight.

When the plane touches down in Sarasota, I'm even more relieved than I usually am when a plane lands. I've had enough of playing babysitter. Which is what I've been doing this whole entire time. Tying shoelaces. Coloring pictures. Answering questions about flying and what the pilot does. (I didn't really know the answers, so I just kind of guessed. They're kids; they don't know the difference.)

"Well," I say as we're getting ready to debark, "it was nice meeting you, girls."

I give their parents a pointed look, hoping they'll at least thank me for taking care of their children while they read and relaxed. (I peeked over at them once, and the dad was reading *Marley and Me*. *Marley and Me*! It was so annoying for some reason. That book is, like, ten years old. He had to spend the time that *I* was taking care of his rug rats reading *Marley and Me*? Couldn't he have picked something a little more current?)

But the parents don't say anything. They don't even give me a smile. They're too busy pulling down their overhead luggage.

Ugh.

God, I'm in a bad mood.

"Can I meet you guys at the luggage carousel?" I ask my mom as soon as we're off the plane. She's wearing yoga pants and a pink Ralph Lauren short-sleeved polo shirt with huge Dolce and Gabbana sunglasses holding back her newly highlighted hair. She doesn't need sunglasses. It's nighttime. I've been resisting the urge to reach over and rip them off her head, maybe taking some strands of hair with them.

"Why?" my mom asks, shouldering her bag. "You have so much luggage. You should be there to pick it up."

"I *am* going to be there to pick it up," I grumble. "I just want to get a coffee first." Coffee always helps my mood.

"Sure, honey," my dad says, not because he's taking my side, but because he wants to piss my mom off. "We'll watch for your bags. You brought the Louis Vuitton luggage, right?"

"Yeah." I wonder if I can sell it to pay off my credit card debt.

I wait in line at Starbucks, ignoring the much shorter line at the Dunkin' Donuts, because I need something strong that's going to, hopefully, jolt me out of my bad mood.

The line inches slowly forward, and I tap my foot impatiently, then pull my phone out and text Brooklyn in an effort to distract myself.

We still on?

She texts back immediately: **Yes! Stop freaking out!!**

My biggest fear is that Brooklyn is going to back out of our plan. She's given no indication that she's going to, but that doesn't mean she won't. She could get strep throat. Or food poisoning. Or a broken ankle. People are always cancelling things. Especially me. I'm a huge canceller. I hope that isn't going to make it more likely that Brooklyn is going to cancel on me. Like cancel karma or something.

When I get to the front of the Starbucks line, I decide to switch it up and order an iced mocha. Skinny, because if I'm going to see Jace tomorrow, I don't want to be all bloated. Of course, all those hamburgers I've been eating for the past two weeks aren't going to help, but whatever.

I don't need to impress anyone. Once I'm in North Carolina, I'll meet a new boy. One who will bring me flowers all the time and take me out to fancy dinners and buy me tons of presents like jewelry and iPads and all sorts of stuff. And not in a skeezy way, either, the way guys do when they're feeling guilty or want to show off how much money they have.

Actually, no, forget that. I'm not going to get all caught up in materialistic displays of affection. In fact, it's better for me to find a guy who doesn't have money. No way do I want to repeat my mom's mistakes. Plus I get the feeling that Jace and his family are kind of well-off. And I need the anti-Jace.

But anti-Jace can still bring me lots of presents. Flowers that he's grown himself. Little notes he's written on beautifully colored paper. Cookies he's baked, and books he's found in used bookstores that he wants me to read because they remind him of me.

Who needs Jace Renault? This is me, totally over him, la la la. This is him, disappearing from my mind.

"Skinny mocha latte," the barista calls out, and I pick up my drink, cheered by my new attitude and impending caffeine rush.

Brooklyn texts me again, and I check my phone.

Can't wait to c u! NC BAYBEE!

I smile and slip the phone back into my bag, then start to make my way through the crowd and over to the baggage carousel where my parents are waiting.

But a few seconds later, I stop short.

Because moving through the airport, coming from the other way, is Jace. He's wearing a cool-looking silver T-shirt, and his hair is pushed back from his face, and he's slouched over with his hands in his pockets and, oh, my God, he looks so hot and what am I going to do if he sees me?

I don't have time to run the other way. I don't have time to do *anything.* My heart is beating fast and the room is spinning and my face is flushing and I don't—

Oh.

Wait.

That's not Jace. It's some guy with a lip piercing and spiky hair who actually looks nothing like him. Well. Okay. Good. False alarm. I mean, I didn't want to see him anyway.

I keep walking through the airport, my heart finally slowing to its normal rate. I guess that whole thing about Jace disappearing from my mind needs a little work. Sigh.

jace before

Friday, June 25, 10:07 a.m.
Sarasota, Florida

The night before the wedding, I can't sleep at all. I know it's ridiculous. I know it's lame. I know it's totally stupid. I know it's because of Peyton.

I toss and turn and toss and turn. Finally at around three in the morning, I give up. I play around on the Internet for a while, but the Internet is boring. I try to read a book, but I can't keep my mind on it. I try to work on my graduation speech, but I've already gone over the stupid thing so many times that if I work on it any more, I'm afraid it's going to end up being worse. Finally, I drift off to sleep at about five a.m. after watching a bunch of reruns of *The Office* on Netflix.

I'm woken up at ten the next morning by my mom knocking on my door.

"Jace?"

I roll over and blink at the clock, wondering what's

going on. My mom never wakes me up, because she thinks I'm the perfect son and therefore trusts me enough to set my own wake-up time. (Which is actually true. I am the perfect son. And I do know when to wake up. Never before eleven, har har har.)

"Yeah?" I call back.

"Someone's here to see you."

Peyton. It's the first name that pops into my mind. She has to be in Florida by now, right? The wedding's tonight at seven, so her flight probably got in last night. Maybe she came to my house to—

"It's Evan," my mom says. "He seems a little . . . worked up."

I sigh and swing my legs over the bed, then pull a sweatshirt on over my shorts and T-shirt. When I get to the door, Evan's standing on the porch, his hands in the pockets of his khakis, his feet shuffling back and forth. His eyes are darting all around, which makes me nervous. I have no idea what's going on with him, but I have enough to be dealing with. Graduation, a wedding, seeing Peyton . . .

"Hey," I say.

"Hello!" he says, immediately pasting a smile on his face. "There's my best friend in the world!"

Oh, Jesus Christ. "What have you done?" I ask immediately.

He looks wounded. "I can't believe you would ask me that."

"Really?" I cross my arms over my chest. "You really can't believe it?"

"No," he says, raising his chin in the air. "I can't. I've been nothing but nice to you, for my whole *life* even—"

"I didn't say you weren't," I interrupt him. "All I said was that it can't really be surprising to you that I would question what kind of scrape you've gotten yourself into that would necessitate you showing up on my doorstep at ten in the morning unannounced."

His look of outrage deepens. "I don't get myself into scrapes!"

"Really?" I ask. "What about the time you signed up to sell wrapping paper for the senior fundraiser and then ended up spending the money yourself?"

"I needed that money—otherwise I wouldn't have been able to afford my prom ticket! And besides, I paid it back."

"What about the time you ended up involved in that vitamin pyramid scheme? The one where you almost got arrested for trying to sell diet pills to all the girls at school?"

"How was I supposed to know you had to be eighteen to take them?" he protests. "And besides, I got decked in the face because of that, remember?" He rubs his jaw, remembering.

"Yeah, because you can't just go around asking girls if they want to buy diet pills! Of course they're going to get pissed."

"That wasn't what—"

"Enough!" I hold my hand up. And then I start to feel bad. "Forget it. I shouldn't have brought all that stuff up."

Evan nods. "You shouldn't have," he agrees. "That stuff was in past, and I've really changed. Especially since I got together with Whitney."

I gape at him. "You guys have only been together for a few weeks."

"A few weeks is enough time. People can change like *that* if they're motivated." He snaps his fingers.

"I guess," I say doubtfully. "So then what are you doing here so—" I'm cut off by the sound of a yelp coming from the yard. I frown. "What the hell was that? If the neighbor's dog gets into my mom's flower beds again, she's going to flip."

I look around, but I don't see the dog anywhere.

"That's kind of what I'm here to talk to you about," Evan says, looking sheepish.

"My mom's flower beds?" I ask with a laugh.

He shakes his head, and then I get it.

"Oh no," I say. "Evan, please don't tell me you—"

"I got a dog." He steps to the side, so that I can see where his car's parked in the driveway. There's a dog in the backseat. When it sees us looking, it immediately starts whining and crying.

"Oh, Evan," I say, my stomach dropping. "You didn't."

"Why not?"

"You can't take care of a dog," I say. "You're too . . ." I'm about to say "irresponsible," but I'm pretty sure that would piss him off. ". . . impulsive."

"Thanks for the vote of confidence, Jace," he says, and

rolls his eyes like it's completely out of the realm of possibility that he would be considered impulsive. He puffs his chest out. "You'll be happy to know, then, that the dog's not for me. It's for Whitney."

"Okay." I peer at the dog gingerly. It definitely doesn't look like the type of dog you'd get someone as a present. Dogs that are presents should be clean and friendly looking, with their ears perked up and a big red bow around their necks. This dog looks . . . well, kind of scruffy. But whatever. If Evan's happy, I'm happy. "That's nice, Evan," I say. "I'm sure she's really going to like it."

"Well, that's the thing," he says. I close my eyes and wait for it. "She's allergic to dogs."

"Why in the world would you get her a dog if you knew she was allergic?"

"Well, *obviously* I didn't know she was allergic when I got her the dog." He shrugs. "But what's done is done."

"So take it back."

"I can't."

"Why not?"

"Because I got it from the shelter."

"And they won't take it back?" Not that I really blame them. If I'd gotten rid of a dog that looked like that, I wouldn't be excited to take it back either. I know that's a horrible thing to say. But it's true. Then I have a thought. "You didn't pay for that dog, did you?"

"Well, you have to give them an adoption fee, Jace,"

he says. "Shelters subsist on adoption fees and donations. Which reminds me, when was the last time you did any charity work?"

I look at him incredulously. "When's the last time *you* did any charity work?"

He nods. "Good point."

"Okay, so what are you going to do with him?" The dog is pawing at the inside of the window now, his front legs leaving muddy prints on the glass. "Is that how you tried to give him to Whitney?" I ask. "Because he's all dirty." She's probably not even allergic. She probably just didn't want a dirty dog.

"I never even got him to Whitney's," Evan says. He starts throwing his keys up in the air and then catching them. "I just told her I was coming over with a surprise, and she jokingly said 'I hope it's not a puppy, because I'm allergic.'"

"And what did you say?"

"I said, 'Of course it's not a puppy, I would never bring you an animal without asking your permission first.'"

"Okay," I say, "so then bring it back."

He sighs. "Jace," he says. "I just told you the problem with that."

"No, you didn't."

"The problem *is* they said all sales are final."

"All sales are final?" I shake my head. "That makes no sense. It's an animal shelter, not a Sears."

"Fine, they didn't say that." He stops throwing his keys up in the air and looks at me seriously. "But I can't take him back, Jace. No one wants him. And if no one wants him, they're going to put him to sleep. That's why I got him. He was on a list, you know, of dogs on their last chance." He lowers his voice at that last part, like he doesn't want the dog knowing about the last chance list.

"So then what are you going to do?" I ask.

"I'm going to find him a home."

"Good for you." I give Evan a good strong pat on the shoulder and then start backing into my house before he can try to involve me in whatever crazy scheme he's come up with to find a home for this dog. I can't help anyway—I don't know anyone who even wants a dog, much less a dog that looks like a big mess.

"But," he says, following me into the house, "I can't find him a home today."

"Why not?"

"Because it takes a long time for a dog to find a home! That's how he ended up at the shelter in the first place."

"Well, you should have thought of that before you got him. And anyway, why can't you keep him at your house?" I walk into the kitchen, then open the refrigerator and pull out the orange juice.

"Can I have some of that?" Evan asks, plopping himself down at the breakfast bar.

"That depends," I say. "How soon after you drink it are you going to leave?"

He gets a wounded look on his face, and I sigh. Just

because the dude was trying to do something nice for his girlfriend doesn't mean I have to be a dick. "I'm just kidding," I say, and pour him a big glass.

"Thanks." He drinks from it noisily. "I really am going to find that dog a home, Jace. I'm going to work very hard and find him a great home. I'll put up posters, I'll post ads on the Internet, I'll even take him door to door."

"Great."

"But I can't start on any of that right now."

"Why not?"

"Because I'm supposed to be going over to Whitney's with a present."

"Yeah, but you just said she's allergic to her present." I reach into the breadbox and pull out two slices of whole wheat, then pop them in the toaster.

Evan opens the pantry and pulls out a box of cereal, then begins fixing himself a bowl. "Yeah, but she doesn't know that. So now I have to bring her something else. And so I need someplace to leave the dog."

"Leave him at your house."

"Right," he says. "Like my parents are going to go for that. Anyway, I was thinking that maybe you could watch him." He settles back down at the breakfast bar and takes a big, slurpy bite of cereal.

"No." I shake my head. "My mom would never let me."

"Your mom would never let you what?" my mom asks, appearing in the kitchen.

"Let Jace have a dog," Evan says.

"Well, that's true," my mom says. "I love dogs but I don't know if it would be a good idea right now, since Jace is getting ready to go off to college."

"Oh, I wasn't talking about him keeping it," Evan says. "I was talking about him just watching one for me."

"Like dog-sitting?" my mom asks. She pulls down a bowl and starts making herself a bowl of cereal too. The same kind Evan has. I sigh.

"No," I say. "Not like dog-sitting. It's not even his dog."

My mom frowns. "Whose dog is it?"

"It doesn't have a home," Evan says sadly. His eyes are watering, which is a total fake. The dude never cries, especially not over a dog that he just met. "He was a shelter dog that they were about to put down."

My mom sets her spoon down and puts her hand over her heart. "That's terrible!"

"They weren't about to put it down," I say, slathering peanut butter on my toast.

"Yes, they were," Evan says. "They're one of those kill shelters, the kind that kill dogs if they don't get adopted."

"It's horrible the way people just discard dogs these days," my mom says, shaking her head. She sits down next to Evan with her bowl of cereal. "You really shouldn't get a dog unless you're equipped to take care of it."

"I know," Evan says, even though he just got a dog that he wasn't equipped to take care of.

"Anyway," I say, draining my juice. "Thanks for stopping by, Evan, and good luck with the dog. I need to go work on my speech for graduation on Sunday."

"I thought your speech was done," my mom says, a look of panic in her eyes. My mom's all worried that I'm going to get up there and blank out on my speech or something. It's, like, her big fear. Which is ridiculous, since all I have to do is read it.

"I just thought I'd put some finishing touches on it," I lie. "And practice reading it out loud."

"You don't want to sound too rehearsed," my mom says.

"She's right." Evan spoons up the rest of his cereal, then brings his bowl over to the sink. "If you sound too robotic, people are going to start tuning out. Of course, people will probably tune out anyway, but you can at least try to make it a little easier for them to listen."

"Thanks." I roll my eyes.

"So, look, can the dog stay with you or what?"

"No," I say at the same time my mom says, "Yes."

"What?" we both say, looking at each other.

"Why the hell would you want to let me have a dog?" I ask. "It's ridiculous. I begged and begged for a dog growing up, and you never let me have one."

"You weren't ready for the responsibility. And with your father and me working so many hours, it wouldn't have been fair."

"I'm not ready for the responsibility now, either," I try.

"I'm very irresponsible." I look at my empty glass of juice. "See how I just leave my dirty glasses around? I'm horrible with responsibility."

She waves me off. "Of course we'll take the dog in. How long?"

"Just a couple of days," Evan says. "Thanks, Mrs. Renault. I'm always telling Jace how lucky he is to have a mom as cool as you."

It's a lie. Well, half a lie. Sometimes he does say that, but it's only because his parents are so strict that anyone else's parents would seem cool by default.

"What about the wedding?" I say wildly in a last-ditch effort to derail this horrible plan. "Who's going to watch the dog while we're at the wedding?"

The wedding is at night, at this super-fancy resort, and so we're going to be spending the night there tonight. I guess they're having some big brunch tomorrow morning, and they gave my mom a major guilt trip when she tried to get out of it. Which means I have to go, too. Which means the night before my graduation is going to be a total waste.

"We can bring him with us," my mom says. "He can hang out in the hotel."

Great. A dog in my hotel room.

Just one more thing to worry about.

the trip peyton

Saturday, June 26, 3:37 p.m.
Ocala, Florida

When Jace's car smashes into whatever it is that's behind us, it takes me a second to realize what happened. It's like my brain can't comprehend or accept the fact that I hit something. I slam my foot down on the brake, which is pretty stupid, since we're already stopped.

From the backseat, Hector gives a little squeal.

I close my eyes. "What just happened?" I croak.

"What the hell do you think just happened?" Jace yells. "You hit someone."

"Are they . . . are they *dead*?" I whisper.

"No, they're not dead, you hit their car, not them." He's unbuckling his seat belt and stepping out of the car. There's man in a button-up shirt with a receding hairline standing behind us, his face so red and so mad that for a second I think he's going to explode into a fireball.

I put the car in park, then unbuckle my seat belt and take a deep breath. Hector is just sitting in the backseat, not making a sound. I check him over before I get out, to make sure he's okay. He looks fine, physically, which is good. But he's just sitting there quietly, which is kind of disturbing. I mean, usually he always wants to whine and wiggle around. The fact that he's being so silent means he knows something bad is going on.

"It's okay, boy," I whisper into his fur, wishing I could just stay in here with him. How could I have hit someone? I know the answer. The truth is, I was distracted. I was thinking about what Jace said in the restaurant, about how running away wasn't going to solve anything. Deep down, I know he's right. It's not going to help anything. It's not going to help me figure out how much of the credit card debt I'm going to be responsible for. It's not going to help me figure out how to confront my mom.

Does this mean I'm a coward? Does Jace think I'm a coward?

"I just need the summer," I whisper to Hector. "I just need the summer to not have to deal with it, and then I'll figure it all out, I promise."

Hector whines and turns his head, then puts his front legs on the back windshield and starts pawing at the glass.

I sigh. I know I should get out and see what's going on. I take another deep breath and then step out of the car.

"What the hell have you done to my *car*?" the man I hit is yelling.

Jace doesn't answer him, just peers down at the cars, looking at the damage. And there's kind of a lot. At least, it kind of looks like there is. The whole back bumper of Jace's car is hanging off. I immediately burst into tears. Something like that is expensive. Extremely expensive. You have to pay thousands and thousands of dollars for bodywork. I know because one time my mom got into a fender bender and it cost like two thousand dollars in bodywork and my dad was so pissed he threatened to take her Navigator away and make her buy something that had lower insurance premiums, like a Corolla.

"Why are you crying?" the man roars when he sees me standing there. "You're the one who hit me! I'm the one who should be crying!" He's waving his arms all around, his face flushed and sweaty. God, he's scary. I look at his car, but I can't see any damage.

"There's nothing wrong with your car," Jace says. He's been inspecting it while I've been crying. "So you can be on your way."

"I will not be on my way!" the man screeches. "We are calling the police."

"Knock it off," Jace says and rolls his eyes. "It's a stupid fender bender. I'll get you my insurance info." He turns and heads toward the car to get his insurance card.

"Were you driving the car, young lady?" the man demands.

I open my mouth to answer, then quickly shut it. He's probably going to try to nab me on some kind of insurance technicality or something. Like say that since I was driving, I have to pay everything out of pocket.

"Because if you were, you need some driving lessons. The first thing I always tell my daughter, the *first thing*, is that you need to check your rearview mirrors. Didn't you take driver's ed?"

I did take driver's ed, but it actually wasn't that helpful. It was four of us all in one car, and you spent most of the time just sitting there, waiting for your turn to drive. It was an hour-long class, so you only got, like, fifteen minutes of driving time once a week.

At the end of the six-week class, you got a percentage off your insurance. Which will come in handy now. Because my insurance will probably have to pay, won't it? Or will Jace's? God, I wonder if I should call my dad. He knows about stuff like this. Of course, I'll have to make something up, something about how I was driving with Brooklyn and crashed the rental car. He's not going to be happy, especially since—

"Here you go," Jace says, shoving a crinkled up piece of paper into the man's hands. "There's my insurance information."

Jace pulls out his cell phone out and snaps some pictures of both of the cars, and the man does the same.

Then the guy grumbles something about "crazy female

drivers," gets back in his car, and drives away. How rude. I mean, couldn't he at least have said something about crazy *teenage* drivers? Why does it have to be female drivers? I'm a very good driver. Well, usually. I mean, I'd never gotten into an accident before this.

When it's time to get back into Jace's car, I know enough to slide into the passenger seat. Hector does a little whine and then lies down in the backseat and stays quiet. Jace climbs into the car next to me, his face dark and stormy looking.

"I'm really sorry," I say. "I should have looked behind me."

He doesn't stay anything, just sits there, looking out the windshield, his hands gripping the wheel.

"I'll pay for it," I say.

He still doesn't respond.

"I'll make sure it all gets paid for, I promise."

He still doesn't say anything.

My eyes fill back up with tears, and after a second, Hector slides his paws onto the back of my seat and starts licking my face. I don't even care about all the disgusting dog germs that are getting all over me.

"You can drive me back to the hotel if you want," I say to Jace. "If you do, I'll understand. Or you can take me back to Courtney's, and she can help me get home."

I can tell he's really mad. After a second, he turns the key in the ignition, makes a big point of adjusting the rearview mirror and then pulls out of the parking lot.

When we get to the highway, I'm sure he's going to start heading back to Siesta Key. But instead, he continues on our route, driving north toward the Carolinas.

Jace doesn't talk the whole rest of the way through Florida and into Georgia. It's actually pretty unnerving. I don't know what he's thinking. I don't know what he's planning. I'm half afraid that maybe he's so mad he's going to drop me off on the side of the road somewhere, leaving me to hitchhike the rest of the way to North Carolina.

When Hector starts whining in the backseat like he has to go to the bathroom, I'm relieved. I have to go to the bathroom, too, but I'm way too nervous to say anything.

Jace reaches over and pulls the GPS out from the little holder on the windshield, and starts punching something in, probably looking for a rest stop.

"I can do that," I offer, trying to sound equal parts apologetic, thankful, and helpful. "It's probably safer for me to use it. You know, since you're driving and all."

He snorts. Which makes sense. I mean, who am I to bring up safety? I'm the one who just got into an accident in a car that wasn't mine before I even started driving. He finds what he's looking for on the GPS, then slides it back into the holder.

Ten minutes later, he pulls into the rest stop, still not talking to me. He gets out of the car and starts walking

Hector over on the grass. I'm not sure exactly what I'm supposed to do, so after I minute, I unbuckle my seat belt and head inside.

I use the restroom, then buy myself the cheapest food I can find—a snack-size bag of potato chips and a can of generic diet soda. Total cost = three dollars. At the last minute, I add a second bag of chips and a bottle of water for Jace. I figure doubling my budget is worth making the effort to keep him happy.

Well, maybe not *happy*, exactly. I mean, even I know that a snack isn't going to make up for the fact that I smashed his car. But maybe we can move past it. Maybe it will become one of those funny little road-trip stories we'll tell people later. Like party conversations, ha ha ha.

But when I get back to the car, Jace is standing behind it, scowling down at the bumper.

"I got you some snacks," I say.

He takes the water from me, pulls off the cap, and takes a long sip. Then he takes the chips.

"You're welcome," I say.

He still doesn't say anything, just keeps looking down at the bumper.

"Okkkkaayyy," I say. "So are you going to just ignore me the whole rest of the time?"

"I'm not ignoring you."

"You're not? Because it seems pretty much like you are."

"Why would you think that?"

"Because you haven't been talking to me for the past four hours!"

"You wrecked my car."

I roll my eyes. "I didn't *wreck* your car," I say. "It still runs, doesn't it?"

"I'm not sure," he says. He picks up the bumper and pushes it up against the frame of the car. When he holds it like that, it almost looks like you could just glue it back on. They probably have some kind of special glue you can buy at an auto parts store for like, ten dollars. That's what happened when Brooklyn got her brakes done. It was going to cost her four hundred dollars if she took it into a shop, but instead she got this kid in our class to do it for eighty dollars after she bought the parts at AutoZone.

"It might be something we can fix ourselves," I say, crouching down. I hold up one edge of the bumper, but when I do, the other side droops down and scrapes the paint. Oops.

"Don't touch it," Jace says, running his hands through his hair. "Jesus."

"Sorry." I feel my eyes start to fill with tears. I blink as fast as I can, not wanting him to know he's having this kind of effect on me.

He sighs. "No, I'm sorry," he says. "I'm being a douche. You didn't mean to crash my car."

"I *didn't* mean it," I say, shaking my head vehemently. "I swear. I should have been looking where I was going. But it was a total accident. And I really am going to pay for it, I promise. I'll send you however much it costs."

Of course, I have no idea how I'm going to get said money, but I'm so desperate for Jace not to not be mad at me anymore that I'll pretty much promise anything. Besides, it's the right thing to do.

"The insurance will probably cover it," he says. He rolls his head around, stretching his neck. "Look, we should probably find a place to stay."

"A place to stay?" Hector is pawing at my legs, so I crouch down and rub his head until he starts to calm down a little.

"Yeah, a hotel. I'm exhausted, and there's no way I'm going to let you drive."

I nod. "That's fair." I take a deep breath. "Can we stay somewhere cheap?"

He nods. "Sure."

I want to ask him if he expects me to pay for his room, too, but I don't. If he says yes, I don't know what I'm going to do.

We all climb back into the car. Hector sits on my lap this time. He smells kind of gross, but I don't mind. It's comforting, having him close to me. Besides, he's just a dog. He has no idea that my life is a disaster, that I'm on a road trip with a guy I can't stand, or that my mom did something horrible to me. All Hector knows is that he's in this car, right now, driving, while I pet him.

And that's enough to make him happy.

I just wish it were enough for me.

Half an hour later, Jace pulls up in front of the Residence Inn in downtown Savannah. It's definitely not the cheapest hotel, but it's one of the only ones around that seemed like it was in a safe area, close to our route, and most importantly, took pets.

When we get inside, Jace walks right up to the front desk.

"We need, um, two rooms please, I guess," he says. He looks at me for confirmation. I nod. "And we have a dog."

"And which room would you like the dog to stay in?" the front desk clerk asks happily. Her nametag says MIA.

"Mine," Jace says. I'm about to protest, because it would be nice to have Hector curled up in bed with me, but then the front desk clerk says it costs an extra seventy-five dollars for the pet fee. Jace hands over his credit card and pays for the rooms, I guess expecting that I'll pay him back later.

"If you want to go out to eat, I recommend the Distillery," the clerk says. She swipes Jace's card and gives us a smile. "It's right around the corner and it's delicious."

"Thanks," I say.

Jace signs the receipt Mia gives him, then goes outside to park the car and bring Hector in. I wait in the lobby with our bags.

When he comes back, we walk through the bar area and

down the hall toward our rooms in silence. Even Hector seems subdued, trotting along next to Jace compliantly, not even noticing the other hotel guests smiling at him and remarking to each other about how cute he is.

"Well," I say as I slide my key card into the door of my room. It beeps and blinks with a little green light. "Um, I guess I'll see you in the morning? And I'll, uh, I'll pay you back for the room then."

"Yeah," he says, sliding his card into the keypad of the room across the hall. "I guess I'll see you in the morning."

He disappears through the door, and I stand there for a second, already missing him. Finally I shake my head to clear my thoughts, and then walk into my room.

jace the trip

Saturday June 26, 7:45 p.m.
Savannah, Georgia

I wasn't that mad at Peyton for crashing my car. I swear to God, I wasn't. Shit, it could just as easily have been me. I've been in a couple of fender benders since I got my license, and it's not like it's that big of a deal. I mean, what does it really matter? No one got hurt. And my insurance is going to cover the whole thing anyway, so it's not like it's going to be expensive.

So no, I wasn't mad at Peyton. I was mad at myself.

Because when she slammed into that car behind us, I realized something. *I didn't want to call off the trip.* She crashed my car, she'd been being kind of bratty to me, I was probably going to miss my stupid graduation because of her, and still *I didn't want to call off the trip.*

And when I thought about it, the only reason I could think of for how that could be was because I wanted to be with

Peyton. I wanted to stay with her. Peyton, who acts like she can't stand me, who acts like she doesn't want anything to do with me, who got into an accident with my car that is probably going to cause my insurance rates to go through the roof, and I wanted to stay with her. What the hell is wrong with me?

This is what's going through my head as I lie on my bed in the hotel room in Savannah. Finally, I can't take it anymore, and so I hook Hector's leash on and take him outside.

There's a field across the street from the hotel, and I walk Hector over and onto the grass. It must have been raining in Savannah earlier, because the grass is wet, and within a couple of minutes Hector's paws are a completely muddy mess.

I say a silent prayer of thanks that the hotel room I'm staying in has two beds. Maybe I can towel him off just enough so that he's not dripping, and then put him in the bed next to me. It's just dirt, right? It's not like it won't come off in the wash. Of course, the sheets are bright white, so . . .

My phone rings, and I sigh and reach into my pocket. It's definitely going to be my mom. Every time she's called, I've sent it right to voice mail, knowing that she's going to be bothering me about how I need to get home in time for graduation. I don't understand why stupid graduation means so much to her. Whether I'm there to give a big speech or not doesn't change the fact that I'm valedictorian.

But it's not my mom calling. It's a number I don't recognize.

"Hello?" I try to balance my phone against my shoulder as I grip Hector's leash with two hands. There's a leaf floating by, and apparently this is a big concern to him. So big that he feels the need to chase it, practically pulling my arm out of its socket in the process.

"Jace!" a girl's voice says. "Thank God! We thought you were dead!"

"Who thought I was dead?"

"I don't know," she says. There's a pause. "Actually, I guess only your mom thought that. I pretty much knew you weren't dead."

"Who is this?"

"It's Courtney!"

"Oh. Sorry. I didn't recognize the number."

"I'm calling from Jordan's phone." She lowers her voice. "Listen, I don't know where you are or what you're up to, but your mom's really worried. She says you have graduation tomorrow night, and she hasn't been able to get in touch with you. She's about thirty seconds away from calling the police."

"I know she hasn't been able to get in touch with me," I say. "I've been sending her calls to voice mail." I pause, waiting for Courtney to tell me that wasn't a very nice thing to do. But she doesn't. "And anyway, I told her I wasn't going to graduation. So I don't know why she's freaking out."

"Okay." Courtney's silent for a minute. I watch as Hector sniffs around, pawing things and eating grass. "So what do you want me to tell her if she calls?"

"She's *calling* you?"

"Well, yeah," she says. "She's worried about you, and she thought that maybe you'd come to hang out with me and my friends."

"Why would she think that?" I ask. "I told her I was—" I shake my head in frustration. "Actually, never mind. Just tell her that I'm safe, okay? And that I'll be home soon."

"Okay." There's a silence again. "Jace?" she asks finally.

"Yeah?"

"Are you with Peyton?"

I hesitate. I don't want to lie, but on the other hand, I don't want Courtney telling my mom any details, either. The less my mom knows, the better. Which is exactly why I'm not taking her calls. "Is this off the record?"

"Off the record?"

"Yeah, like are you going to tell my mom what I'm telling you?"

"No," she says. "I'll tell her you're safe and that you'll be home soon, but that's it."

"Then yes, I'm with Peyton."

"That's what I thought," she says. And I'm pretty sure I can hear a smile in her voice.

I walk Hector around for another half an hour or so, figuring it's probably a good idea to tire him out before I take him back to the room. I feel bad that he's been cooped up in the car all day. Not that he seems to be holding it against me. In fact, just the opposite. He seems totally happy, wagging his tail and trying to meet everybody that walks by.

We have to cross over the grass to get back to the hotel, and so by the time we get to the sidewalk in front of the building, his paws are leaving muddy prints all over the pavement. There's no way I'm going to be able to just towel him off. And if he jumps on the bed like this, it's going to be mess.

It's wishful thinking to expect I can keep him on the floor. Last night at the hotel in Siesta Key he jumped right up on the bed as soon as the lights went out and then nosed his snout under my pillow. Don't ask me why he thought that would be a comfortable position, or why he turned over sometime in the night and slept on his back. Dogs are just weird.

"I really, really don't want to give you a bath," I say to Hector as I slide my key card into the gate that separates the hotel from the sidewalk. "But it looks like that's what's going to have to happen. Do you like the water, Hector?"

He wags his tail and looks at me happily, but I'll bet once he gets into the water, it's going to be a big debacle. Maybe I should just keep him dirty. At least I know what kind of dirt I'm dealing with. I'll just make sure to leave a big tip so that the housekeepers won't—

"Ahhh!" Peyton screams. She's on the other side of the gate, trying to pull it toward her at the same time I'm trying to pull it toward me.

"Oh," she says once she walks through and sees that it's me. "Hi."

"What are you doing?" I ask suspiciously.

She shrugs. "Just going for a walk. I was going to see if there was a gas station or something where I could grab something to eat."

"Why would you want to eat gas station food?" But as soon as the words are out of my mouth, I realize the reason. She's broke. Which explains why she bought those chips and waters at the rest stop, instead of going for something more substantial.

"What the hell happened to him?" she asks, looking down at Hector and ignoring my question about the gas station food. "He looks like a big muddy mess."

"Nothing happened to him," I say, suddenly defensive. I pull Hector's leash back a little bit, so that he's closer to me. "We were just going for a walk. Dogs get dirty on walks sometimes, Peyton." I roll my eyes like she doesn't know anything about dogs.

"Yeah, but he's reeeally dirty." She kneels down on the sidewalk, and Hector puts his front paws on her knees and licks her face. "What'd you do, let him walk through mud puddles?"

"No." Yes. "Anyway, I have to go give him a bath."

"A *bath*?"

"Yes, a bath. Dogs have baths, Peyton, when they're dirty."

She stands up and grins at me. "No, I know that. I'm just surprised, that's all."

"By what?"

"By the fact that you're going to give him a bath."

"Why?" I'm somehow insulted.

"I don't know." She shrugs. "It just doesn't seem like the kind of thing you would do."

"Well, I'm going to."

"Okay."

"Okay."

We stand there, looking at each other for a moment.

"Well," she says finally. "Um, let me know if you need any help."

"I won't."

"Well, if you do—"

"If I do, I'll let you know. But I'm pretty sure I won't."

"Okay. Well, see you tomorrow." She pushes past me through the gate, and even though I'm so annoyed at her, even though I can't stand the fact that she's acting like I'm so incompetent that I can't even give a dog a bath, I have to resist the urge to reach out and pull her toward me.

I shake my head and pull Hector through the gate and down the hall toward our room. This time, as we pass other hotel guests, they wrinkle up their noses and look at Hector like he's disgusting. Which I guess he kind of is, but really. You'd think people would be a little nicer.

He'll be fine after he has a bath. A bath that I can handle on my own, thank you very much. A bath that I definitely won't be needing Peyton's help with.

the trip peyton

Saturday, June 26, 8:17 p.m.
Savannah, Georgia

The gas station in Savannah is surprisingly well-stocked and surprisingly cheap. I don't know if it's Southern pricing or what, but I was able to get Oreos, a Diet Coke, two bags of chips, and some nacho cheese Combos for only six dollars. Six dollars! What a score.

It was so cheap that at first I thought maybe it was one of those things where the food is about to go bad, and so everything's marked down. But I checked the expiration dates, and they weren't even close. So yay for nonperishable Southern snacks!

I walk quickly back to the hotel, munching on a bag of chips as I go. It's a nice walk—it's still a little light out, and the Georgia air is warm and slightly humid against my skin. I decide to take the long way around the building, and go through the front lobby of the hotel instead of the side gate.

For the first time in a few days, I start to feel happy. *It's all going to work out,* I tell myself as I walk through the automatic doors. *It's going to be fine.*

The girl at the front desk, Mia, has her iPod on, and she's dancing to whatever song she's listening to as she enters something into the computer. She smiles and gives me a little wave.

"How's your room?" she asks.

"It's great!" I tell her. "Thanks."

She smiles, revealing the gap between her front teeth. "Let me know if you need anything else."

"I will."

Everyone here is so friendly and relaxed! There are people sitting at the bar as I pass by to my room, and they're laughing and joking around with each other. One of the women gives me a little wave as I go by, and I wave back. I guess this is what people mean when they talk about Southern hospitality. I wonder if this is how it's going to be in North Carolina, too.

I hope so. I could totally get used to it.

I push open the door to my room and dump my snacks on the bed. I decide to have a nice long hot shower, then watch *Jersey Shore* reruns or something equally mindless while I eat.

I grab a pair of fleece pants and a tank top out of my suitcase, bring them into the bathroom with me, undress, and then turn the shower on full blast. I push it as hot as I can stand it, letting the water wash the stress off me as the stream beads down over my body. I stay in there for a long time, and when I finally turn the water off, I feel relaxed and loose.

And honestly, when you really think about it, why shouldn't I be? I'm only one day away from being in North Carolina, only one day away from having my own apartment, only one day away from starting my new life. Who cares what other people are going to think or say? Who cares if I'm making a big mistake? People probably told Bill Gates he was making a big mistake when he dropped out of college. Same with Mark Zuckerberg. Of course, those guys were tech geniuses, and were actually working on something that they were going to bring to market. Or whatever you call it when you make a new product.

But maybe I could bring something to market. One time at the ninth-grade bake sale I made these amazing brownies because I messed up the recipe on the back of the chocolate chip bag. People were raving about them all day. I could open a brownie shop. And then expand into cookies and cakes. I've always wanted to learn how to make cookies and cakes in the shape of things, like on those shows where they build pastries up to look like people or cartoon characters. I could totally do that.

I'm so cheered by my new life as a retail and/or Internet entrepreneur, that I'm humming a little tune to myself as I get out of the shower and get dressed.

I'm just about to turn the TV on when there's a knock on my door. I ignore it, figuring it's probably housekeeping or maybe that nice girl from the front desk, coming to set a chocolate on my pillow or something. They probably do things like that in the South.

I rip open my bag of Combos, and pop one in my mouth.

The knock comes again. Geez. These Southern people might need to learn that being friendly is only friendly when the other person actually wants it.

"Peyton?"

Oh. It's Jace. Well, that explains it. He's definitely not going to be practicing Southern hospitality. He's lucky if he even practices Northern hospitality.

I creep to the door and peer out the peephole. He's standing there in a white T-shirt and a pair of dark green track pants. His hair is all messed up, and there's a big smear of dirt on the front of his shirt.

Hector is standing next to him, wagging his tail.

"PEYTON!" Jace says, and knocks again. "Are you in there?"

I sigh and unlock the door. "Of course I'm in here," I say. "Where else would I be?"

"I've been trying to call your room for the past forty-five minutes," he says. "Why didn't you answer?"

He peers past me into the room, all suspicious, like he half expects that I'm going to be throwing a party or entertaining a gentleman caller or something.

"I was at the gas station, remember?"

"For an hour?"

"No," I say, even though I was probably there for longer that I should have been, picking out my snacks. There were just so many to choose from. "Not for an hour. But then I was in the shower." I cross my arms over my chest, suddenly realizing that all I'm wearing is a thin tank top.

"Well, can you help me?" Jace asks.

"Jace," I say seriously. "I think you're beyond help." I think it's a pretty funny joke, honestly, but Jace doesn't seem to agree.

"Ha ha," he says, rolling his eyes. "But seriously, I need help with Hector. He won't listen."

"What else is new?" I look down at Hector and give him a fond smile, because honestly, how can I not love a creature that is giving Jace a hard time and not listening to him? And that's when I realize that Hector is now an even bigger mess than he was when I saw him outside after his walk.

Now not only is he covered in mud, but the mud seems to have been diluted by water and soap. It's dripping off his fur into dirty, gritty puddles that are collecting on the wood floor of the hallway.

"What happened to him?" I wrinkle my nose. "He's all soapy and dirty." I didn't even know you could be both soapy and dirty at the same time.

"I was giving him a bath," Jace says. "And he wouldn't

sit still. Every time I would try to rinse him off, he would jump out of the tub."

"He jumped out of the tub like *that*?"

"Yeah, and ran all around my room making it a disgusting mess."

I bite back a laugh.

"It's not funny!" Jace says.

"You're right," I say, nodding mock seriously. "It isn't."

Jace sighs. "Are you going to help me or not?"

"I thought you didn't need my help." I give him a challenging look.

He gives me one right back. "We all need a little help now and then, don't we Peyton?" I know he's talking about the fact that I needed him to drive me to North Carolina. Or, as far as he knows, Connecticut. I hate that he's bringing that up. But he does have a point.

"Whatever," I say, holding the door to my room open. "Come on in."

Okay, so giving Hector a bath with Jace was actually kind of fun. Once we let go of the idea that there was any chance that we, Hector, or the bathroom were going to stay clean, and just took it for what it was—a big, disgusting mess—it went a lot more smoothly.

"You hold him while I rinse him, okay?" I tell Jace.

"Okay," Jace says. Hector is in the tub, just standing there, looking at us like we're crazy. He doesn't seem to mind the water, but you never know when he's going to get excited and want to play or cause mischief.

Jace holds Hector gingerly around the stomach, and I pull down the shower sprayer to rinse Hector off. "It's okay, boy," I say. "It's just some nice warm water, it'll feel good."

Hector acts like he understands me, and raises his head up to the water. "Good boy," I tell him.

"You know he can't understand you, right?" Jace asks.

"Yes, he can," I say, even though I know it's not true. "He's a very smart dog."

Jace scoffs at me.

"He is!" I say. "And he doesn't like you saying that he's not smart, do you, boy?"

As if on cue, Hector works his way out from Jace's hands and puts his front paws up on the side of the tub.

"Hey, hey, hey," Jace says, lowering him back down into the water. "What are you doing?"

"I told you," I say. "He didn't like you saying that he doesn't understand English." And then I add, "And also you were hardly holding on to him. You don't have to be afraid of him, Jace, he wouldn't hurt a fly."

"I'm not afraid of him!"

"Then what's the big deal?"

"Nothing." He shrugs. "I just don't like him."

"Why not?"

"Because he's a pain in the ass."

"God, you are really mean, you know that?"

"I'm mean?" he says, and shakes his head. "Okay, fine, Peyton, you want to know why I'm being weird around Hector?" He takes a deep breath and then looks away from me and down at the bathroom floor.

"Yes!" I say. "I do want to know why you're so weird around Hector." I take the showerhead and point the stream of water down around Hector's back legs. He wags his tail, shooting little drops of warm water onto my arms.

"Fine," Jace says, "But don't say I didn't warn you." He takes another deep breath in and then closes his eyes for a second. "When I was seven I had a dog. He was a golden retriever named Mork. That was the year I was getting teased at school, and Mork, he . . . he was always near me. He was the only one didn't care about my speech impediment."

"You had a speech impediment?" I ask, frowning.

"Yeah," he says. "That's why I got teased."

I frown. "You don't have it anymore."

"I had to work with a speech therapist," he says. He sounds annoyed. "But anyway, back to Mork. He was my best friend." He gets a faraway look in his eyes, and I'm not sure, but I think he's even getting a little choked up. "At least, he *was* my best friend. Until that year's Christmas morning."

"What happened on Christmas morning?" I ask. My stomach is already clenching in dread, anticipating where this story might be going. I cannot deal with stories that have to do with animals dying.

But I can't just tell Jace to stop. Obviously this is something that has scarred him for life, something he feels like he needs to get out. And more importantly, he's decided to pick *me* to talk about it with. It makes me feel connected to him, and I can't help it, but I love that feeling.

"On Christmas morning, I came downstairs." He shakes his head, getting that same faraway look on his face. And I know it's not my imagination now—he really *does* have tears in his eyes. "And I immediately ran to look in my stocking. There it was, on the fireplace, with Mork's stocking right next to it." He swallows hard, and as if by instinct, I reach over and take his hand. If he's surprised that I did that, he doesn't show it. His fingers tighten around mine, and my breath catches in my chest. I don't know if it's because the moment is so emotional or because we're holding hands, but my body suddenly feels like it's on fire.

"And I immediately called for him. Mork! Mork! But he didn't come. I looked at my parents, you know, and asked them where he was. Usually he slept with me in my bed, but I'd been so excited about Christmas that when I woke up, I hadn't thought to look for him." He sniffs. "And then my parents told me he went to the farm. But he wasn't at the farm, Peyton. He . . . he *wasn't at the farm*."

"Oh, my God," I say. A lump rises in my throat, making it hard to breathe. "That's horrible. What did he die from?"

"Cancer."

"Cancer?" I frown. "And you didn't notice he was sick?"

"No." Jace shakes his head. "I was only seven, after all." It's very brief, less than a second even, but I think I saw the sides of his mouth twitch. Almost into a smile. Which makes no sense. Why would Jace be smiling? Unless he's thinking about Mork and remembering him fondly. Or unless . . . I snatch my hand away from his.

"You're lying!"

"No, I'm not." He shakes his head sadly. "Poor little Mark."

"You said his name was Mork."

"That's what I said . . . poor little Mork." But I can still see the smile playing on his lips.

"You jerk!" I say. "I cannot believe you would make up a story about a dog with cancer!"

He laughs. "Oh, come on," he says. "It was funny. You should have seen the look on your face."

"Of course there was a look on my face," I say, throwing my hands up in the air, exasperated. "Anyone would have a look on their face when they heard about some poor kid losing their dog."

Hector whines.

"See?" I say. "You're upsetting him with all this talk of dog diseases. Have a heart."

"I have a heart!"

"No, you don't."

"Yes, I do," he says. "Look, I'll prove it to you." He reaches into the tub and wraps his arms around Hector, suds and all. "Oooh," he says in a baby voice. "Ooooh, Hector, you're such a good boy, oooh, I love you, Hector."

Hector's tail immediately starts wagging, and he pushes his snout into Jace's face and starts licking it. "Oh, Hector, you're so sweet," Jace says. "You're just the best dog."

Hector moves and Jace's elbows slip, causing Jace's whole upper body to slide over the side and into the tub. For a second, everyone freezes. I'm afraid Jace is going to be mad, since now he's soaking wet, but instead he just says, "Oooh, Hector, that's okay," and then slides his whole body into the tub, clothes and all.

Hector gives a happy bark, glad to have a friend with him, and then plants his front paws on Jace's chest.

"Oh, my God," I say, laughing as water sloshes over the side and onto the bathroom floor. "You're soaked."

"Oh, you think that's funny?" Jace asks me playfully, and then before I know it, he's pulling me into the tub with them. But there's not really enough room for the three of us, and so Hector jumps out and then starts running back and forth in front of the tub, getting soap suds and water all over the bathroom.

I'm laughing hysterically now, my pajamas and tank top totally soaked.

When I catch my breath a few moments later, I realize that I'm lying on top of Jace. I can feel his chest underneath me, and the warmth of his breath on my cheek. Our legs are tangled together in the water, and my whole body flushes hot.

"Sorry," I say. I don't know why I'm saying it. He's the one who pulled me in here with him, not the other way around. But he pulled me into the tub as a joke, as a way to get back at me for laughing. He was just messing around, and the last thing I want is for him to think I planted my body on top of his on purpose.

"What are you sorry for?" Jace asks. His voice is deep and husky, and I pull my gaze toward his face. He's looking right into my eyes, and then he reaches up and slides a finger down the side of my face, over my cheek, and down over my collarbone. His touch is soft and sends shivers exploding through my body. My heart is beating so fast and my stomach is turning and I feel like I should say something—anything—but I can't.

Which turns out to be okay. The fact that I can't talk, I mean.

Because before I can say anything, Jace pulls my face toward his and kisses me.

before jace

Saturday, June 25, 6:58 p.m.
Siesta Key, Florida

I am going to be totally cool. I am going to be totally cool and totally in control of the situation. There is nothing to get all worked up about. It's just a stupid wedding. Yes, a stupid wedding that a girl I have a history with is going to be attending. But fuck that. My history with Peyton was a long time ago. Well. If you consider three months a long time ago. Which I do.

When the ceremony starts, I sit there with my parents, scanning the rows of people, trying to look for Peyton without being all obvious about it. I'm so distracted that I don't even hear the vows. Not that I really care. In my opinion, weddings are pretty much bullshit. I'm not saying that I don't believe in marriage—I just have a hard time understanding how you're supposed to be all happy and excited for the couple getting married when you're pretty sure their marriage is going to end up completely shattered.

Take Courtney's dad, for example. Here he is, getting married, taking vows, promising that he's going to love and cherish this woman forever. When really, he already promised to love and cherish Courtney's *mom* forever. Which he obviously didn't do. And now he's pledging his undying devotion to another woman? Why should I believe him this time?

But whatever. No one wants to hear that shit. They just want to be all weepy and blather on about how beautiful it all is.

After the ceremony, everyone files into the huge ballroom at the Siesta Key Yacht Club for the reception. Of course my parents are among the first people to get there. My mom has this obsessive need to be on time for everything.

"Did you make sure you fed Hector, Jace?" my mom asks as we walk in. "Because it's very important that we get him into a routine."

"Yes, Mom," I say, struggling to keep the annoyance out of my voice. "I fed Hector." It's true. I did feed him. Of course, I don't mention that I forgot to bring his dog food, so he had to make do with a McDonald's quarter pounder. He loved it. I never saw a dog eat something so fast. I guess they don't get much beef at the pound.

"Good," she says, not even suspecting that he wasn't

eating his special, wheat-free, sugar-free, organic-whatever dog food that she picked up for him. I don't know why she's so concerned about Hector and his routine. It's not like we're keeping him.

A waiter wearing one of those long-tailed tuxedos passes by with a tray of hors d'oeuvres, and I reach out and snag two of them. You always have to make sure to take double food at these kind of fancy-pants events, because if you don't, you end up hungry. You never know when the waiters are going to come by again, or when dinner is going to finally be served.

I start inching away from my parents little by little, heading toward the bar. The one good thing about weddings is that if there's open bar, no one's ever IDing. And I'm definitely going to need a cocktail to calm my nerves.

Finally, my parents run into some couple they know, and start chattering away. After an awkward introduction ("This is our son, Jace; he's graduating tomorrow, can you believe it, he's valedictorian!"), I excuse myself and start walking toward the bar.

But before I can get there, a voice calls my name. A female voice.

"Jace!"

My stomach flips.

I turn around.

But it's not Peyton.

It's Courtney.

"Courtney," I say as she runs up to me and gives me a hug. "You look great."

"Thanks." She's wearing a long red dress. I guess she decided to change out of her bridesmaid dress before coming to the reception. Which I think might have been a good choice. I don't know anything about fashion, but I'm assuming that huge bows and green fabric aren't exactly what a nineteen-year-old girl wants to be wearing.

"It's so nice to see you!" she says. "Have you met my boyfriend, Jordan?"

"Not officially. We never really got a chance to talk at the Christmas party." I hold my hand out to the guy standing behind her. "What's up, man?"

"Not much," he says. His eyes are darting around the room, and he seems distracted.

I wonder if this is really weird for him. He's Courtney's boyfriend and also the son of the bride. Yup, Courtney's dad married Jordan's mom. Courtney and Jordan were together before their parents were, but still. That's got to be so weird. Are the four of them all going to live together now or some shit? I want to ask, but honestly, it's really none of my business.

"Don't mind him," Courtney says. "He's just looking for his friend B.J."

"What the hell," Jordan says, his eyes settling on something over my shoulder. "I told that asshole not to wear white!"

I turn around to see a kid about our age walking through the door, wearing a tight white suit, a white tie, and a white fedora. He's even got on white shoes. When he sees Jordan, he tips his hat and gives him a big smile.

"Excuse me," Jordan says. "I have to go talk to him. But I'll see you guys later—you're sitting at our table, right, Jace?"

"He is," Courtney says. Jordan gives her a kiss on the cheek and then heads over to the kid in white, who's now doing the moonwalk on the dance floor, even though no one else is dancing and the music that's playing is definitely not moonwalk appropriate.

"Should we get a drink?" Courtney asks.

I nod, then take her arm and lead her through the crowd to the bar. She orders a Diet Coke, and after a second, I order a Sprite, mostly because I don't want to seem like the jerk who ordered alcohol at her dad's wedding when she was drinking soda.

"So are you excited about graduation tomorrow?" she asks. She takes a sip of her drink.

"Not really." I plop down onto a bar stool. "It seems kind of pointless."

"Graduating?"

"Not *graduating*, just the graduation ceremony itself. Most of those people I never want to see again in my life."

"But then isn't it a good thing?" she asks. "To celebrate moving on?"

"I guess." I shrug. "But it's like we're all supposed to be moving on to the real world, celebrating this big achievement together. I don't know, it all just seems melodramatic and over the top."

"Yeah." She looks down into her drink thoughtfully, swishing the little red cocktail straw around in the liquid. "Your mom said your speech is amazing."

"My mom told you that? Jesus." I take another sip of my Sprite, then signal the bartender. Fuck this soda shit. I need something stronger.

"Well, she told my dad," Courtney says, "who told me."

I cringe. "Sorry."

She shrugs. "It's okay."

Ever since Courtney started dating Jordan, her dad hasn't exactly been thrilled. I don't really know the particulars, but for some reason, he doesn't like Jordan. I don't know why. Courtney's always struck me as someone who has her head on straight when it comes to things like relationships, and I don't think she'd be with a bad guy.

Anyway, Courtney's dad doesn't like Jordan, and it seems like lately he's been doing this weird thing where he's always trying to talk up other guys to Courtney, namely me. As if she and I are going to end up together or something. Which is ridiculous. Courtney's a really pretty girl, but there's never been anything like that between us. Ever. She's like my sister.

"I just wish my dad would stop trying to get me

interested in other guys. He needs to realize that I love Jordan, and that we're going to be together whether he likes it or not."

"Why doesn't he like him?"

She sighs. "It's complicated." She bites her lip. "But the thing is, he can't make my decisions for me. Especially when it comes to relationships. Hell, *I* have a hard enough time controlling who I fall in love with."

"I hear ya," I say. I understand exactly what she means.

Right then more than ever.

Because at that moment, Peyton walks into the ballroom.

Her dark hair is pulled back on the top, the rest of it loose and flowing around her shoulders. She's wearing a blue-green dress that's tight and yet sophisticated at the same time.

Her body has always driven me crazy.

She looks even better than I remember.

My body feels numb and my mouth goes dry.

"Bartender," I call again, louder this time. "I need a drink."

peyton before

Friday, June 25, 8:10 p.m.
Siesta Key, Florida

I walk into the reception late, which is a bit of a tactical error on my part. Actually, a lot of a tactical error. I thought that if I got there early, if I got there *first*, I'd be forced to sit at some table with my parents, waiting and wondering when Jace was going to show up. Definitely not good for my mental state.

So I decided that arriving late, when I was pretty sure he'd already be there was a good strategy—that way I could just come in and find my seat and not have to worry about watching the door every five seconds, wondering when he was going to show up. Then, when I was finally ready, I'd very casually scan the room until my eyes landed on him, and then I'd just make sure to ignore him for the whole night.

Of course, this plan had not been decided on lightly. At first I thought maybe I should be the bigger person, that I should go up to him and at least say hello. Brooklyn and I even spent a whole afternoon in my room coming up with opening lines. It was like a scene from a movie, where the heroine keeps practicing what she's going to say when she finally gets up the nerve to talk to the guy she likes. Of course, in those scenarios, it's usually a guy she's never talked to in her life, not a guy who she has a kind of history with and thought she was in love with. *Thought* being the operative word. As in, past tense.

After we came up with the perfect opening line ("Hi, Jace, it's nice to see you. You're looking very well," which would be followed by me pushing past him and going to talk to some imaginary person whom I just noticed was at the wedding), I realized that was a horrible plan. To be the better person, I mean. After all, he never replied to my text. And taking the high road is overrated anyway.

So I changed my plan to just ignoring him.

As you can see, I've spent way more time thinking about this than I should have.

Anyway, getting to the reception a little bit late meant my parents left their hotel room before I left mine. And so I had to walk into the reception alone, which was kind of intimidating, and a little bit humiliating. What if Jace saw me and thought my parents weren't even at the wedding and I'd come by myself just because I wanted to see him so badly? Like some kind of stalker or something?

I do my best to ignore the butterflies in my stomach, then walk with my shoulders back and my head held high right to table eight, which, according to my place card, is where I'm sitting.

There's no one at my table yet, which makes no sense since I got here late. Shouldn't people be seated? But it seems like everyone's at the bar, eating hors d'oeuvres and ordering drinks and having a grand old time. Damn. I should have come later. Or at least made sure someone was sitting at my table before I sat down.

God. What a disaster.

I sip water from my goblet, then grab an hors d'oeuvre from one of the tuxedoed waiters as he goes by. The thing I've learned about hors d'oeuvres is that you have to get them while you can—otherwise, you end up having to wait forever just to get some food.

I pop the pig in a blanket into my mouth, wondering why they'd have pigs in a blanket at such a high-level affair. Then I realize that if Jace lays his eyes on me now, he's going to see me sitting here all by myself, eating a hot dog. Which is *so* not the first impression I want to give him. I quickly swallow what's in my mouth and decide not to eat any more until other people sit down.

But now I don't know what to do with my hands.

I take another sip of my water.

"Our table's over here!" someone shouts. I look up to see a guy about my age dressed in a white suit and white shoes weaving his way through the crowd. He plops down into the seat next to me.

"Howdy!" he says. "Who are you? And are you here for the bride or the groom?" He sticks his hand out to me, almost knocking my water glass over in the process. I can't tell if he's drunk or just crazy.

"Um, I'm Peyton," I say, moving my glass to the other side of my plate and safely out of his reach. "And the groom is my uncle."

He nods. "I'm here with the bride." He pulls a sparkling white handkerchief out of his pocket, blows his nose, and then stuffs it back in his pocket. Ewww.

"I'm sorry," I say. "Are you Jocelyn?"

"Jocelyn?"

"Yes," I say. I point down at the card in front of him. "Because the place card says I'm supposed to be sitting next to someone named Jocelyn."

He peers down at it. "Oh, no, that's my girlfriend." He leans in toward me, like he's about to let me in on a secret. "Actually, she's my ex-girlfriend as of 12:17 a.m. last night. Or this morning, whatever." He reaches for his water glass, and downs the contents.

"I'm sorry," I say. "Um, that you guys broke up."

"Yeah, it was really horrible," he says. "I just . . . I don't understand what women want, you know? " He shakes his head sadly. "Do you?"

I'm about to say that of course I understand what

women want, that I *am* a woman, but then I realize that would be a lie. How can I know what women want when I hardly know what I want myself? "No." I sigh. "I don't think anyone knows what women want."

"That's what I've been trying to tell people," he says, gesturing around the wedding, as if maybe he's been going up to each and every guest, trying to convince them that no one knows what women want. He points a finger at me. "You're smart, I can tell."

"There you are!" Another guy comes up to our table, sounding a little frantic. "Jesus, B.J., can you stay in one place for one second?" This new guy sets a white ceramic cup full of coffee in front of B.J. "Here, drink that." He shakes his head, and I recognize him as Courtney's boyfriend, Jordan.

"Hi, I'm Jordan," he says, holding his hand out to me.

"I'm Peyton."

"Oh, right," he says, his face breaking into a smile. "Courtney's cousin. She talks about you all the time."

"She does? Good things, I hope."

"Always." He smiles again, and slides into the seat on the other side of B.J. And then, suddenly, Jordan's smile fades. "Ah, shit," he mutters.

I follow his gaze to where Courtney's crossing the room, walking toward us with another girl. They both look stunning—Courtney's in a floor-length red gown, and the girl she's with is wearing a tight baby-blue dress that hits just below her knees, her hair swept to one side.

"What?" I ask.

"That's Jocelyn," B.J. says morosely into his coffee. "That's my ex-girlfriend."

"Oh." I clear my throat. "Um, so you guys are both going to be at this table, then?"

"Yup," B.J. says. He leans in close to me. "Listen," he says, "I might flirt with you, you know, to make her jealous. I want her to know that I'm desirable and that other girls are interested in me." He inches his chair toward mine.

"Oh, I'm sure she already knows that," I say.

"No, she doesn't. So if I kiss you or something, just know that it's all part of the show."

Great.

"You're in my seat," Jocelyn says to B.J. when she gets to our table.

"I'm sorry," he says, looking around like he doesn't know where her voice is coming from. "I thought you weren't talking to me."

"I'm talking to you," she says. "I'm just not dating you. Now move."

"No." B.J. shakes his head. "I want to sit here." He scoots his chair even closer to mine and gives me a smile, like he wants to sit there so that he can be close to me.

"Who the hell are you?" Jocelyn asks. She puts her hand on her hip and glares down at me.

Lovely. Now I'm going to get my ass kicked by some girl

I don't know, over some guy who I don't know, and don't even *care* to know. "Um, I'm Peyton."

"Jocelyn," Courtney says, grabbing her arm, "come on, you can sit over here with me."

"I don't want to sit over there with you," Jocelyn says. "I want to sit there, in my seat."

"You heard Courtney," B.J. says, waving Jocelyn away like she's some kind of gnat. "You go sit over there. I'm going to sit with Peyton." He puts his hand on my arm and gives me another smile.

I smile back tentatively. I don't know what's worse—pretending to be going along with B.J.'s flirting and maybe getting into a fistfight with Jocelyn, or not going along with it and dealing with whatever craziness B.J. might come up with to punish me.

Joceyln's eyes widen when she sees B.J.'s hand on my arm, and for a moment, I'm pretty sure she's going to hit me. Or him. Or both of us. But at the last second she changes her mind, and her face breaks into a wide smile. But it's not the kind of smile you give when you're happy. It's the kind of smile you give when you're up to something bad.

Sure enough, a minute later, she's heading off to the dance floor, where she grabs some random guy and starts grinding on him. It's kind of a spectacle, actually, since no one's really even dancing yet. And Jocelyn's kind of rubbing all over the guy. And he's definitely older than her. Like, twenty-five at least.

Jordan looks at Courtney, but Courtney just shrugs. "We have to let them work it out," she says.

"We're not going to work it out!" B.J. declares. "You two need to stop babysitting us. We're breaking up." He motions for a waiter who's holding a tray of champagne flutes, grabs one, and downs it in about one second.

Great. Somehow I've ended up at the crazy table. Why is this stuff always happening to me? Why aren't I sitting with my parents, over in some corner somewhere, listening to adults talk about property taxes and kitchen renovations and school districts and all the other ridiculous things parents talk about?

Then again, this is a lot more interesting. At least I won't be bored. In fact, I realize I haven't thought about Jace in, like, ten minutes. That must be some kind of record or something. I guess being about to get your ass kicked will do that to you.

Courtney slides over to me and smiles. "I like your dress," she says.

"Thanks. I like yours, too."

"How's everything going?"

I paste a smile on my face. "It's going great."

"Really?" she says. "Because—"

"Excuse me," a voice on the other side of Courtney says, "but I think you're in my seat."

I look up. And there he is. Jace. The wind immediately gets knocked out of me, and red-hot lust shoots through my body. He looks amazing, even better than I remember. Tall. Dark hair. Blue eyes. He's wearing a white button-up shirt and gray pants, and his tie is loosened around his neck. His sleeves are rolled up a little bit, showing off his forearms, which are tanned and muscular.

"Oh." Courtney sounds surprised. She looks at me. "This is . . . I mean, this is *my* seat." She points to the place card. "And I was talking to Peyton."

"Yeah," Jace says. "But I want to sit there."

Courtney looks at me, her eyes asking me if it's okay. And what can I do? I can't say no. If I say no, Jace is going to realize that he's having an effect on me. And what is it that they always say? The opposite of love isn't hate, it's indifference?

Well. I will show Jace Renault that I am totally indifferent to him, thank you very much.

"It's fine," I say, and shrug.

And then, before I know what's happening, Courtney's getting up, and Jace is settling into the chair next to me. He reaches out and grabs my water glass, then takes a swig.

"That was my water," I say.

"Sorry." He holds it out to me. "You want it back?"

"Not *now*."

He shrugs and then takes another sip. "So how are you doing?"

He looks at me, and I look at him, and something about the way he's doing it, something about the way he's looking at me is sending shivers up my spine. He's looking at me the same way that I've been wanting to look at him. Like maybe he wants to take me into the coatroom and get me naked or something.

And that's when I know.

It is definitely not over between me and Jace Renault.

jace the trip

Saturday, June 26, 9:29 p.m.
Savannah, Georgia

I don't know how or why that happened. One minute I was telling that stupid story about my fake dog having cancer (which was pretty scummy, I'll admit), the next minute I was goofing off and splashing around in the bathtub with Hector, and then somehow, I was kissing Peyton.

I couldn't help myself. It was like I had to have her. Her body was pressed against mine, and I *needed* to kiss her. If I'm being totally honest, I've been wanting to kiss her all damn day. I'm actually surprised I lasted as long as I did.

And the kiss was good. Really, really, *really* good.

I pull her down closer to me, my hands on her face and in her hair. I want the kiss to go on forever. But after a little bit, she pulls back.

"Hi," I say, giving her a lazy smile.

"Hey," she says. She rests her head on my chest, and for some ridiculous reason, we just stay like that, me holding her in a bathtub while I stroke her hair.

Hector is gone—I don't really know where he is, but it definitely cannot be anywhere good. He's probably messing up the room. But I don't care. Right now all I care about is Peyton, about making this moment last forever. It sounds cheesy, but I don't give a fuck.

We stay like that for maybe twenty minutes or so, alternating between kissing and just lying there. Finally, she props her head up on her elbow. "We should get out of this tub," she says. "My clothes are soaking wet."

I grin. "Or you could just take them off."

"Funny." She pulls herself up and out of the tub, and after a second, I follow. She hands me a fluffy white towel off the rack in the bathroom, and I get to work drying off my hair.

"I need some dry clothes," I tell her. "I'll be right back."

I head back to my room and change into a clean T-shirt and a pair of track pants. When I get back to Peyton's room, she's sitting on the edge of the bed with Hector. She's changed into a soft pink T-shirt and a pair of black yoga pants, her hair hanging in curly tendrils down her back.

"Hi," she says.

"Hi." I sit down next to her. But suddenly, something feels . . . I don't know, *different.* Like the spell was broken or something. Now that we've kissed, I'm not sure what I'm supposed to do. Kiss her again? Turn on the television? Act like nothing happened?

"So," she says.

"So." I look at Hector. "You dried him off."

She nods.

"He looks clean."

"Yup." She nods again.

Wow. Talk about awkward. This is what I hate about things like this. It's like they can't ever just be normal. They always have to be some big deal. Like, we just kissed. So what? Let's kiss again, that's what I say.

"So, are you hungry?" I try. "Maybe we should order food or something."

"I got food from the gas station."

"Oh. Right. Well, what do you want to do?"

"I think . . ." She twists her hands in her lap nervously. "I think that maybe I should go to sleep."

I blink at her, unable to believe what I'm hearing. "You think that you should go to *sleep*?"

She nods.

"But it's not even ten o'clock!"

"We need to get on the road early tomorrow."

"Bullshit."

"What?" She looks at me, sounding shocked that I would say such a thing.

"I said bullshit," I say. "I just kissed you, and you're

freaked out by it, and so now you want to do what you always do. Just run away and pretend it didn't happen."

Her eyes widen, and flash with anger. "Are you kidding me?"

"No." I cross my arms over my chest. "I'm dead serious."

"You think I'm freaked out because you kissed me?"

"Yes."

"I'm not."

"You are!"

"I'm not!"

"Then why are you acting like it?"

She springs off the bed, like there's too much anger in her body to keep it still. "Okay, fine," she says. "I am freaked out, Jace. I'm freaked out because for some reason, I can't stop thinking about you. I can't stop thinking about how it feels to kiss you, about how happy I was when I thought we were going to be together, about how even though I feel like I should hate you, my heart knows that I don't."

"You don't have to be freaked out about that."

"Yes, I do," she says. "I do have to be freaked out about it!"

I stand up and go to put my arms around her, but she pushes me away. "No," she says. "Every time I let myself get close to you, I end up getting hurt."

"Every time?" I ask. I'm still standing close to her, and it's taking every ounce of my self-control not to reach out and kiss her again. "I don't think we've gotten close enough times for there to be an 'every time.'"

"Yes, we have!" she says.

"Name one time."

"Last night." She crosses her arms over her chest. "We . . . I mean, we . . . you know what happened between us last night, and then I found out that you lied to me."

"I didn't lie to you," I say.

"A lie by omission is still a lie," she counters.

"Oh, really?" I say. "Because if we're counting lies by omissions as lies, then I'm not the only one we should be talking about." It's kind of a horrible thing to say. It's not fair to her to bring up what I'm talking about.

"What are you talking about?" She frowns.

"Nothing," I say. "Just forget it." I shake my head and grab Hector's leash off the nightstand and clip it onto his collar. He's just sitting there on the bed, his head down, almost like he knows we're fighting. It actually makes me kind of sad. Just because me and Peyton are pissed at each other doesn't mean we should be scaring poor Hector.

"No," Peyton says. "I don't want to forget it." She stands in front of me, blocking my way to the door.

"Peyton," I say. "Stop. I don't want to talk about it. I'm going back to my room."

"Of course you are," she says, giving me a bitter laugh. "That's what you do, right, Jace? Everything's always some kind of big joke, you never want to talk about anything real, like why you kissed me last night, or why you lied to me, or why you just stopped talking to me after Christmas."

"You think that's what happened?" I say. "That I just stopped talking to you?"

"You didn't?" She crosses her arms over her chest, daring me to contradict her.

"No! I mean, I did, but it wasn't . . ." My thoughts are spinning around now, making my brain all confused and crazy. I take a deep breath. "It's not that simple. And besides, I told you I didn't want to talk about it."

"Of course." She steps out of the way, and I'm halfway to the door before she speaks again. "Don't worry about tomorrow, Jace," she says. "I can find my own way home."

Suddenly, I'm super pissed off. Like, *really* pissed off. I don't know why, since it's not like she said anything horrible, and let's face it—her giving me an out is going to make my life a whole lot easier. I might even be able to make graduation.

But it's just the way she says it—in this completely detached voice, like she's taken all her anger and hurt and folded it up into a little square and then deposited it into some box somewhere that's out of reach. It's the same shit she pulled with me over the spring, the same shit that caused her to be the only girl who's ever broken my heart.

"Oh, really?" I say. "You can find your own way home?"

She nods. "I wouldn't want you to have to express your feelings or anything. We all know what a horrible thing that would be."

"Right," I say. "And you know all about expressing your feelings, right, Peyton?"

"More than you."

"Really?" I counter. "Then why didn't you tell me your parents were getting divorced?"

Her face changes in an instant. Her eyes go wide and her skin goes pale and I want to take the words back, I would do *anything* to take the words back, but it's too late—they're hanging there, over us, their meaning permeating the room.

"Peyton—" I take a step toward her.

"No." She puts her hand up, stopping me, and the look in her eyes tells me she's serious. "How did you know about that?"

"Your uncle told me."

"My uncle told you? But that's—" She bites her lip, so hard that it starts to turn red. Her eyes narrow. "Just. Go."

"Peyton, let's—"

"I'm serious, Jace," she says. *"Go."*

"No." I shake my head. "I'm not leaving you. I'm not giving up on this again."

"Fine." She grabs her key card and her purse off the nightstand. "If you're not going to leave, then I will."

"Peyton." I try one more time, but it's useless.

She walks out, leaving me standing there, alone, in a hotel room that isn't even mine.

the trip peyton

Saturday, June 26, 9:47 p.m.
Savannah, Georgia

By the time I get outside the hotel, tears are streaming down my face. They're the worst kind of tears—the kind that are hot and angry and devastating, the kind that slide silently down your cheeks and leave salty tracks on your skin.

For the first time, I realize the drawback to the weather in the South—it's never cold enough that your tears will freeze on your face before they have a chance to fall down your cheeks. And so you can't deny that you're crying.

I don't know where I'm going or what I should do. I'm alone in downtown Savannah, and it's probably not a good idea for me to be wandering the streets alone at night. I have no phone, and I hardly have any money, either.

And then I remember the restaurant the front desk clerk recommended—the Distillery. She said it was within walking distance, and she made it seem like it was a popular place. I don't know what else to do, so I start walking toward downtown, and sure enough, a couple of blocks later, I see it.

There's a big neon sign outside, with umbrellaed tables set up on the sidewalk. The inside looks warm and welcoming, so I brush my tears away and walk into the restaurant.

"Welcome to the Distillery," the hostess says, picking up a menu and giving me a smile. "One tonight?"

Her voice has a gentle tone, and the fact that she says "one tonight" instead of "just one" makes me feel like I'm out enjoying some time to myself, and not like a big loser who has no one to go to a restaurant with.

"Yes," I say. "One tonight."

She shows me to a cute little table in the corner of the restaurant, and puts the menu down in front of me.

When the waitress, a gorgeous African American girl with short hair and a bright white smile, comes over, I order a Diet Coke and the Southern chicken tenders.

While I wait for my food, I think about Jace. I wonder what he's doing—if he's back at the hotel, if he stayed in my room, if he went back to his own, if he left. He said he wasn't going to, but come on. Why would he really stay?

I cannot believe he knew this whole time that my parents were getting a divorce. Does that mean Courtney knows, too? Does that mean it's really happening? I feel the tears starting up again and I swipe at them angrily with my napkin.

I am not going to start crying in here. I can't—someone would definitely ask me what was wrong. The vibe in here is a cheerful one. Pretty much everyone is hanging out and talking, clinking their glasses together as they order more drinks and toast to whatever it is they're all so damn happy about.

When the waitress sets the chicken fingers down in front of me, at first I'm not that hungry. But I force myself to take a bite, and they're so good that by the time I'm on my third or fourth bite, I'm inhaling them.

And as I eat, I keep thinking about Jace.

I think about every single thing he's ever done to me. Every single time he let me down. And yes, when he said he hasn't let me down enough to make it an "every single time," he was right.

But when you're in love with someone—or at least, when you think you are—once is enough.

I met Jace over Christmas, which I think gave us kind of a weird start to begin with. Christmas is such a magical time. The lights, the sparkliness, the tinsel, the cold and snow outside mixed with the warmth inside.

Okay, that was cheesy, but it really is true. Who wouldn't want to fall in love around Christmastime? It was like the deck was stacked against me right from the beginning.

I'd just found out that my parents were getting divorced.

At the beginning of December, they sat me down in the dining room over a dinner of roast chicken and potatoes (made by my mom—I should have known something was up when she offered to cook dinner) and told me.

Not like it was a shock. I mean, I live in the same house with them. I could hear their screaming fights and my dad had been sleeping in the guestroom for months. But it still hit me like a sucker punch in the stomach. Which is weird now that I think about it—that I had that reaction—because on some level, I didn't really believe them.

I remember calling my sister at college, and she seemed to agree with me. "They've been talking about divorce for years," she said. "I doubt it's really going to happen."

Of course, Kira was completely out of the loop—she'd been away at NYU for two years, and she'd spent the summer in Europe, backpacking around with her friends. On the rare occasions she did come home for a weekend, she'd end up spending most of the time out somewhere with her high school friends, or holed up in her old room, studying.

My parents would put on a great face—making sure not to fight when Kira was around, making sure we all ate dinner as a family on the nights she was home.

Looking back, I probably should have seen that as odd. Why would they need to put on some kind of show when their older daughter was in the house?

Anyway, there's no way Kira could have had any idea how bad things had gotten between my parents. She didn't know they were up late into the night, having screaming fights that would last forever. She didn't see me when I'd sneak out of bed and put on my iPod so I wouldn't have to hear the yelling. (Eventually, I started plugging my iPod into the outlet by my nightstand, putting my playlist of soothing pop songs on repeat, and falling asleep with it on, so I wouldn't have to hear my parents at all.)

But even though things were bad, I still didn't really believe they were going to divorce. They were always threatening each other with divorce. They'd yell at each other all the time about how they were going to leave each other.

True, they'd never actually sat me down and *said* they were getting divorced before this, but still. It somehow seemed more like another show they were putting on instead of a major marital decision. My mom even dabbed daintily at her eyes with a cloth napkin while they were telling me, and my dad reached over and gripped my hand like he was afraid I was going to start crying or something. The whole thing just seemed so staged and fake.

Anyway, after the big divorce reveal, my mom decided that she and I were going to Florida to spend Christmas with Courtney and her dad. I wasn't all that psyched to go—not that I cared that much about Christmas, but I wanted to spend the school vacation hanging out with Brooklyn. But my mom was insistent.

I felt bad and guilty about leaving my dad alone on Christmas, and so before we left, I pulled the box of

Christmas decorations out of the attic, and dressed the mantel with our stockings. Then, right before my mom and I left for the airport, I stuffed my dad's stocking with the things I knew he would like—Lindt chocolates, butterscotch truffles, a new pair of socks, and a gift card to his favorite sports store. I signed everything as being from Santa.

The first day we were in Florida was, I think, the first time I realized the whole divorce thing might actually be real.

Courtney and I were sitting out by her pool, enjoying the fact that it was almost eighty degrees and sunny—in December!—when we heard the sound of my mom crying coming through the kitchen window.

"It's going to be fine," Courtney's dad soothed.

I'd never heard my mom cry like that before. It gave me a weird sort of twisting feeling in my stomach, and anxiety bloomed in my throat. Courtney turned the page of her magazine loudly, pretending she hadn't heard them, and after a moment, I did the same.

That night, she invited me to come to a Christmas party at her boyfriend Jordan's mom's (Jordan's mom was also Courtney's dad's new girlfriend. Awkward.) house.

"I don't think so," I said, shaking my head. "I think I'm just going to stay here."

"And do what?" she said. "Read? Watch TV?"

I didn't know that the big deal was—both of those seemed like wonderful options, especially since I was in the middle of watching the first season of *Downton Abbey* on Netflix and it was really starting to get good. I loved all those English accents and regency clothes. Or frocks, as they called them.

"Yeah." I shrugged. "Or maybe wrap some presents." It was a lie. I'd wrapped all my presents back in Connecticut, and brought them to Florida like that.

"You're coming," Courtney said.

"I have nothing to wear."

"You can borrow something of mine."

I shook my head.

"Come on," she said. "You can't just stay inside all night, you're only here for a few days. Don't you want to take advantage of the weather?"

I didn't really see how standing around inside Jordan's mom's house was any different from sitting around in Courtney's dad's house, but whatever. I needed to snap out of my funk, and I knew she was right—staying home wasn't going to do it.

"Fine," I said, shooting one last longing look toward where my computer was sitting on the nightstand in the guestroom. "I'll go."

"Yay!" She grabbed my hand and pulled me into her room so we could find something for me to wear.

I figured there'd be no way I'd be able to fit into any of Courtney's clothes, but surprisingly, she had this really pretty red dress that was perfect. It had a slightly poofy bubble skirt and a fitted top that plunged down in the front and gave me just the right amount of cleavage. I looped a long silver jingle-bell necklace around my neck, slid my feet into a pair of Courtney's strappy silver sandals (they were only a little bit too small), and lined my eyes with a sparkly gold shadow. By the time we left, I was a feeling a little bit better and a lot more festive.

The party was in full swing when we pulled up. We walked right into the house and through the great room, through the sliding glass doors and to the back, where most people had spilled out onto the lanai and were standing around, mingling and drinking champagne.

I'll admit that I noticed him right away—he was sitting on an expensive-looking lounge chair, and the light from the pool was illuminating his face, and I thought he was cute. Okay, fine, I thought he was gorgeous. He took my breath away in a way that no guy had ever done before.

I couldn't take my eyes off him all night.

"That's Jace," Courtney said finally, when she caught me looking. "Do you want me to introduce you?"

I shook my head. One, I wasn't that bold. And two, guys who looked like that didn't usually go for girls who looked like me. It wasn't that I thought I was ugly—I knew I was cute, passably pretty. I didn't have guys falling all over me, and I wasn't going to win any beauty pageants, but still—I did okay. Jace, however, seemed like he was way out of my league.

But when Courtney went off with her boyfriend, Jordan, leaving me to fend for myself, Jace decided to introduce himself.

I was over by the veggies and dip tray, working my way through a piece of celery, when he came over and picked up a plate.

"You're not double dipping, are you?" he asked, giving me a mock serious look.

I shook my head, not trusting myself to speak. First, I had a mouthful of vegetable, and second, he was even cuter up close than he was far away. My heart started pounding in my chest, my body flushed hot, and I had to take two big deep breaths to calm myself down.

When he was done loading his plate, he popped a tomato into his mouth and then reached out and tweaked my necklace. The jingle bell rang.

"Cute," he said. "I like jingle-bell necklaces."

"Oh," I said. "Me too." I realized how stupid it sounded, so I quickly added, "I borrowed it from my cousin." I licked my lips, which were suddenly completely dry. "Courtney's my cousin. I'm here visiting her from Connecticut."

"Cool," he said. He wiped his hand on a napkin and stuck it out for me to shake. "I'm Jace Renault. My mom's best friends with Courtney's mom. And my dad's best friends with Courtney's dad."

"Wow," I said, shaking my head. "That's gotta be awkward."

He nodded. "Super awkward." He leaned in and whispered in my ear, like we were sharing a secret. "Although if you ask me, I think it's pretty dicky for a dude to leave his family for another woman." His breath tickled at my skin, making every nerve in my body stand on high alert.

"Well," I said, "on the surface, yeah, it seems like an asshole move. But what if it's true love?"

"True love?" He was still standing close to me, although he'd moved back just a little bit, and now his eyes were on mine. "You really believe that?"

"In true love? Or that Courtney's dad found it with another woman?"

He cocked his head. "Both."

I bit my lip and thought about it. "No," I said. "I don't believe that it's true love. But I do believe in it. At least, I think I do."

"Why don't you think it's true love between them?" he asked. "Have you ever seen them together?"

I shake my head. "Just an instinct. Besides, haven't they only known each other for, like, less than a year?"

He nods. "So, you don't believe in love at first sight?"

I shook my head no. "But I do believe in lust at first sight." I was shocked that I had the nerve to say this, and my face felt warm.

"Really?" The sides of his mouth slid up into a grin. "Interesting."

My heart was racing now. While we'd been talking,

we'd moved a few steps over to the side, and now we were a little bit removed from the party, almost like we were there together.

"So what's your name?" he asked.

"Peyton," I said.

He looked at me, seemingly taking it in, like my telling him my name was one of the most important things he'd ever heard. He nodded. "Peyton," he said, and I couldn't help but think that the way he said my name was super sexy. "That's a really nice name."

Yes, I thought as I took a sip of my ginger ale. I definitely believed in lust at first sight.

We ended up talking for the rest of the night—sitting in the corner, sharing one of the big chaise lounge chairs that dotted the lanai. He sat next to me so casually, just sort of leaned back next to me so that our legs were touching, like it was the most natural thing in the world for us to be sitting on the same chair.

He was wearing khaki pants and Nike sandals, which was so not appropriate for a party like this, but he somehow managed to pull it off.

Every time the bare skin of my ankle brushed against his, he set me on fire.

We didn't talk about anything important, really, that first night. Mostly just gossiped about the other people at the party. A couple of times I caught Courtney and her boyfriend, Jordan, over in the corner, glancing at us and whispering, and I knew what they were thinking: that something was going to happen between me and Jace.

I knew it wasn't true—like I said, guys like Jace never really gave me the time of day. He was probably just bored at a party where he hardly knew anyone, and had found someone his own age to pass the time with. That didn't stop me from getting a secret thrill out of the fact that Jordan and Courtney were talking about us.

But when we left that night, I thought that was it. I dodged Courtney's questions, rolling my eyes at her suggestions that Jace was flirting with me. She asked me if I thought he was cute, and I copped to it, because honestly, it wasn't really a matter of opinion. But that was it, I told her. I was never going to see him again.

I had a hard time falling asleep that night.

But by the next morning, I'd forced myself to forget about him.

Until Courtney and I were out shopping for bathing suits—so not my favorite activity, but she was determined that we were going to go to the beach. (Of course, I hadn't brought a bathing suit specifically because I wanted to avoid the beach, but Courtney was insistent.) She'd offered to let me borrow one of hers, but there was no way that I was going to set myself up for that kind of humiliation. A party dress was one thing, but a bathing suit was another story.

I was in the dressing room of this place at the mall called Swimming with Sharks, trying on a particularly unflattering tankini—wearing a tankini in the first place is kind of like putting a big sign on yourself that says you don't feel comfortable in a bikini—when my cell phone rang, flashing a Florida area code and a number that I didn't recognize.

Figuring it could be my mom calling from my uncle's house or something, I picked it up.

"Hello?" I balanced my phone against my shoulder as I tried to slide the top of the tankini over my body. It wasn't working. My boobs were slipping out of the sides, and the front gave me that weird smooshed-boob thing that sometimes happens with sports bras.

"Peyton?" It was a male voice I didn't recognize.

"This is Peyton," I said, preparing myself for a telemarketer. I had put my number on that no-call list, but I heard it took a few weeks for it to kick in. I didn't even *have* the ability to switch my cable provider or anything like that, but did these telemarketers care? No. They kept calling and pushing, and of course I was way too nice to just hang up because I figured their job must really suck, sitting in a hot call center all day and probably earning about eight dollars an—

"Hey, it's Jace."

"Who?" I asked. Not because I didn't know who it was, but because I was sure I'd misheard. The bottom of the tankini fell to the floor, leaving me standing there in just my underwear and the top of the bathing suit.

"Jace Renault? We met last night at the party."

"Oh," I said. "Right." There was an awkward pause, and I tried to come up with something brilliant to say. I couldn't, so he forged on.

"I hope you don't mind that I called you—I called Courtney's house and your uncle gave me your cell number."

"No, I don't mind." Mind? Now that the shock had worn off, my heart was beating in my chest, and all I could think about was that Jace was on the phone. He called Courtney's dad to get my number! I sat down on the little bench in the dressing room, trying not to think about whatever kind of germs were lurking on there.

"So what's up?" he asked. "Are you busy?"

"Busy? No, I'm not busy." There was a pause. God, he must have thought I was some kind of idiot, incapable of making conversation. "Are you?"

"Am I busy?"

"No. Yes. I mean, what are you doing? What are you up to?" God, this was going from bad to worse.

"Not much," he said, and I heard what sounded like the squeak of springs, like maybe he was lying down on his bed or something. I tried not to think about his body, stretched out on his bed, his shirt slipping up just a little bit, showing his rock-hard stomach. I wasn't sure his stomach was rock hard, but I had an idea it would be. I blushed.

"So why are you calling?"

He laughed. "Getting right to the point, are you?"

"No, I just meant . . . I mean, if you went to the trouble of getting my number from my uncle, you must be calling for a reason."

"I was wondering if maybe you wanted to grab lunch in a little while."

My heart caught in my chest. Before I could answer, there was a knock on the dressing room door. Courtney. "Hey," she said. "Are you in there? How does it look?"

"Is that Courtney?" Jace asked.

"Um, yeah." I was about to add that we were at the mall trying on bathing suits, but I was afraid if he knew I was out, he would take his invitation back. I knew that wanting to go to lunch with him so bad was pathetic. But what was even more pathetic was letting him think that I didn't have a life, so I said, "We're out shopping for bathing suits."

"Really?" he said, sounding interested. "That's kind of hot."

"We're not in the same dressing room," I said, rolling my eyes. Why did guys always get so turned on by the thought of two girls being naked together? Couldn't they be satisfied with just one?

"I wasn't thinking about Courtney."

"Oh." I was breathless. I couldn't help it. He had a hot voice.

"Peyton?" Another knock on the door. "Are you on the phone?"

"Yeah," I called. "Just a second."

"I should probably let you go," Jace said. "It seems like you're busy."

"Yeah," I said, holding my breath and hoping that he'd bring up having lunch again.

"So what time are you going to be done shopping? Do you want to meet for a late lunch or something? Like maybe around three?"

"That sounds great."

"Okay." I could hear him smiling through the phone, and that made me smile. "I'll pick you up at Courtney's?"

"Sounds good," I said, trying to act like it was no big deal, that I always got asked out by super-hot guys a day after meeting them.

We hung up, and I opened the door to the dressing room, forgetting that I was wearing only the top of a bathing suit and my underwear.

"Oh," Courtney said, frowning. "You're not dressed."

I grabbed her arm and pulled her into the dressing room. "Jace Renault just called me."

She smiled. "I knew it!"

"Shhh!" My grip on her arm tightened. "Do you swear you didn't tell him to?"

She shook her head. "I would never!"

I knew it was true. Courtney would never do something like that, ever.

"Okay." I bit my lip. "We're going to have a late lunch."

"Well," Courtney said, tossing my clothes at me. "That

settles it. Forget bathing suits. We need to get you something for your date."

So we did. I bought a pair of skinny jeans and this shimmery off-the-shoulder top with a matching spaghetti-strap tank top that was sexy and casual and perfect.

I bought new lip gloss and a sparkly mascara and I spent two hours getting ready. And by the time Jace came to pick me up, I felt beautiful.

He took me to this really cool Hawaiian fusion restaurant, and I had fish tacos that were so good I could hardly stand it. When we were done eating, we walked around Siesta Key Village, poking into souvenir shops until we got bored, and then headed down toward the beach. We talked about everything and anything, and it was pretty much perfect.

As the sun went down, we sat on the beach, letting the warm water lap at our feet. Honestly, it was the most romantic thing that had ever happened to me.

As the sun dipped down, Jace turned toward me.

"Make a wish," he said.

"Why?"

"You always make a wish when the sun goes down," he said, inching toward me on the sand.

He smelled like the ocean, and when he pulled me close, electricity zinged through my body, setting my nerve endings on fire.

"Did you just make that up?" I asked.

"No." He shook his head. "It's, like, a thing."

"Okay." I shut my eyes tight as the sun disappeared, looking like it was dipping right into the water. When I opened them, I turned and looked at him. His eyes were shut tight, his hair ruffling in the breeze. After a moment, he opened them.

"What did you wish for?" I asked.

"If I tell you, it won't come true." The sides of his mouth pulled up into a grin.

"I won't tell anyone."

He looked at me seriously, pretending like he was thinking about it. Then he shook his head. "Nope."

"Fine." I shrugged. "Then I'm not telling you mine."

"I don't want to know yours." His face was moving closer to mine, and now his lips were right there, teasing me.

"Yes, you do."

"How do you know?"

"Because it was a really good wish."

"Really?" He was even closer to me now, so close that I could feel the warmth of his skin against my cheek, the whisper of his breath against my forehead. He reached down and took my chin, tilted it up toward him gently.

"Yes," I said, almost unable to speak. "Really."

"So you're not going to tell me?"

"I'll tell you mine if you tell me yours."

He smiled. "Deal." And then, before I knew what was happening, his mouth was on mine. The kiss was delicious, soft and perfect and amazing, the kind of kiss you read about in books but don't think could ever happen to you, especially not from an amazingly hot guy you've only known for a day.

We kissed for what felt like forever, falling back onto the sand as the last slip of light dipped below the horizon.

When we finally stopped, my lips wanted his to come back, wanted to feel them forever. I know it sounds ridiculous, but it was true. He held my hand all the way back to the car.

I was going to be in Florida for the next few days, but he was leaving the next morning to spend Christmas skiing in Colorado with his family.

He told me he'd text me, but I didn't believe him.

But as I was climbing into bed that night, my phone was already ringing.

"Hello?" I said as I slid under the sheets in the spare bedroom of Courtney's house.

"It's me," he said, and I smiled.

We talked all night, until he had to get off the phone and head to the airport. When I got home to Connecticut, we picked up right where we left off. Talking all the time. Emailing. Texting. We even talked about visiting each other over spring break.

I felt like maybe I was falling in love with him. Brooklyn thought I was crazy—she didn't understand how I could be so caught up in a guy I'd only spent a few hours with, a guy who was thousands of miles away, a guy who I had no idea when I would see again.

I understood her point, but I couldn't stop it. It was a force bigger than me. And whenever a voice in the back of my head would whisper that it wasn't real, I would ignore it. I wanted so badly to believe that it was.

In January, when my parents' fighting started getting worse, I'd bundle up in sweatpants and cozy socks, then take my cell out onto the deck and talk to Jace, the cold night air nipping at my lips.

We talked about everything. And yet, for some reason, I never told him that my parents were getting divorced. I don't know why. It wasn't that I thought he would judge me—we'd told each other plenty of personal things. Looking back now, I would have to say that it was because I was in some kind of denial. I didn't want to admit to *myself* that my parents were getting divorced, so why would I tell Jace that they were?

We went on like this for two months.

Until one day.

He just stopped.

Stopped returning my calls.

Stopped emailing me.

Stopped texting me.

It was like he just disappeared.

Finally, I broke down and told Courtney, asked her if she had any idea what might have happened. She called and asked him. It made me feel pathetic, but I didn't know what else to do. I was desperate.

All she could offer was that he said it was complicated, and that he wouldn't tell her any more than that.

So I did my best to forget him. And failed miserably.

The waitress brings the check over, snapping me out of my reverie.

"Here you go, hon," she says as she sets it down and picks up my empty plate. "Can I get you anything else tonight?"

"No." I shake my head. I'm not ready to go back to the hotel, but what choice do I really have? I can't just stay here all night drinking sodas. So I pay my bill and head out of the comfort of the cozy restaurant and back onto the street.

I'm sure it's just my mood, but the streets of Savannah somehow seem dark and dirty now, the people not as happy. The few that are out this late move past me, their hands in their pockets, not making eye contact. It's a little cooler now than it was before, and the wind kicks up a little, forcing me to keep my head down as I walk.

As I approach the hotel, I know I should go in the side entrance—the door that's the closest to my room, the door that will take me right back to where I need to go. It doesn't make sense to go around to the front—it's a longer walk.

But I want to see if Jace's car is still in the parking lot

across the street—if he's still at the hotel or if he took off, leaving me here alone. Not that I would blame him.

But still. He said he wasn't going to.

And I can't help it. I want him to be here. I need to find out if he is.

So I circle back around to the front of the hotel, keeping my eyes down on the cobblestone pavement until the very last moment. And then, right when I'm almost at the door, I look up, over to the parking lot.

The lot is full, and I scan the cars for his. But it's not there. I know it, even though I keep looking. There's an empty spot—the same spot where he parked earlier. It's the only empty spot in the lot, which means that it must have just recently been vacated.

He left. Even though he said he wasn't going to, Jace left.

the trip jace

Saturday, June 26, 10:27 p.m.
Savannah, Georgia

I left. Yup. I took Hector right back to my room, packed up the little stuff I had, headed out to my car, jumped in, and left. I didn't even care that I didn't check out. Let them charge me or whatever they fuck they want to do.

In fact, I hope they do charge me. I hope they give me some kind of bullshit no-checkout fee, or an expensive room-cleaning fee since I ended up leaving the room a big mess from Hector's bath. I don't care. I'll sue them. I'll get a lawyer and I'll sue them for whatever dumb charges they want to try to stick me with. There has to be some law against that, some kind of FCC regulations or some shit.

I reach over and turn the radio on angrily. I have no idea where I'm going. I just know that I have to get away from here, that I have to get away from Peyton.

Hector's sitting next to me on the front seat, looking at me quietly.

"What's wrong?" I ask him.

He whines a little and then inches over until his nose is on my lap. I swear this dog can sense people's emotions. It's crazy.

I reach down and give him a rub on his muzzle. "I'm sorry, boy," I say. "I shouldn't be taking my bad mood out on you. You didn't do anything."

In fact, when I think about it, Hector's the only one who's actually been supportive of me. He's just been happy to be by my side, not asking for anything except some attention and some food once in a while. He's very low maintenance, and he doesn't put any expectations on me. He doesn't keep secrets from me. He doesn't expect me to go to some stupid graduation and give some big speech. He doesn't expect me to just accept it when he doesn't tell me his parents are getting divorced. He just loves me no matter what. Even though I've been treating him like I don't care.

"I'm sorry, boy," I say again, and scratch his ears some more. He sighs in happiness, snuggles up closer to me, and then closes his eyes and immediately falls asleep. I shake my head, wishing my life were as easy as his.

I don't bother turning the GPS on. I just follow the signs and head south, figuring that at some point I'll end up back in Florida. I'm not in any rush to get back there, anyway.

My mom will be ripshit and I'll have to figure out what I'm going to do about graduation.

But I keep driving. Even though going home is going to suck, and even though I don't know exactly where I'm going, I need the miles to keep adding up, to keep putting distance between Peyton and me.

jace before

Friday, June 25, 8:18 p.m.
Siesta Key, Florida

I wanted to play it cool. I wanted to sit here at this stupid wedding reception, next to Peyton, and just pretend that she didn't mean anything to me.

But it's that fucking dress she's wearing. It's low-cut and tight and just . . . Jesus. Why would she wear a dress like that? Is she doing it just to torture me? I like the idea that maybe she had me in mind when she picked it out. Of course, she might be wearing it because she wants to get attention from other guys.

I look around the wedding suspiciously, trying to see if anyone is looking at her. I don't want to have to punch someone out, but I'll do it if I have to.

"So what's up?" I ask her. "How have you been?"

I see the indecision flick through her eyes—she's trying to decide whether or not to tell me to fuck off, to turn her back and keep talking to Jordan and Courtney. But instead, she just shrugs. "Fine. How have you been?"

"I'm good." I take another sip of her water, still wishing I had some kind of alcohol. I never did get a chance to get the bartender's attention.

"Getting ready for graduation?"

I nod. "Yup."

"That's nice." Her eyes slide past me, scanning the room, almost like she's looking for someone to get up and go talk to. I'm desperate to keep her near me, and so I say, "I'm giving a speech."

"You got valedictorian?"

I nod.

"That's amazing, Jace, congratulations." She smiles, and I can tell she's really happy for me. And even though I don't care about the stupid speech, even though I don't care about being valedictorian, I smile too.

Because the way she's looking at me makes me realize something—it is definitely not over between Peyton Miller and me.

Talking about my speech seems to somehow break the ice between us, and all through dinner, we're talking and laughing and kind of flirting.

I can't take my eyes off her. I think about why I stopped talking to her, about why I stopped replying to her emails and her texts. And suddenly, I'm so, so sorry. It's like my biggest regret in my whole entire life. I want to tell her that I'm sorry, I want to tell her that I didn't mean it, I want to tell her that I take it back, that we need to talk, that we need to be together, that now that she's here I never want her to leave me again. But I can't do that in front of all of these people.

Shit like that only happens in movies.

"Do you want to dance?" I ask Peyton as the plates get cleared.

"With you?" She looks at me skeptically.

"Yeah." I push my shoulders back in a false show of bravado. "I'm an excellent dancer."

"Oh, really?" She rolls her eyes, but she's smiling. "I wouldn't peg you for an excellent dancer."

I puff my lip out, pretending to be hurt. "Why not? You don't think I have moves like Jagger?"

"They weren't talking about Jagger's dance moves," she says, grinning.

I stand up and hold my hand out to her. "Come on," I say. "I'll show you."

She hesitates, and for a second I think she's going to say no. But then she takes my hand, and I pull her out onto the dance floor.

We dance for a long time, letting ourselves get caught up in the music. Most of the songs are fast, which is good. It keeps us from having that awkward moment where we have to decide if we're going to dance a slow dance, or if we're just going to go back to our seats.

But when the inevitable moment comes, and a slow song starts and the lights dim even more, it's not awkward. There's not even a hesitation on her part. She slips right into my arms, and it feels right. Perfect.

"Hi," I murmur into her hair, knowing it's a corny thing to say. But I can't help it. For some reason, whenever I'm around this girl, she turns me into some kind of lovesick fool.

"Hey," she says back. We dance the whole song, and when it's over, she pulls away from me slowly, almost like it's too much for her body to be away from mine. I know how she feels, because I feel the same way.

When another fast song starts, we decide to take a break and head back to the table.

I ignore the knowing looks that Courtney is giving me, and I ignore it when she leans over and whispers something to Jordan and he grins. They're probably making jokes about how Peyton and I are going to have sex or something tonight. I want that. Not to have sex with Peyton—although, actually, that's not really true, because of course I would love to have sex with Peyton—but to be like Jordan and Courtney. A couple who's giving each other knowing looks and sharing private jokes about other couples.

I know that at some point, Peyton and I are going to have to talk about what happened between us, about how

I stopped talking to her, about why she never told me her parents were getting divorced if we were supposedly so close. But I don't want to think about that right now. All I want to think about is how I'm never, ever going to let her go again.

When the waiters start to pour coffee, and everyone stands up so they can watch Courtney's dad and his new bride cut the cake, Peyton grabs my arm and pulls me toward the back of the room.

We stand there together, watching.

"If they smash it into each other's faces, it means they don't really love each other," Peyton reports.

"What?" I look at her, shocked.

"It's true." She shrugs. "Would you smash cake into the face of someone you really liked?"

I think about it. "No. Probably not."

We watch as the bride cuts the cake, and then the bride and groom each hold a piece, feeding each other daintily.

"Well," I say, "I guess they're really in love."

Peyton shakes her head. "Give it a minute."

So I do. And just when I think I'm in the clear, Jordan's mom takes her piece of cake and shoves it into Courtney's dad's face. Then he shoves his piece into hers. The crowd whoops and claps.

Peyton turns to me, grinning. "See?"

"So they don't really love each other."

"Nope." She shakes her head, and then the grin slips

from her face, and she's looking down at the ground. I wonder if she's thinking about what happened between us, and the fear that she might decide she wants to get away from me slides up my spine.

"Hey," I say, clearing my throat. I put my hand on her arm. "Do you want to go back to my room?" She looks at me in surprise, like she can't imagine I would suggest such a thing, and I put my hands up in surrender. "No, no," I say. "I just mean so that we can talk. About, um . . . you know, what happened."

She takes in a deep breath, and then she nods. "Okay," she says finally. "Let's go."

We slip quietly out the back of the ballroom, the crowd still hooting and hollering.

peyton before

Friday, June 25, 9:45 p.m.
Siesta Key, Florida

This is so not a good idea.

Going back to Jace's room, I mean.

I know he's a jerk. I know he just stopped talking to me after making me feel like maybe he was falling in love with me, after making me feel like maybe all those emails and text messages and late-night phone calls and the way he kissed me on the beach at Christmas really meant something.

And after Jace stopped talking to me, I made a promise to myself that no matter how much I was hurting, no matter how much I cried, that I wouldn't ever let him suck me back in.

I broke that promise, obviously, when I texted him. And now I'm really breaking it, by dancing with him, by talking to him, by letting him take me back to his room.

But I can't stop myself—it's like a wave of emotion that's bigger than I am. It's wrong and perfect and delicious and warm and cold at the same time.

Is this what love feels like?

When we get back to his room, he unlocks the door and turns the light on.

The room's a mess. Not dirty or anything, just messy. His suitcase is open on the bed, and a bunch of clothes are strewn around the room, on the floor, on the bed, even on the chair that's sitting in the corner.

"Wow," I say. "Someone needs housekeeping. Why'd you throw your clothes all around the room?" I realize I don't really know Jace that well. Maybe he had some kind of anger-fueled fit or something. "Did you . . . did you have a fit?" I whisper.

"No," he says, rolling his eyes. "I didn't have a fit. I had a Hector."

"A what?"

The sound of jangling comes from the bathroom, and then the cutest dog I've ever seen comes running out, a red T-shirt in his mouth. His little tail is wagging, his ears are perked up, and when he sees me, he drops the shirt and rushes up to me like we're long-lost friends.

He jumps, putting his front paws on my super-expensive dress, but I don't even care.

"Hi, buddy," I say, falling to my knees on the floor. "Oh, you're so cute!"

"Yeah," Jace says, sitting down next to me and giving Hector a pat on his head. "If by cute you mean a total menace."

"Awww, how bad can he be?" I ask, burying my face in Hector's fur. "He's adorable!"

"Adorable can mean trouble," Jace reports.

I snort. "Don't I know it." I look up at him, hoping he can hear the accusing tone in my voice, hoping he knows that I'm talking about him.

"Peyton," he says quietly. And I can tell he knows exactly what I'm talking about, exactly what I mean when I said that if you're cute you can be trouble. "We need to talk."

I nod. Suddenly there's a twisting in my chest. I'm scared. Scared that whatever he says isn't going to be enough, that whatever explanation he gives isn't going to make up for the fact that he broke my heart, smashed it to pieces, and didn't even stick around to make sure I'd be able to be put back together.

He takes my hand and pulls me up onto the bed, and once we're sitting there, he doesn't let me go. Hector lies on the floor, chewing on one of Jace's socks.

Jace takes a deep breath. "I'm sorry I just stopped talking to you like that," he says. "It wasn't right."

I nod, waiting for the explanation. I'm looking down at the floor, but there's just silence. He doesn't say anything, and it's almost like maybe he's waiting for me to say something.

But I'm not going to. I'm not going to let him off the hook like that, I'm not just going to tell him that everything's okay because that would be a lie. Everything *isn't* okay—it's one thing to dance with him, to feel his arms around me, to go back to his room with him. But let's face it, this is just me losing my self-control for a little bit.

At some point, he's going to have to give me an explanation about what happened, about why he just disappeared, about why he just stopped responding to me. And it's going to have to be a good reason. Otherwise I'm going to have to walk out of this room, I'm going to have to leave him here, I'm going to have to move on with my life, even if it's hard.

I look up at him, praying he has some amazing explanation. Okay, fine, right now I would take any kind of explanation, anything that would allow me to understand why or how he could do something like that, why or how it was that I had him all wrong.

But instead of saying anything, he leans down and brushes his lips against mine. Sparks and warmth flood through my body.

"Peyton." He whispers my name, and his eyes are asking me if this is okay. And when I don't stop him, he kisses me again. This time the kiss is deeper, more delicious, more searching.

His tongue moves against mine, and his hands are on the back of my neck, his fingers sending shivers up my spine. I kiss him back, my mind a complete mess, my body on fire. I'm not thinking about anything but this kiss.

We stay like that for a while, just kissing, until finally, we fall back onto the bed. I'm breathless, my thoughts spinning and turning and jumbling, taken over by the feelings that are rushing through me. The moment swallows me whole, and it's only me and Jace, here, on the bed, together. It's endless and perfect and beautiful and I never want it to end.

"Wait," Jace says. He sits up and shakes his head.

"What?" I ask, trying to catch my breath.

"We should . . . I mean . . ." He runs his fingers through his hair, brushing it back from his face. I love the fact that I have this effect on him, that I might be driving him as crazy as he's driving me. "We should talk first."

"Okay." I sit up and lean back against the heavy cherry headboard of the bed, trying to hide my disappointment. All I want to do is keep kissing him. But I know he's right—it's better if we talk first, if we get to the bottom of things. And the fact that he's the one that's bringing it up just makes me want him more. It's like a double-edged sword.

From his spot on the floor, Hector begins to whine.

"So," Jace says, taking a deep breath and standing up. "I'm going to take Hector out, and then you and I can talk."

I nod. "Sounds good."

He cocks his head. "Are you hungry?"

"Hungry? We just ate at the wedding."

"Yeah, but that food doesn't count." He wrinkles his nose. "Too fancy. You want to order pizza?"

I didn't think I was that hungry, but now that he's said it, pizza sounds amazing. "That sounds really good," I admit.

"Okay." He nods. "Walk first, then I'll come back and order us some food. And then we'll talk."

"Perfect."

He walks out the door and I let out a happy sigh, running my hands up and down over the sheets. As I do, my hand accidentally brushes something off the bed and onto the floor. At first I think it's the TV remote, and I reach down to pick it up. But it's not. It's Jace's cell phone. It must have fallen out of his pocket.

I go to set it on the nightstand next to me, but when I do, my eyes fall onto a text message on the screen.

From someone named Kari. Miss you, it says.

Miss you.

Miss. You.

The two words reverberate through my head, through the room, getting bigger, taking over everything.

Miss you miss you miss you miss you ruining everything miss you.

Before I can even think about what I'm doing and whether or not it's right, I open the text history between the two of them.

Kari: Hey cutie, when will you be back?

Jace: **Tomorrow morning.**

Kari: **Am I still going to graduation with you and your family?**

Jace: **Yup. Can't wait!**

Kari: **Miss you.**

My heart squeezes, and I set the phone down on the bed and then sit there for a long moment, staring at it.

Maybe it's a relative, I tell myself. *A cousin, or an older aunt or something. Miss you* could mean *miss you and your family* and *cutie* could be like if you were talking to a kid or something.

My fingers are on autopilot, and they scroll through Jace's phone until they land on the name.

Kari.

I hit call.

It only rings once before she picks up.

"Hey, sexy," a voice says.

A girl's voice.

A girl who's my age.

I hang up the phone.

Tears prick at my eyes, but I blink fast, and then, just like that, the sadness is gone. I shut it off, the way I've shut off all kinds of things these past few months—my parents getting divorced, my mom using my credit card, everything.

And then I walk out the door of Jace's room, and force myself not to look back.

before jace

Friday, June 25, 10:29 p.m.
Siesta Key, Florida

I walk Hector down behind the restaurant of the yacht club, hoping that he doesn't poop on the grass. I have a bag, but the last thing I really want to be doing is picking up dog poop. And this is definitely the kind of place where if you don't, someone will notice and say something, like, "Hey, shitbag, clean up after your dog."

I let Hector sniff around for a while until finally he lifts his leg and pees.

"Come on, boy," I say, running him back up the hill to my room. I want to get back to Peyton. I want to kiss her more, and I want to talk to her about why she didn't tell me her parents were getting divorced, about how much that hurt me, about how even if she *did* hurt me that not talking to her was a stupid thing to do, about how much I regret letting my idiotic pride get in the way.

But when I get back to my room, she's not there.

"Peyton?" I call out. But there's no answer. I knock on the door to the bathroom, but she's not in there either. "Where is she, boy?" I ask Hector, before realizing that's a really stupid thing to do, since (a) Hector wasn't here when she left and (b) he's a dog, and therefore can't talk.

My phone's sitting on the nightstand, and I pick it up so that I can call her. Maybe she had to go tell her parents she was leaving the wedding, or maybe she decided to order the pizza and go pick it up herself.

When I pick up the phone, though, I see there's a new text from Kari.

Miss you.

My heart jumps into my throat. But there's no way Peyton could have seen it. She wouldn't have looked in my phone. She wouldn't have done something like that.

But then where is she?

I try calling her, but she doesn't answer. In fact, it goes right to voicemail. I don't know what room she's in, so I call the front desk.

"Hi," I say. "I'd like Peyton Miller's room, please."

The operator connects me, and I listen as the phone rings on the other end, over and over and over, until finally a recording picks up and says that the person I'm trying to reach isn't there.

Okay, so she's not in her room. Which is actually a good thing. She must have gone and picked up the pizza.

I look at my phone, thinking about Kari. Shit. I'm going to have to break up with her. And I should probably do it before Peyton comes back. I'm going to have to tell Peyton about it, too, which is going to suck.

I shake my head. Whatever. Peyton and I will make it through this. Yes, it's going to be messy and mixed-up and we're going to have a lot of talking to do, but I don't care. If we're ever going to work out, we're going to have to start being honest with each other.

I sigh and then pick up the phone and call Kari.

"Hey," she says when she answers. "Why are you pranking me?"

"What are you talking about?" I ask.

"You just called me a few minutes ago, and then you hung up."

"No, I didn't."

"Yes, you did."

"No, I didn't."

"Jace!" She laughs. "You did."

"My phone must have called you by accident," I say.

"I don't think so," she says. "It rang, and I picked up the phone and said 'Hey, sexy' and then you hung up on me. It wasn't very nice."

Bile rises up in my throat. I pull the phone away from my ear and scroll through the call log. And there it is. An outgoing call to Kari, made ten minutes ago. An outgoing call that must have been made by Peyton. Shit, shit, shit.

"Hello?" Kari's saying. "Jace, are you there?"

"Yeah," I say. "I'm here." I'm already on my way out the door, grabbing my keys and shutting the door behind me, shrugging on a sweater and walking down by the fountain and the garden path, scanning the area for Peyton.

"Is everything okay?" she asks. "You don't sound like yourself."

I take a deep breath. "No," I say. "Everything's not okay."

before peyton

Friday, June 25, 10:31 p.m.
Siesta Key, Florida

When I leave Jace's hotel room, I don't really know what to do, so I go to my parents' room (my mom gave me a key just in case I needed it), and grab the keys to the rental car that got us here from the airport.

I slide my phone into my purse, shutting it off just in case she decides to call and yell at me for taking the car. Although even if she does, who cares? I mean, what's she going to do? Call the police? Big deal, I'll call the police on her for stealing my identity. I get behind the wheel of the car and drive. I don't really know where I'm going, just that I need to get away from Jace, need something to keep my mind occupied until tomorrow, until Brooklyn comes, until I can escape to North Carolina and forget about Jace Renault for good.

jace before

Saturday, June 26, 10:41 p.m.
Siesta Key, Florida

She took it well. Kari, I mean. Of course, she didn't understand what the hell I was talking about at first, mostly because I was babbling, but also because I ran into Courtney's grandma while I was walking, and she stopped me and wanted to have this big discussion about iPads.

Seriously. I'm enmeshed in the biggest emotional drama of my life, and the lady started asking me about *iPads* and if I thought she should get one. Like I'm fucking Steve Jobs or something. I was perfectly polite to her, but she seemed a little miffed that I couldn't give her more info on the specs. I really don't understand why old people always think everyone from the younger generation is some kind of tech genius.

Anyway, Kari couldn't understand why I hadn't mentioned Peyton before, and at first I'm pretty sure she thought

I was making the whole thing up just to have a reason to break up with her. But by the end, it seemed like she believed me, and she was cool about it. "Jace," she said. "I hope we can still be friends. Because honestly, we were better that way." On some level, she definitely must have felt the weirdness between us too.

So now I'm roaming around the grounds of the yacht club looking for Peyton, not really sure where the hell I should go or where she might be. I finally end up ducking into the main building, not because I think Peyton is going to be there, but because I spot Courtney's grandma lurking around outside, and I really don't want to have another run in with her.

I look around the lobby, but obviously Peyton's not there. Why would she be hanging out in the lobby of the hotel?

And then, suddenly, I have a brilliant idea. An idea so obvious that it's actually not even that brilliant. I'll just find out what room Peyton's in, and then go and find her! Even if she's not at her room right now, she's going to have to come back to it sometime, right?

I make my way over to the front desk clerk, a twenty-something guy wearing a nametag that says WADE. It would be much better if Wade were a woman. Women I can sweet talk—you give them a sob story, a little smile, compliment them on their looks, and you can usually get what you want. (Not that I usually manipulate women like that, of course.

That's way too douchey. But desperate times call for desperate measures.)

"Hello, sir!" Wade says as I approach. Okay. So Wade is perky. Hopefully, he's perkily going to do what I ask him.

"Hey," I say. I shake my head and try to look sheepish. "I forgot my room number."

"No problem, sir!" he chirps. Seriously, he chirps. I've never really heard a guy chirp before, but whatever. To each his own. He puts his fingers over the keyboard of the computer that's in front of him. "Can I have your name, please?"

"Well, see, that's the problem," I say. "The room isn't in my name."

"No problem, sir," he says. Only this time he doesn't sound so sure. I take this as a very bad sign. "Just tell me the name of the person under whom your room is booked."

I rack my brain, trying to remember Peyton's mom's first name.

"Michelle," I say. "Michelle Miller."

Wade clacks across the keys. "Hmm," he says. "Are you Peyton?"

"Am I . . . ?" For a second, I'm confused, but then I get it. The room is in Peyton's mom's name, and Peyton must be listed on the account as the only other person who's allowed to have access to it. And since Peyton can be a boy's name too, I guess Wade here just assumes that I'm Peyton.

"Why, yes," I say, puffing out my chest. "Yes, I am Peyton. Peyton Miller, yup, that's me."

"Okay, Mr. Miller," Wade says, "I'm just going to need to see your ID."

Fuck.

"Um, my ID's in the room." I hold my hands out and shrug, like, *Oh, well, what can you do?*

"Oh no!" Wade puts on a really upset face, like he can't take the fact that now he's going to have to tell me some bad news. "That's really too bad, Mr. Miller, because unfortunately we are not allowed to give out room information or replace keys unless we have identification." He pushes the desk phone toward me. "Is there anyone you can call who can come down here and help? The person who booked the room, perhaps?"

"No." I shake my head sadly. "The person who booked the room is . . . unavailable."

I stare at Wade, waiting for him to do something.

But he doesn't.

He just folds his hands in front of him and stares at me.

"So, what am I supposed to do?" I persist. "I need to get in my room. My dog, Hector, is in there, and he probably really needs to go out."

I figure I can get him with the dog story for sure—after all, I seem to be the only person on the face of the planet who doesn't fall to pieces when Hector gets brought into it—but instead, Wade gets a shocked look on his face.

"Sir," he says, and then takes in a deep breath, like there's a situation that now has to be dealt with. "Dogs are not allowed at this hotel!"

Shit. "Oh," I say. "Well, um . . ." I rack my brain desperately for something that can save the situation. But I can't think of anything. And now Peyton and her mom are probably going to get some sort of bullshit pet charge on their bill or something.

I wonder if I can offer Wade some money to just forget about this whole thing. He doesn't seem like the type to take a bribe, but you can never really tell now, can you?

And then my eyes land on his bracelet. It's one of those plastic bands that come in all different kinds of bright colors—his is yellow—and on it are the words I'M A BELIEBER.

I've been on Facebook and Twitter enough to know that this means the dude likes Justin Bieber. So I quickly turn on the charm.

"Oh, my God!" I say, pointing at his bracelet. "You like Justin, too?"

He looks at me, then puffs his chest out. "Justin who?"

"Is there more than one?" I scoff.

His mouth drops. "You? *You're* a belieber?"

"Um, yeah," I say, "for years." I'm not sure if Justin has even been around that long, but whatever. "I love his music, and honestly, I don't understand why more guys don't like him."

"That's what I always say!" He looks around then motions me forward, like he wants to let me in on a secret. I step closer to the desk, and he lifts up the cuff of his sleeve and shows me a tattoo. It says JB in curly script.

"So cool!" I gush, when in actuality, all I want to do is lunge across this dude's desk and grab his keyboard so that I can find out what room Peyton is in. "Anyway, aren't beliebers supposed to look out for each other?"

He hesitates.

"Come on!" I say. "You know Justin would want it."

He sighs, then looks around to make sure we're alone. "Fine," he whispers. "I'll tell you the room number and I'll even forget about the dog. But I'm not doing this for you, I'm doing it for Justin!"

I'm so thankful that I almost reach across the counter and hug him. "Thank you, thank you, thank you," I say. "Dude, you have no idea how much I appreciate it."

He gets to typing, but then, like some kind of nightmare, all of a sudden from behind me comes the sound of someone screaming my name.

"Jace! Hey, Jace!"

I don't turn around, willing whoever it is to just go away.

"JACE!" The person is really screaming now.

I just keep grinning at Wade.

"I think that guy is looking for you," Wade says, looking at something over my shoulder. He wrinkles his nose in disgust.

"Oh, no," I say. "He must think I'm someone else."

"JACE RENAULT, IT'S ME B.J. FROM THE WEDDING!!"

The voice is getting louder, and I lean in toward Wade, trying to get a peek at the computer screen. "Did you find the room number yet?" I'm about to start sweating.

Wade goes to open his mouth, but before he can say anything, I feel a pair of arms wrap around my shoulders from behind and grab me tight. What the *hell*? I struggle to get out of the embrace.

"Jace!" B.J. says, and grins. "You're here!"

I shake my head, trying to communicate to him with my eyes that I'm in the middle of a scheme, and that he should just go away.

But of course he doesn't get it.

"Jace! It's me, B.J.! From the wedding?" He frowns. "Are you okay? You don't look so good."

"Excuse me," Wade says from behind the computer. His eyes, which had brightened up a little when we were bonding over being (albeit fake) beliebers, are now dark and stormy. "I'm going to have to ask you to leave this desk, otherwise I'm going to have to call security."

I think about protesting, about trying to convince him that I really am Peyton Miller, but I'm smart enough to know when I'm licked.

I sigh and move away from the desk as Wade starts mumbling something about how I'm not really a belieber, how a real belieber would never be so deceptive. Shows what he knows. One time I was at a Barnes & Noble when a new Justin Bieber book came out and I got run over by two eleven-year-old girls who were so excited to buy it that they lost all sense of real decorum.

"What's up, my man?" B.J. says, and claps me on the back like we're old friends. "Why did that guy want to call security on you? Did you try to sneak alcohol into your room?" He nods sympathetically, like he's been there, done that. Which is not that hard to believe.

"No, I didn't try to sneak alcohol into my room," I say. I resist the urge to start screaming at him, and then maybe throttle him around the throat for good measure.

"Then what is it?" He lowers his voice. "Drugs? Because that's not cool, dude. Crack is whack!"

I shake my head, my anger starting to dissipate. How can I be mad at someone who's so obviously clueless? "No, it's not drugs," I say. "It's a girl."

"Pffft!" he says, shaking his head. "Chicks! They're crazy, aren't they?"

"Not this one," I say. "I'm the crazy one. The crazy one who fucked everything all up."

"Man, that sucks," B.J. says. He crosses his arms over his chest. "So what are you going to do?"

"I don't know," I say. "I have no fucking clue."

He looks thoughtful for a moment, his lips sliding over to the side, pursed in concentration. Then his eyes light up.

"I know!" he says. He reaches into his pocket and pulls out his phone. "I'll call Jordan!"

"Jordan?"

"Yeah, you know, Courtney's boyfriend? He's the best when it comes to figuring out chicks."

"Um, no, that's okay," I say. The last thing I need is people who are pretty much strangers trying to help me with my emotional problems. I mean, talk about humiliating.

But B.J. doesn't seem to want to listen, and ten minutes later, Jordan's walking into the lobby. Wade is still giving us death looks, so I herd everyone over to the lounge on the other side of the room.

"Oh, sweet," B.J. says, his eyes lighting up. "They have a pool table."

He picks up a pool cue and starts swinging it around like a samurai sword. "So what's up?" Jordan asks, reaching out and taking the pool cue out of B.J.'s hands. "Why did you guys ask me to come down here?"

"Jace needs women advice," B.J. reports. He starts racking up the balls.

"No, I don't," I say.

Jordan nods. "Peyton, huh?"

I nod sheepishly. "Yeah. Courtney told you?"

"Yeah. So what's the deal?"

"Yeah, what's the deal?" B.J asks, then leans over the pool table and breaks the balls. One goes flying over the side of the table and onto the floor. "Oops," he says. It rolls across the marble floor until it hits the side of a man's foot. "Sorry," B.J. says.

The man gives him a dirty look, but B.J. isn't fazed. He just puts the ball back on the table. "Do over," he says. "Okay, guys?"

"Fine with me," I say.

"Whatever." Jordan says. He grabs a pool cue and I do the same. "So what's going on?"

"Well," I say, really thinking about it. "We met at Christmas, and then I broke up with her."

B.J's mouth drops open. "You *broke up* with her? Dude, are you crazy? Peyton's hot."

"There's more to relationships than hotness, B.J." Jordan says. He leans over and shoots the orange solid into the side pocket effortlessly.

"Don't I know it," B.J. says. He shakes his head. "Jocelyn's hot, and that's not even close to being enough." He looks at me like he's letting me in on a secret. "With girls, you have to worry about their emotions."

"So why'd you dump her?" Jordan asks me.

"Because I found out she'd been keeping a secret from me."

Jordan and B.J. exchange a glance.

"Been there," Jordan says.

"Courtney kept a secret from you?"

"No, *he* kept one from *her*," B.J. reports. He bends over the pool table to take his shot, but the ball only goes about two inches before rolling to a stop on the felt.

"So what happened?" I ask.

"I broke up with her," Jordan says. "Because I was a pussy."

"Yeah," I say. "Been there, dude." It's my turn, so I lean over the table and concentrate on the shot. I put all my energy into sinking the yellow ball, and it works. It goes right into the pocket. "So what happened?"

"I made myself miserable because I couldn't tell her how I felt," Jordan says, shrugging. "And finally, she found out the secret on her own."

"She found out on her own?"

"Yup. And she was totally pissed."

"So what did you do?"

"I had to make it up to her," he says. "And she didn't want to forgive me, so I had to work at it." He shakes his head. "If there's one thing I've realized, it's that you have to be honest. Even if you're scared, even if you're worried that you're going to get your heart stomped on, even if you think that the truth is going to ruin everything, you have to put it out there. Because otherwise, you're fucked." He leans over and sinks the solid blue ball into the middle pocket. He says this whole thing completely matter-of-factly, and the thing is, I believe him. I believe he knows what he's talking about.

I've seen him and Courtney together. I've seen the way they look at each other like they're the only people in the room. They seem connected. I want that with Peyton. And I know Jordan's right—in order to have that kind of relationship, you have to put it all out there, you have to be willing to let yourself be vulnerable. Otherwise, there's no way you're going to be able to have anything real.

"Now," Jordan says, "the only question is, is she worth it?"

"She's worth it," I say. God, is she worth it.

"Then you have to go find her."

And again, I know that he's right.

peyton | the trip

Saturday, June 26, 10:53 p.m.
Savannah, Georgia

When I get back to my hotel room in Savannah, I'm starting to consider maybe having a mini meltdown. I mean, I have no clue what I'm going to do. I don't know how the hell I'm going to get to North Carolina. I don't have a car. I hardly have any money. I don't even have a *phone*.

I plop down on the bed, wondering if maybe I should just call my mom and have her come get me. Or maybe my dad. I could tell him about why I wanted to run away, about what my mom did to me.

But doing that would mean I would have to speak the words out loud, and I really don't know if I'm ready for that. Besides, I don't *want* to go home. I want to go to North Carolina. I want to get my apartment in Creve Coeur. I want to stay there for the summer until I can figure out what the hell I'm going to do.

I stare up at the ceiling. Maybe all I need is a good night's sleep. Maybe tomorrow morning I'll be able to come up with a plan. I mean, there has to be a way. People are always finding ways to do things with little to no resources. It's, like, the basis of civilization. Maybe I can take a bus, or maybe I can find one of those cash-advance places that are super shady and charge you, like, triple the money when you go to pay it back.

I turn on a rerun of one of the Real Housewives shows, and then slide under the covers, determined to just fall asleep. But it's not working. I can't stop thinking about him. About Jace. About how he knew my parents were getting divorced, about how that was the reason he stopped talking to me.

I'd spent so much time obsessing about what went wrong, and the possibility that maybe he'd somehow found out about my parents had never crossed my mind.

Of course, the absolute worst part about it is that I'm the one who did this. I'm the one who pushed him away. I'm the one who didn't tell him something important that was going on in my life. All that time we spent on the phone—all that time I spent getting to know him, making plans, getting close, and I didn't tell him. I should have told him.

Even so, I can't put all of the blame on myself. He's the one who just blew me off like it was nothing. He didn't even bother to ask me about it.

And what about the fact that he was kissing me last

night, while the whole time he had a girlfriend? A girlfriend who was texting him all "I miss you" and blah blah blah. And yeah, I was kissing him in the bathtub tonight even after knowing that. But you can't really blame me. I mean, it was a physical reaction that couldn't be controlled.

Anyway, that's two strikes against Jace. Two strikes and you're out. I mean, when you think about it, that's how it should be. Who wants to stick around for a third strike? Anyone can have one slip up, but after the second, it's probably not an accident.

My thoughts swirl around my head, keeping me awake and driving me crazy, until finally, at around three in the morning, I fall into a fitful sleep.

I'm woken up by a knock on the door. It's so loud and violent that at first, I think it must be coming from the TV. But when I blink my eyes open, the clock on the nightstand says 10:07 a.m., and the TV is off. I must have turned it off at some point during the night.

I sit up in bed. Shit, shit, shit. This is not how my morning was supposed to go. I was supposed to be awake by six or seven, showered and clean, my stomach full of free continental breakfast. I was supposed to be bright-eyed and bushy-tailed, ready to come up with a brilliant plan for my future. But instead, I'm still in bed, being assaulted by aggressive knocking on the door. Probably housekeeping. Don't they know that checkout isn't until noon?

I throw my legs over the bed and pad to the door,

yanking down the right leg of my pajama pants, which has slid up to my knee.

"I'm still in here," I call. "I'll be out at noon, you know, when it's time for *checkout*."

"Oh, no, you won't!" a voice says. "You will open up this door right now, young lady."

My heart pounds in fear. Whoever that is sounds like they mean business. Real business. The only other times I've heard a tone like that is when I'm watching reruns of police shows, and there's some wanted man in a house somewhere who won't come out. But I'm not a criminal. And I don't have a warrant. Unless . . . we never called the police after we got into that accident earlier. Maybe they traced the car or something back to me, and now I'm going to get in trouble for leaving the scene of a crime!

I tiptoe to the door and peer through the peephole, expecting to see a policewoman or two, uniformed and holding handcuffs, ready to take me to jail. Then I would definitely have to call my parents. No way do I have enough money to bail myself out of jail.

But there's no police officer on the other side of the door. There's just a tall woman, with perfectly highlighted light brown hair that's pulled back into a low bun. She's wearing a cream-colored T-shirt, dark jeans, a sheer black cardigan, and gold ballet flats. Maybe she's undercover? She doesn't look like the type of person who would be sent out to pick up criminals.

"Can I help you, ma'am?" I ask politely. Something shady is definitely going on here, and if she doesn't identify herself, well, then, I'll just call 911 and the real police department can get to the bottom of this.

"Yes," she says. "I think you can help me. I'm looking for Jace Renault."

"Oh." I think about it, not sure I want to admit that I know Jace, that he was just here with me last night. What if he's in some kind of trouble? Of course, he left me, so if law enforcement is looking for him, it would serve him right if I turned him in. But if it *is* about the car, then there's a good chance I could get in trouble, too. "Who am I speaking with, please?" I ask.

I watch through the peephole as the woman in the hallway takes a step back, like she can't believe I've asked such a question. "Who am *I* speaking to?" she asks, moving back toward the door and pounding on it again with her fist. Yikes. We've got a live one here.

"I asked you first," I counter, not wanting her to know that I'm secretly terrified.

"My name is Piper Renault," she says. "I'm Jace's mother."

Oh. Well. I guess that explains it.

Mrs. Renault isn't at all like what I imagined. I know it's stereotyping, but I thought she'd be this really stuffy, sort of boring, plain-looking woman. She's a professor of women's studies, so I'd just assumed—I mean, aren't all those women's lib people always kind of crunchy-looking? I thought they didn't like it when women wore makeup or bras or anything that put their sexuality on display.

But Mrs. Renault is really pretty. She's wearing this amazing shade of lipstick, and I kind of even want to ask her what it's called, but she's definitely not in a mood to talk makeup.

When I unlocked the door and let her in, the first thing she did was start barging around my room like she owned the place. "Jace!" she called, opening the bathroom door roughly and peeking in. "Come out! The jig is up!"

Yikes. The jig is up, even. She opened the closet next, but of course Jace wasn't in there.

"He's not here," I say. "Um, he left." I wish I had some more information to give her because she seems like maybe she's about to start really tearing this place up, and I don't want to be the one to get in trouble for it.

"Ha!" she says. She gets down on her hands and knees and looks under the bed.

"I swear," I say. "Mrs. Renault, Jace isn't here."

"Then where is he?" She taps her foot against the floor impatiently, waiting for me to tell her where her son is.

"I don't know," I say. "I don't . . . I mean, I think he's probably on his way home."

"On his way home! I truly doubt that." She looks around the room one more time, and then her gaze settles on me. "So what is this? You two decided to run away together or what? You want to get married or something?"

"Married?" I'm shocked she would even think that. "God, no. We weren't running away to get married."

"Then what? Tell me why Jace would skip out on his graduation to be with you!"

"Jace . . . what? He skipped out on his graduation?" I frown. That makes no sense. "Why would he do that?"

"I don't know!" She throws her hands up in exasperation. "But it's tonight. Tonight at seven o'clock. Which means that if he's not on his way home right now, he's going to miss it!" She looks at the clock and then crosses her arms over her chest.

I take a deep breath. "Mrs. Renault, I'm sorry about Jace and his graduation. And I swear, if I knew where he was, I would tell you. But I don't. He left here last night, late. He, um . . . we . . . we got into a fight."

She looks at me and opens her mouth like maybe she's going to yell at me again, or tell me that she doesn't believe me, or demand that I tell her everything I know. But at the last moment, her face crumples. She sits down next to me on the bed, just looking down at the floor. After a moment, she wordlessly reaches over and grabs the bag of Combos that's sitting on my nightstand. She slides her hand into the bag, pulls out a few, and pops them into her mouth.

There's an awkward silence as she just sits there and eats, and I just sit there being nervous. She holds the bag out to me, and I don't really want any, but I feel like it would be rude not to take some, and so I eat a couple.

"I was probably too hard on him," she says. "I pushed him, I know that I did."

"No," I say, shaking my head. "I'm sure you were fine."

"No, I wasn't. He doesn't care about school. Yes, he's smart, and that's great, but he's not into all the accolades, all the trappings and things that go along with it. He doesn't need to impress people." She dips her hand back into the bag. "Unlike his mother."

I want to tell her it's okay, but I don't. Because honestly, it's kind of not. I mean, look at my mom—she's so concerned with putting on a good face, with making people think that she has all kinds of money, and for what? It definitely put a huge burden on her relationship with my dad, and it's basically ruined our relationship, even though she might not know it yet.

Jace's family actually has money, so it's funny how his mom just picked something else to focus on—she wanted everyone to know that Jace was super smart, to parade him around like he was some kind of golden child or something.

"I'm sure you did the best you could," I say, figuring I need to give her a break. At least she's here, and at least she's admitting what she's done.

Jace's mom blows out a big breath and then hands me back the empty bag of Combos. "Sorry I ate all your Combos," she says. "I'll buy you a new bag."

"That's okay," I say. "I was done with them anyway." I set the empty bag back on the nightstand. "So you drove all night to get to Jace?"

"No." She shakes her head. "I took a flight first thing this morning. As soon as the credit card showed the charge at this hotel, I headed for the airport. I was going to drag him back on a flight this afternoon, then get him home and ready for graduation tonight."

"How did you know what rooms we were in?"

"I told the woman at the front desk that Jace was using my credit card and that it was technically a stolen charge that could be disputed and cancelled unless she told me."

I nod. "You're a good mom."

She sighs. "It doesn't feel like it." She reaches into her bag and pulls out her cell phone. "He won't answer my calls."

"Well, I'd call him for you, but he probably won't answer my calls, either."

"Because you guys had a fight?" she asks.

"Yes."

She nods, thinking about it. "So if you're not running away to get married, then what are you doing?"

"Didn't he tell you?" I ask. "I didn't have a ride home from the wedding. My ride got—" I grope around for a word. Delayed? Cancelled? "My ride kind of ditched me. And so Jace said that he would drive me home."

She frowns. "That's what he told me," she says. "But don't you live in Connecticut?"

"Yeah," I say. "How'd you know that?"

She waves her hand like it should be obvious. "Of course I know where you live, Peyton. Over the winter you were all Jace could talk about. Peyton this and Peyton that." She looks at me out of the corner of her eye. "What happened between you guys, anyway?"

I swallow, not sure how much I want to reveal to her. She is Jace's mom after all, and pretty much a total stranger. But then I think, whatever, screw it. Keeping things from people hasn't gotten me all that far—I'm stranded in a Savannah hotel room with no money, after all—so maybe it's time to turn over a new leaf.

"I kept something from him," I say. "Something pretty big. And when he found out, he got mad and just stopped talking to me."

She nods. "That sounds like Jace. Unfortunately, he's a product of his parents. Stubborn like me. Shuts down and avoids conflict like my husband when he really cares about someone." She gives me a thin smile. "Do you really think he's on his way home?"

"I really do."

"Not because he's excited about graduation, though."

"No," I say. "Not because he's excited about graduation."

"Ah, well." She stands up and shoulders her purse, then turns around and looks at me. "Do you . . . I mean, are you okay here? Do you need a ride somewhere?"

I think about asking her to take me to the airport, but then what would I do once I was there? I have no money for a flight, and as soon as that became obvious, she'd most definitely call my parents. Same if I asked for a ride to the bus station. She'd start asking me all those annoying questions adults love to ask, like where I'm going and who's going to meet me and blah blah blah.

"No," I say. "My friend's coming to pick me up."

"You sure?" She's standing up now.

"I'm sure."

"Okay." She sighs, then turns around and heads to the door. "Thanks, Peyton," she says. And then she's gone.

I look at the clock next to my bed. Ten thirty. Only an hour and a half until I need to be out of here. Ninety minutes to come up with some kind of plan. I can do it.

But first, I reach over and pick up the phone. I hesitate for a second, then dial the number that no matter how many times I deleted from my cell, I could never delete from my heart.

It rings, and I hold my breath, hoping against hope that he'll pick up. But he doesn't. It goes right to voicemail.

"Jace," I say. "Hey, it's Peyton. I wanted to let you know that your mom was just here. She, um, wanted to make sure you were still going to graduation, but she . . . she seemed like maybe by the end of it she wasn't mad at you. She was just happy that you were okay. At least, I kind of led her to believe you were okay, even though I'm not really sure if you are. Are you okay? I hope so. You should . . . I mean, maybe you should call your mom."

I hang up the phone.

And then, after a moment, I take a deep breath and head for the shower.

jace the trip

Sunday, June 27, 10:53 a.m.
Richmond Hill, Georgia

I haven't left Savannah. Well, that's not exactly true. I've left Savannah, but I haven't gone that far. I drove around for a while last night, going in circles, not knowing exactly what the hell to do. Go back and get Peyton? Say fuck it and go back home? Finally, I ended up at some diner about twenty miles away, where I've been sitting for most of the night.

Every five seconds, I change my mind. Go back and get Peyton. Go home and go to graduation. Fuck everything and just sit here for the whole day, then deal with everything later. Why the hell am I suddenly so indecisive? Usually I know exactly what I want and how to go after it.

My phone has been blowing up with phone calls from my mom all night and all morning. So when I'm ordering what seems like my fifteenth cup of coffee, and my phone buzzes with a voicemail, I don't really give it much thought. Until I look down and see that it's from a Savannah area code.

Peyton. Maybe she wants me to come back and get her, maybe she's going to tell me she's sorry she ever lied to me, that she needs me, that she can't believe what a horrible thing she did.

I pick up the phone and play the message.

"Jace," she says. "Hey, it's Peyton. I wanted to let you know your mom was just here . . ."

What the *fuck*? My *mom* was just there? The thought of Peyton and my mom hanging out makes me want to break out in hives. Also, why did my mom drive all the way to Savannah to find me?

I knew I shouldn't have used my credit card to pay for the room! She probably tracked it and found out what hotel we were at. I can only imagine how pissed off she must be.

Although from what Peyton said, it seems like maybe my mom isn't all that mad about graduation—that she's actually just worried about me. I sigh, feeling like an asshole. I should have at least texted my mom to let her know I was okay.

I pick up my phone and tap out a quick text. **Mom, I'm okay. Not going to make graduation, obviously. But I'll be home soon, and we'll talk then.**

The reply comes almost immediately. **Thanks for letting me know, Jace. I love you and I'm so glad you're okay.**

I hold my phone in my hand, wondering if I should call Peyton. She did call me, after all. And even though she didn't *specifically* ask me to call her back, it would be rude not to. Wouldn't it?

Before I can talk myself out of it, I call the hotel and ask for her room. But when they connect me, it just rings and rings. The thought of her leaving makes my throat hurt. I don't want her wandering around Savannah by herself, with no money and no idea where she's going. I should never have left her.

I look down to where Hector's sitting at my feet. He was in the car for the first couple of hours I was here, but when the waitress peered through the window and saw him, she told me I could bring him in as long as none of the customers complained. He's been chill, Hector—just lying still, his head on his paws. The waitress brought him a plate of sausage biscuits and gravy, which he wolfed down in about two minutes. I think he's in a food coma.

I don't know what to do. Go back? Don't go back?

What I need is some advice. But who can I call? I dial Evan, but he doesn't answer.

I scroll through my phone until I find Courtney's number, and before I can think about whether or not it's a good idea, I push call.

"Hello?" she answers, her voice sleepy. "Jace? Are you okay?"

"Yeah, I'm okay," I say.

"Jesus!" she says. "Do you know your mom's been going crazy? She found out you're in Georgia, and she's on her way there. I tried to call you, but you weren't picking up."

"Yeah, I know. Listen, are you with Jordan?"

"Yeah, he's right here next to me," she says. "Why?"

"Can I talk to him?"

"Oh, no," she says, sounding wary. "Why? Are you involved with drugs or something?"

"No." I shake my head. "Just . . . can I talk to him?"

"Sure." I hear the sound of her waking Jordan, the blankets rustling, and then his voice comes over the phone.

"Yo," he says.

"Hey," I say. "Remember how you told me about how I had to be honest with Peyton, no matter what?"

"Yeah." There's another rustling sound, like maybe he's sitting up in bed or something. He sighs. "You didn't do it, did you?"

"How'd you know?"

"I could just tell. You weren't ready."

"Well, I think I'm ready now."

"How do you know?"

"Because I can't stop thinking about her."

"Not enough."

"I would do anything for her."

"Anything?"

"Yes."

"Even put yourself out there, giving her the opportunity to tell you to fuck off and stomp all over your heart?"

"Yes."

"Okay," he says simply. "Then you need to go get her."

"But what if—"

"What if nothing," he says, cutting me off. "If you love her, if you really mean it, then there's nothing else to talk about."

"There isn't?"

"No," he says, sounding exasperated, like maybe I still don't get it. "You have to just go get her. Enough talking. It's time for action."

I swallow. Just go get her. I know he's right. So instead of even saying goodbye, I hang up the phone and throw some dollar bills onto the table. Then I grab Hector's leash and slip out the door.

No more talking. It's time to go get Peyton.

the trip peyton

Sunday, June 27, 11:07 a.m.
Savannah, Georgia

I thought I heard the phone ringing while I was in the shower, which made my heart jump and leap, thinking that maybe it was Jace calling me back. I'll admit that part of the reason I left him that message was because I wanted him to call me back.

I wanted him to call me and be all—"Hey, Peyton, thanks for telling me about my mom, what exactly did she say?" And then I would be all, "She was really worried about you, Jace, but I told her not to be, and then I calmed her down, and by the end, it seemed like maybe she'd even grown as a person." And then he'd be all, "Oh, my God, Peyton, you're amazing and way better than my stupid girlfriend Kari, will you marry me?"

I mean, it's not like I did anything amazing when his mom showed up here, but still. If I'd wanted to, I could have gotten her all riled up and told her Jace and I were getting married because I was pregnant with his love child.

Which actually would have been pretty funny. If she'd been in a different frame of mind, I'll bet she might have even thought it was a funny joke.

I towel-dry my hair and then dress in a pair of jeans and a red tank top, pulling my still-a-little-damp hair up and twisting it into a loose ponytail. Then I head down to the lobby to grab one of those carts so that I can load all my luggage up onto it.

I have to be out of my room at noon, but no one ever said anything about being out of the *hotel*, now, did they? My plan is to sit in the lobby with my computer, Googling and researching until I figure out some kind of plan.

If worse comes to worst, I might have to call Courtney or Brooklyn and ask them to wire me some money. Although I probably won't have to do that until I get to North Carolina. I mean, I should have enough for a bus ticket, at least. On the East Coast, you can get a bus ticket from New York to Boston for, like, nineteen dollars. Nineteen dollars! And it seems like prices are definitely a lot lower in the South.

When I get back to my room with the cart, I load it up and then slide it out into the hall. Jace might have been right when he called me high maintenance. Why the hell am I bringing all this stuff to North Carolina? Did I really think I was going to wear all of it? Not to mention that all these bags make it super inconvenient to travel.

Of course, I couldn't have foreseen the way things turned out—I thought I was going to be driving in a car with Brooklyn, not having to carry all this stuff onto a bus.

But still. I really did not need all this junk, I think, as I make my way to the lobby, carefully pushing the cart in front of me. I didn't need the matching shoes and earrings for each outfit, I didn't need all those different colors of nail polish and all those different summer dresses. I could have packed a bunch of shorts and tank tops, which would have fit nicely into one bag. Where the hell did I think I was going for the summer anyway, the Riviera?

The thought is actually kind of disturbing—that I might be the type of girl who has to bring all her stupid, overpriced designer clothes with her everywhere she goes. I don't even like half of these clothes, and only wear them because it's what my mom wants me to wear. And I'm not actually even sure if *she* likes them, or if she just thinks she *should* like them because they're expensive.

I push the cart angrily into the lobby as fast as I can, hating the idea that I might be like my mom in any way.

"Whoa," Mia, the girl from the front desk, says when she sees me coming. "Do you need any help with that?" She doesn't wait for my answer, just comes over and starts helping me steer the cart into the lounge.

"Thanks," I say.

"Are you checking out?" she asks. "Because if you are, you can take the cart outside, you know."

"I am checking out," I say, pushing a strand of hair out of my face. "But I thought maybe I'd hang out in the lounge here for a little bit, just do some work on my computer before I get on the road." Hopefully, she can't tell that I'm going to be spending that time figuring out exactly *how* I'm going to be getting on the road.

"That's cool," she says, shrugging. "Stay as long as you want." She hesitates a second, then leans in close to me. "Did, uh, everything work out? With that woman?"

"That woman?"

"Yeah, your friend's mom? She seemed a little worked up. I'm sorry I gave out your room numbers like that, but she said she was going to call the police."

I smile. "No, it's fine. You did the right thing."

She smiles. "Good. Do you want any breakfast? It's free."

"Sure," I say nonchalantly.

She waves at the buffet—it's small, just some bagels, coffee, and cereal, but still. It's food. And it's free.

"I'll check you out, and just let me know if you need any help with your bags." She grins again. "We can get one of the guys to do it for you next time."

She starts walking back toward the front desk, then stops and turns around. "Is your friend checking out too?"

"My friend?"

"Yeah, the guy you were with. The hot one."

"Oh," I say. "Yeah, he's checking out, too."

I almost say he checked out last night, but then I catch myself. Probably doesn't give the best impression if I checked in with a guy, and then he left in the middle of the night. I mean, talk about sketchy. She'll probably think I'm some kind of prostitute or something. I'm not even sure they have those in the South. Isn't it all religious and conservative down here?

She disappears back behind the front desk, and I sit down and open my laptop.

After about twenty minutes, I'm starting to feel a little bit defeated. Yes, there are some cheap bus tickets, but the next two buses aren't leaving the station until three o'clock. Which means I'll have to find something to do here for the next four hours.

And then I'll have to figure out a way to lug my bags all the way to the bus station. Either that or spend money on a cab.

And *then,* when I get to the bus station in North Carolina, I'll still be thirty minutes away from my apartment in Creve Coeur. Which means another taxi. Not to mention that the bus doesn't get to North Carolina until nine o'clock tonight, and I can only pick up the keys to my apartment at the rental office between eight and eight. Which means I'm going to have to find a place to stay in North Carolina for the night. Which means I might have to sleep in the bus station.

I take a deep breath in, then search some different bus lines, but it's all the same story. Okay, I think. I can sleep in the bus station. It's not *that* horrible, when you really think about it. People do it all the time. And who says I actually have to sleep? I could just stay up all night, read a book or something. Not that I have a book. Why didn't I bring a book? And of course I don't have a phone, so if there were some kind of emergency, I'd be in trouble.

But I'm sure they have pay phones there. Maybe I could call Brooklyn or something, and get her to call me right back. Then we could stay up all night talking. I should probably call Brooklyn anyway. She's got to be worried about me. She's probably tried calling me like three million times by now.

Okay. I can do this. It's really just about changing your mind set, about not looking at the negative side of things. When you think about it, is a day or so of travel challenges really going to make me scrap my whole plan? I've come so far already. I just need to figure out the safest way to do things without spending a lot of money.

Just take it a step at a time, I tell myself.

Okay.

Step One.

Get from here to the bus station.

I could take a cab, but that definitely wouldn't save money.

And then I have a brilliant idea. Why not take a *bus* to the bus station? There has to be a city bus that goes there, right?

I Google the Savannah city bus schedule, my fingers flying over the keys. The nearest bus stop is about half a mile away. And the next bus to the Greyhound station comes in twenty-five minutes. Not bad. So I can walk the half mile to the bus stop, take the bus to the bus station, then hang out there until it's time to go to North Carolina. Of course, I have all my bags. And it's like, almost ninety degrees out.

But whatever. How bad can it really be? A little exercise will invigorate me!

Cheered by my new plan, I grab a bagel from the restaurant, and slather it with peanut butter. While I'm eating it, I take two cartons of orange juice and put them in my purse. I'm going to need the hydration.

"Bye!" Mia says as I wheel my stuff through the lobby. She's smiling, but her face turns doubtful as she looks at the big pile of suitcases I have. "You need some help?"

"No thanks!" I say brightly, and continue wheeling. I don't want her to ask any questions. The last thing I need is for her to figure out that I'm going to be wheeling my bags half a mile in this heat. She'd probably think I'm crazy.

"Okay," she says. "Well, thanks for staying with us! Good luck on the rest of your trip!"

"Thanks," I say, wondering if she'd still be wishing me luck if she knew I was going to be stealing this luggage cart so that I can wheel my stuff to the bus stop.

Probably not, but I decide to pretend she still would. If there's one thing I'm going to need, it's luck.

the trip jace

Sunday, June 27, 11:37 a.m.
Savannah, Georgia

I'm trying my best not to speed. I really am. The last thing I want is to get a speeding ticket or get into an accident. But I'm so anxious to get back to Peyton that I can't help it. I keep the car at five miles over the speed limit, reminding myself that speeding isn't going to get me there that much faster, and that if I get pulled over, it's going to take even longer to get back to Savannah.

By the time I pull into the parking lot of the Residence Inn, it's all I can do to keep from jumping out of my skin. Checkout isn't until noon. So I'm betting she's still here. Where else would she be? She *has to* still be here.

The thought that I'm going to miss her sends me into a panic, and I run from the parking lot and across the street to the hotel, jumping up onto the curb, rushing through the automatic doors and down the hall to Peyton's room. But when I get there, the door is open, and two women in maid uniforms are stripping the bed.

"Can I help you?" one of them asks, turning around and looking at me.

"Um, no," I say. I head back down the hallway and into the lobby, looking around. *Think*, I tell myself. Where would she have gone? To the airport? The bus station?

"Hey!" the girl at the front desk says. Mia, I think her name is. "You're back!"

"Yes," I say. "I'm back. I'm, um, I'm looking for my friend."

"The girl you were with?" she says. "She left about half an hour ago."

"She left?" My heart sinks. "She didn't . . . I mean, did she tell you where she was going?"

Mia shakes her head. "No. But she stole one of our luggage carts. I don't care or anything, I mean, I'm sure she had her reasons. But just to let you know if she doesn't return it, they're going to charge your credit card three hundred dollars."

"Thanks," I say, my mind racing.

If Peyton took one of the luggage carts, it means that she's probably walking somewhere. But where would she go?

"How far away is the bus station?" I ask Mia.

"Five miles, maybe?" she says. I guess Peyton could have tried to walk five miles, if she was desperate. "But there's a bus stop about half a mile from here."

"Can you tell me how to get there?"

She pulls a piece of paper out from behind the desk and draws me a little map, giving me directions to both the bus stop and the bus station itself.

"Thanks," I say. "I owe you one."

"No problem," she says. "Good luck."

I'm going to need it.

I'm back to my car in a flash. Hector's sitting in the front seat now, his ears perked up like he knows something's going on.

"We're going to find her, boy," I say as I put on my seat belt. "Don't worry."

I pull out onto the street and head for the bus stop. It's relatively easy to find, although a lot of the way is uphill. I can't imagine how hard it would be to push a whole cartful of suitcases in this heat.

I see the bus stop sign at the end of the street.

But when I get there, there's no sign of Peyton.

I park the car and get out, looking up and down the street, searching for any sign of her. But there's nothing. I walk into the two cafes that are on that road, scanning the tables for Peyton. But she's not there.

I get back in the car and lean my head against the seat.

Hector does a little whine next to me, and I reach over and scratch his ears. "What do you think?" I ask him. "Where's Peyton?"

He wags his tail at the mention of her name.

I sigh.

I don't know what else to do. Maybe I should call Courtney. Or Peyton's parents. Maybe I should drive to the airport. Or the bus station.

I put my car into drive and start to head toward the bus station. But I don't have far to go.

Because a few blocks over, I find Peyton.

She's sitting on the curb, crying.

the trip peyton

Sunday, June 27, 11:49 a.m.
Savannah, Georgia

I missed the bus. I walked all the way here, pushing that stupid cart that I stole, and when I turned the corner, I saw the bus pulling away from the station.

I was so far down the street that I couldn't even run after it. It was kicking up dust, groaning on its wheels and emitting exhaust into the June heat. I stopped pushing. I leaned my head against the cool metal of the luggage cart.

Then I pushed it to the side of the street, walked into the café that was on the road, and bought a bottled water. I wanted to sit inside for a little while, because I was hot from the walk, and the air conditioning felt nice. But I was afraid someone was going to steal the stuff on my luggage cart. I'd already seen a few people pass by on the street, and look it up and down, like maybe they were thinking of waltzing off with it. And the stupid thing was too big to bring in with me.

So I headed back outside to guard my stuff. No one seemed to know when the next bus was coming, but they did tell me where the bus station was.

So I decided to walk.

I got about three blocks before I realized it was time to sit down and have a good cry.

And so now here I am. Sitting here. Having a good cry. I told myself it was only going to be for a few minutes, but I think I've definitely been here for at least ten or so.

There's the sound of a car pulling up to the curb, and I look up, half expecting to see a cop or a meter maid or someone standing there, telling me to get the hell off the street.

But it's not a cop.

And it's not a meter maid.

It's Jace.

He's stepping out of his car and walking toward me. His hair is all rumpled and he's wearing the same T-shirt and track pants he had on last night and there's a little bit of stubble darkening his cheeks. He looks, as always, amazing.

"What are you—" I start.

"Stop," he says, and shakes his head. "Don't talk." He sits down on the curb next to me.

"Don't talk?" I repeat dumbly, even though he just told me not to.

"No. I mean, yeah, you can talk, but—" He shakes his head again like he's trying to clear his thoughts, and then he stares down at the pavement. He's so close that our knees are touching. "I need to say some things," he says, moving his eyes up so that he's looking right at me. "And I don't want you to say anything until I'm done."

My pulse starts to quicken. "Right," I say. "Now you want to talk and I'm just supposed to—"

"Peyton," he says, putting a finger on my lips. "Please." His eyes are on mine, and he's looking at me so longingly, like he really needs to say what he came here to say. So after a second, even though I'm mad, I nod.

"I should have never stopped talking to you the way I did," he says. "It was stupid. *I* was stupid. I found out that you hadn't told me about your parents, and I freaked out." He sighs. "It was my stupid pride. I let it get in the way, and I've been paying for it ever since."

"Why?" I ask.

"Why what?"

"Why did you freak out?"

He hesitates for a second, and I hold my breath, praying he's going to say what I want him to say. "Because I was falling in love with you."

Electricity zings through me, and my heart leaps. "If you were falling in love with me, then why did you stop talking to me?"

"I told you. It was my stupid pride. I . . . I was afraid." His eyes are still on mine, and whatever's passing between us is so intense I'm having a hard time looking at him. "I was afraid that maybe it was real. And I was looking for any excuse for it not to be. And so as soon as I found an out, I just took it."

"Why, though?" I ask. "Why didn't you just ask me about it?"

"Why didn't you just tell me?"

I think about it. Really think about it. "Because saying it out loud would have made it true," I say. "And then I'd have to think about all kinds of other fucked up stuff, like my mom's issues with money and how my parents were still both living in the same house, not even thinking about how that might effect me."

He nods, then finally pulls his gaze from mine. He looks down at the ground. Tears fill my eyes, remembering the betrayal, remembering how much I did—*do*—love him. I want him to tell me we can forget it, that we can move on, that we can just be together. But I know it's not that easy.

"We can't do that to each other," he says finally. "We can't go around keeping secrets like that."

"I know," I say. "I think . . . I mean, I've always known that. I think that's maybe why I told you about my mom and the whole credit card thing."

He nods, then kicks at some gravel on the road with his shoe. "So now what?"

"I don't know." I shake my head. "It's too . . . it just seems like every time we're together, everything gets so complicated."

He takes a deep breath. "So the question is, can you deal with complicated?"

"We live so far away," I say. I feel the familiar twinge of hope stirring in my chest, and my first instinct is to squash it, to tell him that there's no way we can work out, that we don't make sense, that we've screwed everything up way too much to ever go back.

I look away, squinting in the sun. I take a deep breath in. And then I remember something. Something I haven't told Jace. "I wasn't really going home," I say. "I was going to trick you into taking me to North Carolina."

His eyes widen in shock, and then he nods. "It's that bad at home, huh?"

I nod.

"So maybe . . . maybe you can stay in Florida for the summer," he says.

"Right," I say. "Like my parents are going to go for that."

"How can they really stop you?" he asks.

"Where would I stay? I have no money, no job . . ."

"Well, you could maybe stay with me," he says slowly. "Or Courtney. You know her dad is going away for the whole summer on his honeymoon." He gets a thoughtful look on his face as he reaches into his pocket and pulls out his phone.

"Who are you calling?" I ask.

"My mom."

"Your *mom*?" I ask. "But she's—"

He holds a finger to his lips, motioning for me to be quiet. "Mom," he says. "It's me." I hear her start to yell at him on the other line, and then she must catch herself, because she lowers her voice. "Yeah, I know," Jace says. "We can talk about it when I get home. But Mom, can Peyton come to graduation with me? And if we get home in time, can she stay with us for a few days?" He rolls his eyes. "Of course separate rooms, Mom, geez."

A second later, he's off the phone. "It's all set," he says. "We'll fly back to Florida tonight, and worry about my car later. You can go to graduation with me."

I shake my head. "I want to," I say. "I do. But . . ."

"But what?"

"But what about all the stuff you said, about me running away from things?"

He tilts his head, thinking about it. "When we get to Florida," he says, "we'll call your dad. We'll tell him everything that happened, and we'll come up with a plan."

The thought twists my stomach into a ball of anxiety. But Jace reaches out and squeezes my hand, and I immediately feel better. I nod slowly. "What about Kari?"

He shakes his head. "Kari and I broke up."

I narrow my eyes at him. "When?"

"Last night. When you took off, I called her and ended it." He shrugs. "It's always been you, Peyton. Always."

I feel my eyes fill with tears, and I look down at the ground. We just sit like that for a few moments, in the middle of the Savannah summer, him holding my hand, me thinking about what all of this means.

"So I go to Florida with you now," I say slowly, "and stay for a few days. And then what?"

"And then we'll figure it out," he says. "You can talk to Courtney, talk to your parents." He squeezes my hand. "It'll all work out."

I'm not sure if he's talking about me and him, or about the whole situation. I raise my eyes to his, and he reaches out and wipes away the tear that's sliding down my cheek.

"Peyton," he says. "It's going to be okay. I'm going to take care of it, okay? And I'm never going to let you go again."

And for the first time in a really long time, I believe it.

All of it.

That everything's going to be okay.

That he's going to take care of me.

That we're going to be together.

And then he kisses me.

And it just might be the best feeling ever.

Don't miss this sneak peek of Lauren's newest novel,

through to you

through to you

LAUREN BARNHOLDT

author of *two-way street* and *sometimes it happens*

Harper

This is how it starts:

In world history, with a note, on a random Wednesday afternoon.

Penn Mattingly puts the note on my desk as he's walking to his seat in the back of the room.

Instantly I'm suspicious.

We're in high school. High school boys are notorious for leaving weird notes and other paraphernalia around, and usually whatever they've left doesn't say or represent anything nice or appropriate.

"What's that?" my best friend Anna says. Then she reaches across the aisle and plucks the note off my desk.

"Hey!" I don't know why, but suddenly I feel very protective of that note. I'm sure it says something totally ridiculous and/or bordering on sexual harassment. One time sophomore year a senior left a note in Anna's locker that said, *I like your tits in that shirt.* If *I'd* gotten a note like that, I would have died. But Anna just smiled and took it as a compliment. And then she started dating that boy, which was kind of an unconventional way for a relationship to start. But whatever.

"What?" Anna asks as she starts to unfold the piece of paper. "We're best friends. We're supposed to share everything."

I reach over and steal it back. "I'll let you read it," I say, "but I should get to read it first."

But I don't open the paper, at least not right away. Instead I just hold it in my hand. In that second a shiver, almost like a premonition, runs up my spine. I feel like if I read what's on that piece of paper, I'm going to be starting down a road I can't turn back from.

"Open it!" Anna stage-whispers.

"Okay, okay." But still I don't. I turn around and glance back at Penn. He looks the same as always—shaggy dark hair that's just a little bit too long and flops over his forehead; broad shoulders; dark eyes. There's a little bit of stubble on his cheeks and chin, and he's wearing baggie jeans and a red hoodie.

He's joking around with Emmett Wilson and acting completely normal. I marvel at how different guys are from girls. How could Penn have left a note on my desk five seconds ago and now be pretending like it never happened?

Meanwhile Anna and I are sitting here making a huge deal about it before we've even read what it says.

"This is ridiculous," Anna says, rolling her eyes. She reaches out and grabs the note again.

I grab it back.

And then the bell rings and Mr. Marks walks in, and everyone faces front and gets quiet.

I spread the paper out on my lap.

It has one line on it, scrawled in boy handwriting.

I like your sparkle.

My hand reaches up and instinctively touches my hair, lingering on the piece of tinsel threaded through my ponytail. I didn't even want to wear the stupid tinsel, but it's senior spirit week, and Anna insisted we at least do something. So we met in the bathroom this morning and wove strands of tinsel through our hair. Green and blue, our school colors.

I didn't feel very sparkly at the time, but now, knowing Penn has noticed, my face feels all hot. I turn around and look at him again, but his eyes are on his notebook.

I catch Anna's eye and give her a disinterested shrug. Even though my heart is beating superfast, I have this weird feeling, like I shouldn't make a big deal of it to Anna.

So I mouth, "So stupid," and then pass her the note.

I know it's silly, but as soon as it's out of my hands, I want it back.

I'm not the kind of girl who gets notes like this from boys. No one has ever called me sparkly before.

Anna reads it, her eyebrows raised, then shrugs. "Kind of sweet?" she mouths.

She hands the note back to me, and then, suddenly, Mr. Marks turns his attention to us. "Something important, ladies?"

"What do you mean?" Anna asks in this half-snotty, half-fake-innocent voice. Anna's not scared of teachers. I'm scared of everything. Included, but not limited to, spiders, the dark, flying, and blood.

"I *mean* that you're passing notes in my class," Mr. Marks says. He holds his hand out. "Would you like to share it?"

My face burns.

"We weren't passing notes," Anna lies.

Mr. Marks's eyebrows knit together, and he glares at her. I guess what Anna's saying isn't technically a lie. *Technically* we weren't passing notes. At least not ones we'd written ourselves. Is Penn going to get in trouble too? I fight the urge to look back at him to see how he's reacting to this whole thing. I pretty much already know—the type of person to put a note on someone's desk that says *I like your sparkle* isn't the type to get all freaked out if they get in trouble for it.

The classroom phone buzzes on the wall.

Mr. Marks sighs and walks over to it.

"Yes," he says into the receiver. "Yes, she's here." His gaze turns to me, and I sit up straighter in my chair. Mr. Marks hangs up the phone and gives me a glare. "It seems you will be saved from my wrath for the time being, Ms. Fairbanks. You're wanted in the nurse's office."

Crap, crap, crap.

Anna gives me a sympathetic look as I gather up my books and leave the classroom. Once I'm in the hallway, I just stand there, not sure what to do. The period just started. Which means I'm going to have to wander the halls for the next forty-five minutes and hope I don't get caught.

Here's the deal with me and the nurse:

She's kind of stalking me.

I know that sounds crazy, but it's completely true. You'd think that someone who'd completed a bunch of medical training wouldn't have the capacity to be a stalker, but it just goes to show you that you can never tell what's lurking under the surface of someone's mind.

Okay, so maybe I'm being a little bit dramatic. The nurse isn't, like, restraining-order stalking me. It's just that there's some ridiculous rule that all seniors need to have a physical before graduation. It's, like, for some kind of state statistics or something, to make sure everyone's healthy. Most kids get them at their family doctors, or when they sign up for a sport. But one of my biggest fears is doctors and needles. So I haven't gone.

Unfortunately, if you don't show the school proof you've

had one, they call you down to the nurse's office when the school doctor is in and try to give you one there. Um, no thank you. I've seen the school doctor. He has beefy fingers, and he smells like pepperoni and Swiss cheese. It's a ridiculous rule anyway. Why should the school get to dictate your, like, *health*?

I pull Penn's note back out from where I slipped it into my notebook and read it again.

I like your sparkle.

Was he being nice? Or is it one of those jerky things boys do just because they can? Was he making fun of me? I have no experience when it comes to this kind of thing. It's the first note I've received from a boy since the second grade, when Charles Dawcett put a note on my desk that asked me if I would be his girlfriend. I said yes, but by the time recess rolled around, he'd moved on to Addison Roach.

Whatever, I tell myself. *It's just a stupid note. It means nothing.*

But part of me can't help but wish it was something more.

And it's at that exact moment that Penn Mattingly appears behind me and tugs on a strand of my hair.

Penn

It was just a stupid note.

I wrote it on a whim, because I'd seen Harper walking into world history with that one friend she's always with, the one with the spiky hair. And Harper's tinsel sparkled in the light, and she reached up and smoothed her ponytail down, and something about the way she did it made it seem like she was wearing that tinsel ironically. I don't know why, but it was like she'd done it as an afterthought, like maybe someone had convinced her to wear it, like she couldn't even be bothered to wear a blue or green shirt for senior spirit week, so someone had to be like, "Hey, Harper, maybe you should wear this tinsel."

And that kind of killed me.

All these people walking around in their stupid school spirit shirts, thinking that any of this means anything, and there she was wearing this tinsel in this completely ironic way.

So I ripped out a piece of paper from my notebook and wrote that I liked her sparkle. It was just a stupid note I dropped onto her desk. It wasn't supposed to *mean* anything.

But then I noticed she was looking back at me, and I kind of got a little bit nervous that maybe she *thought* it meant something more than it really did, so I pretended to be talking to the kid next to me.

And then I watched Mr. Marks catch her with the note, and I saw her fidget and get all uncomfortable, and in that moment, for some reason, I *wanted* him to read the note. Out loud. To the class. I hadn't signed my name, so no one would have known it was from me.

That's fucked up, I know. But I wanted Harper to be embarrassed. Actually, no, that's not completely true. I didn't want her embarrassed, per se. I just wanted to have an effect on her. I *liked* that I was having an effect on her.

So when she got called down to the nurse's office, I immediately jumped up and asked for the bathroom pass.

I thought I'd have to go running around looking for her, but she was just standing there in the hallway, looking down at something. When I got closer, I saw she was reading my note.

A feeling of trepidation came over me. Why was she

reading my note again? Maybe she was a stalker. I seized her up. Long dark hair, average height, wearing jeans and a pink tank top with a sheer white shirt over it.

She didn't look like a stalker. And besides, I was the one who'd put a note on her desk. If anything, *I* was the one who could be considered a stalker.

But still.

You can never tell. What do stalkers really look like? You'd expect them to be girls who aren't all that cute, girls who are desperate for male attention. But from my experience—and honestly, not to sound like an asshole, but I have kind of a lot of it—the ones you need to worry about are the ones who *are* good-looking. It's like they're so used to getting what they want, they can't take no for an answer.

Is Harper good-looking? I wasn't sure yet.

"Whatcha doin'?" I ask, and lightly pull on a strand of her hair.

She turns around, startled, and drops the note I gave her.

We both bend down to pick it up, and then we both stop when we see what the other one is doing, and so we end up just kind of crouched down over the floor together. I stay like that for a moment longer than necessary, because I can tell she's flustered. I know it's fucked up, but like I said, I like that I'm having an effect on her. Finally she grabs the note and we both stand up.

"Um, I'm not doing anything." She smoothes her ponytail, and her tinsel shimmers. "What are you doing?"

I shrug. "Why do you have to go to the nurse?" I ask. "Are you sick?" She doesn't look sick.

"I'm not going to the nurse." A look of panic crosses her face.

"But you just got called down."

"So?"

"So then why aren't you going?" It's almost funny, me asking someone why they're not doing something. I never do anything I'm supposed to.

She shrugs and shifts her weight from foot to foot. "I don't know."

"Liar."

"Whatever." She pushes her hair back from her face and looks at me defiantly, like she's waiting for me to say something. So I don't.

"Okay, well. I guess I'm just going to go walk around," she says finally.

"The *school*?"

"Yeah."

"Why?"

"Because I just told you, I'm not going to the nurse."

I have no idea what she's talking about. She definitely might be a crazy person. Not, like, a dangerous crazy person or anything. Although, usually if people are nuts in one way, they have the potential to be nuts in all sorts of other ways. But I kind of like it. I like that she's always been quiet in world history, and now here she is, talking nonsense.

"What do you have against nurses?" I tease. I start walking down the hall, just in case Mr. Marks decides to come out and make sure I'm actually going to the bathroom.

Harper follows me.

"Nothing, really."

"Well, you must have *something* against them." Is it possible she doesn't know the amazingness that is the nurse's office? "You know if go down there and tell them you threw up in the bathroom, they'll let you go home. It's, like, a rule."

"She wants me to have a physical," Harper says, "and I have a phobia."

"Of physicals?"

"Of all things medical." She looks at me and raises her chin, challenging me to call her crazy. But I don't. A girl who can admit what she's afraid of is refreshing.

"It's just a school physical, though. You know that, right? They don't take blood or anything." It's true. I've had a million sports physicals for baseball, and if you're not, like, five minutes away from dying or have scoliosis, the physicals are totally useless.

She shrugs. "It's all the same to me."

I'm still walking down the hall, and she's still following me. "So you're just gonna wander around the school?"

She nods. "Until the end of the period, yeah. Then hopefully they'll have forgotten they want to see me."

What a horrible plan. Everyone knows that if you're trying to get away with skipping class, you don't hang around at *school*. "That's the worst idea ever," I tell her. "Someone's going to catch you."

"No, they won't," she says. "I'm going to hide in the bathroom."

"Oh my God," I say, rolling my eyes. "That's the first place they look!" It's such an innocent, ridiculous plan that I can't help think that maybe she's joking. But there's no sign of a smile on her face. I shake my head and then look her up and down. She bites her lip, and she looks so damn cute and kind of like a lost puppy that I can't resist. "You wanna get out of here?"

She looks shocked. "Leave the school?"

"Yeah."

"With *you*?"

"Yes."

"And do *what*?"

"I don't know. Eat. Walk. Have an adventure." I give her my patented smile, the one I use when I want to get my way.

She taps her foot against the floor. "I don't even know you."

"Penn Mattingly." I put my hand out, and she gives me a look like she can't believe I'm trying to pull bullshit on her.

"I know your name."

"So what else do you need?" I pull my wallet out and hand her my license. "Name, date of birth, address . . ."

She looks down at it doubtfully. "That's a horrible picture of you."

"Really?" I cock my head. "I kind of like it. It was after this crazy party, and this girl had . . ." I trail off for a moment, then reach out and take the license back. "Well. It was just a rough night. So given the circumstances, I think I look pretty good."

"Are you always this cocky?"

I shake my head and pretend like she's got me all wrong. "It's a real shame," I tell her, "that you would think that about me."

"You just told me you think you look good in that picture, and that you had some kind of random sexual escapade with a girl. What else am I supposed to think? I mean, I haven't ever spoken to you until today. You're not exactly making the best first impression." She turns on her heel and starts walking away from me.

I chase after her, wondering how I've suddenly become the follower instead of the followee. "That's awful," I say. "That we've been in the same school all this time and we've never even talked. I mean, what if we're soul mates?"

She turns on her heel and gapes at me. "Me and *you*?"

"What, like you're too good for me?"

She shrugs, like maybe she thinks she is. I'm annoyed for a second, and then I realize she's probably right. I might have never spoken to her until today, but I know she's smart. I know she's quiet. I know she always eats lunch outside when the weather is nice. All those things make her too good for me, because the truth is, pretty much any girl who has their shit together is too good for me.

But I push that thought out of my head as best I can, because if I let myself think about that, I won't be able to convince her to come with me. And I don't know why, but I really, really want her to.

"Anyway," I say. "Now that we've explored that possibility, we really shouldn't waste another moment. Let's get out of here."

She tugs on her hair again, and I can see her mind working. She *wants* to go with me, but she's a good girl. Her instinct is probably to be afraid and cautious. *My* instinct is to give her another grin and make a witty comment, but some part of me has a feeling that's not going to work.

So I just wait.

And sure enough, after a moment Harper shrugs. "Okay," she says. "Let's go."